Lauren had never liked surprises.

Even good ones, she thought, though there were few to reference.

Jason drove toward Glendale. Not too far from home, but not a part of town she was familiar with. The sights intrigued her, and she felt a sense of anticipation.

Finally, Jason pulled into a large parking lot filled with pickup trucks. The neon sign on the roof of the bar shone bright orange, casting a glow over everything.

Lauren had never been to any place like this, and her anticipation threatened to morph into anxiety. Jason squeezed her hand and gave her another of those smiles.

"Come on," he said, climbing out and coming around to her side of the car. As they walked across the parking lot, he took her hand again, and she let him. It seemed...right.

His hand was strong, warm and callused, and any uncertainties she'd had fled. She let herself smile back at him and relaxed for the first time that night.

Dear Reader,

As a kid, I was always fascinated with people whose lives were different from mine. I read any biography I could get my hands on. Helen Keller and Annie Sullivan were two people I always admired.

A couple years ago, I was given the opportunity to take sign language classes at work and, through that class, I met someone who left a lasting impression. The instructor for those classes made me think and work hard to learn this new language. She taught us more than the signs, she also showed us a whole new fascinating culture.

As always in new situations, my brain came up with ideas for characters, and a story that scared me enough to make me question my ability as a writer and my sanity. I wanted to show this new culture I'd come to respect and like. This story touched my heart, but proved to be the hardest one I've ever taken on.

I hope you'll enjoy getting more acquainted with the third brother in the Hawkins family, Jason, and the woman who steals his heart, Lauren Ramsey. I also hope to share a respect and understanding of the challenges the hearing-impaired face. Any inaccuracies are purely things I still have to learn in this lifelong journey.

Angel Smits

ANGEL SMITS

The Ballerina's Stand

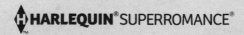 HARLEQUIN® SUPERROMANCE®

Recycling programs
for this product may
not exist in your area.

ISBN-13: 978-0-373-60996-3

The Ballerina's Stand

Printed in U.S.A.

Angel Smits lives in Colorado with her husband, daughter and puppy. Winning the Romance Writers of America's Golden Heart® Award was the highlight of her writing career, until her first Harlequin book hit the shelves. Her social work background inspires her characters while improv writing allows her to torture them. It's a rough job, but someone's got to do it.

Books by Angel Smits

HARLEQUIN SUPERROMANCE

A Message for Julia
Seeking Shelter
A Family for Tyler
The Marine Finds His Family

Other titles by this author available in ebook format.

This book is dedicated to some very amazing people. My critique partners, Pam McCutcheon, Karen Fox and Jodi Anderson, who slogged through this with me. And my husband, Ron, who had to listen to me all the way through. But mostly to Lauraan, who showed me what a strong person can do in this world. Thank you all.

CHAPTER ONE

APPARENTLY, MOST OF Jason Hawkins's siblings had been bitten by the love bug. Standing here in the basement of the church, listening to a local country band, a warm beer in hand, Jason simply watched and shook his head.

His younger brother, DJ, looked as handsome and happy as ever in a black tuxedo. Tammie, the newest addition to the Hawkins clan, glowed in her lacy confection of a wedding dress as DJ spun her around the dance floor.

Those two didn't even seem to notice there was anyone else in the room—except their son, Tyler, who, at the age of nine, took his duty as best man very seriously. He'd banged a spoon on the drinking glasses so many times, to get his parents to kiss, that Jason was getting a headache.

Wyatt and Emily, Jason's older brother and his fiancée, were busy gathering all the silverware to get it to the church ladies in the kitchen and out of Tyler's reach.

Jason considered helping, but they were having entirely too much fun doing it together.

One of his younger sisters, Mandy, sat nearby,

her little one, Lucas, asleep in her arms. She was smiling and swaying to the song's beat as if she wished she were out on the dance floor.

Not like she hadn't been out there plenty. Lane, Mandy's boyfriend, and Lucas's father, had done his due diligence. Now the poor guy was running to get drinks for them at the bar. Mandy and Lane hadn't announced anything official about their relationship yet, but the entire time Jason had been back home, Mandy had stayed at Lane's place. The man didn't look one bit put out about it, either.

Jason figured he'd have yet another wedding to attend soon. He just wasn't sure whose first. Wyatt's or Mandy's?

"I don't see you taking anyone out for a spin, brother dear." His youngest sister, Tara, sidled up to him.

He gave her his best outraged glare. "I danced with Addie, *and* you."

"Obligatory dances with your sisters don't count." They both watched Addie glide by on the arm of one of the ranch hands. Paulo, if he remembered correctly. Jason couldn't keep all the guys straight. He only came back to the ranch a couple times a year and the staff always changed. Chet the ranch foreman, and his wife, Juanita the cook, were the only constants. They, too, were out on the dance floor.

Jason grinned. He'd always enjoyed Tara the most of his siblings. Logical and straightforward, she was the most like him. If he could say *anyone* in this family was like him.

Otherwise, if it weren't for the physical family resemblance, he'd think he was adopted. Wyatt was a rancher. DJ a soldier, although medically retired now, who worked with Wyatt on the ranch. Addie taught school. And Mandy was a stay-at-home mom, working in the ranch office part-time and helping Lane with the Hot Shot fire crew he worked on. All hands-on, active, people.

Jason looked at Tara, who was nursing a beer of her own. Even she liked to get her hands dirty, working with food as a chef. "What about you, sis? Anyone on your horizon?"

"No! And don't jinx it. I'm too busy. I have a restaurant to open, remember, oh mighty lawyer-from-hell with all the paperwork?"

He laughed. She'd grumbled at all the contracts, signatures and forms he'd had her fill out. But she'd be much better off in the long run—and protected. He'd made sure of that.

Even she fit in better here than he did. She wanted to settle in Texas. Near enough to the ranch and family, but far enough away to have her independence.

He understood that last point—it's why he'd moved to California. He glanced around at the simple church basement, contrasting it with his usual surroundings—his office and his Los Angeles apartment.

Contemporary was more his style. Chrome and clean. Linear.

Addie flopped down in the chair next to him. "Okay, Tara, your turn." She panted, giving her sister a pointed look.

"I'm not dancing with Paulo again," Tara said as softly as she could and still be heard. "The man's not light on his feet, or mine."

"Well, I'm not, either. Jason, it's your brotherly duty to protect us from cowboys with big clumsy feet, right?"

"How did I get involved in this?" He looked from sister to sister. "I'm sure as hell not dancing with him." Their laughter, while warm and welcome, didn't let him off the hook, and he knew it.

He was the last unclaimed male over eighteen in this family. He glanced at his watch. Didn't he have a flight to catch?

Damn. Not for twenty-four more hours.

Three of those hours later, the wedding reception finally wound down. Jason made sure he was nowhere around for the bouquet toss by heading to the ranch house for shelter. He had no intention of being anyone's target when they caught the thing, nor for the garter throw. Let a ranch hand or some local hang the piece of silk from the rearview mirror of their truck.

"So, this is where you snuck off to." Tara's voice came through the screen door before she opened it and stepped into Wyatt's big homey kitchen.

"With you right behind me," he told his little—amend that—younger sister.

"You making coffee?" She pointedly glanced at the familiar green canisters behind him that had come from Mom's house. "'Cause there's a whole plate of Addie's cookies that need a cup of warmth to wash them down."

"Thinking about it." He looked at the heaping plate, amazed there were still some left.

"Well, quit thinking and get it done."

He laughed and set to work. Tara sat in the big captain's chair at the head of the table, the soft blue fabric of her bridesmaid's dress rustled loudly. Her high heels thunked to the floor.

"You realize this is just the first one, don't you?" He sat in the next seat.

"Yes. Lord. Are we going to survive six of these?"

"Hey, at least one of them will be yours." He grinned at her.

She groaned as she crossed her arms on the table-top and rested her head on her forearms. "Not any time soon, I hope."

The coffeemaker gave off a last gasping sputter. Jason rose to get them each a cup.

They'd just taken a sip of the rich brew when more footsteps sounded on the walk outside. "You'll have to make another pot," Tara predicted. "Should we hide the cookies?" She took a big bite of the one in her hand.

Jason laughed, snagging one more for himself as the rest of the family came through the screen door. Addie made the best cookies and the comfort they gave wasn't something any of them would give up.

Wyatt entered the kitchen and made his way to the stairs, a sound-asleep Tyler draped over his shoulder. The boy would be staying here while DJ and Tammie went to South Padre Island for their honeymoon. Addie and Emily settled around the table with the rest of them.

Jason served the last of the pot and made the second. The decibel level in the room rose, though that didn't seem to faze baby Lucas. He was sacked out in a swing in the middle of everything.

Jason leaned against the counter, watching and listening to the big rambunctious family. It felt good to be home. Wyatt soon joined him as they both sipped their coffee.

"You're really going to go through this insanity yourself?" Jason asked Wyatt. The engagement ring on Emily's hand still sparkled with the newness of gold and diamond.

"In time," was all Wyatt said. It had taken him forever to propose, so Jason figured the wedding would take just as long. Jason was fine with that.

A knock at the door surprised them all, and Wyatt went to answer. A cowboy, not one of Wyatt's men, stood there. "Come on in, John." Wyatt pushed the screen farther open and the tall, lanky man stepped inside. He hastily yanked the Stetson off his head and nodded toward the room's inhabitants.

"What can I do for you?" Wyatt lifted a cup, silently offering the man some coffee.

"No. I'm good. Gotta get up early and that'll keep me awake. I'm here to see the lawyer."

The room grew quiet, and every head turned to look at Jason. He frowned. He wasn't here to work. Besides, what would a cowpoke need with a corporate attorney? "Uh, that's me." He pushed away from the counter.

"Good. Good." The man twisted his hat in his hands. "Can we talk in private?"

Jason looked around, and Wyatt shrugged. Jason followed the man out into the yard. The big lights were still on, bathing everything in a white glow. Night sounds and a soft breeze broke the prairie quiet.

"What can I help you with? John, right?" Jason knew the man was seeking help—he'd seen that desperate look in too many clients' eyes.

"It's not me, sir." The man twisted his hat around again. "My boss sent me."

"Who's your boss?"

"Pal Haymaker."

Jason cursed. Jason didn't want anything to do with Haymaker, a man who'd tried to run Wyatt out of business and had nearly killed Lane and Mandy with his stupidity.

"I'm not interested in working for him." Jason didn't even try to keep the contempt out of his voice.

"Please, sir." The man stepped forward. "He's not doing so good." The man looked up at the sky as if hoping to see an answer written in the heavens. "I know he ain't been good to you and yours. But he asked me to tell you it's not about your family." The cowboy swallowed and Jason saw the man's Adam's apple bob. "He said he don't trust no one but you with this."

Jason cringed. He hated when a potential case piqued his interest this way. It made it hard to keep his distance and objectivity and turn it down.

"You have any idea what it's about?"

The cowboy shook his head. "He asked me to have you come see him tomorrow mornin'. If you can."

Jason sighed. What could it hurt? "I can be there around nine?"

The cowboy grinned. "Thank you, sir. Thank you very much." Relief rolled off the man's broad shoulders.

Jason watched the cowboy amble away and climb into a battered pickup. A cloud of smoke rose up behind the vehicle as it left the yard.

What would Haymaker have done to the guy if Jason hadn't agreed? He didn't want to know.

"What the hell was that about?" Wyatt spoke from the now-open screen door.

Jason slowly walked back to the house. "Apparently, Pal Haymaker has a legal matter he only trusts me to handle."

"He's up to something."

"Yeah. But I'm curious enough. I think I'll go see him."

"You're not going by yourself."

"Why not? I meet with clients on my own all the time."

"I don't trust Pal and you know why. You might need a witness."

Wyatt did have a point. "Well, you can't go—he'd probably shoot you on sight. And same goes for Lane, especially since their last go-round after the fire. And DJ's not exactly available."

Wyatt laughed mirthlessly. "Yeah. Take Chet with you. He and Pal go way back. He's the only one of us the old man won't try to blast into the next county."

Jason nodded. "I can do that."

"John give you any idea what it's about?"

"No." Jason stared at the empty driveway, a frown on his brow. He was usually good at reading people, and that cowboy hadn't just been doing his boss's bidding. He'd been scared.

"I thought Pal was half-dead."

"Yeah, well, until he's actually six feet under, don't count that bastard out. He's still powerful around here."

The silence settled around them, comfortably. Jason had always respected Wyatt. Only in the last few years had Jason gotten the chance to get to know his older brother better. Man to man.

Wyatt had stepped into the role of parent when their dad died. Wyatt had been fifteen, while Jason had been eleven. Those roles still permeated their relationship.

"How're things going out there in LA?" Wyatt tried to sound casual. Jason almost laughed. Wyatt couldn't fathom the idea of living in a city. Jason loved the pace, the pseudo privacy, the beauty of the big, active city.

"You and Emily should visit. I'll show you around."

"That'd be nice." Emily's voice came out of the darkness, as she stepped outside to lean against Wyatt. His arm went around her almost as a reflex. They were as comfortable as any long-married couple.

And then it hit him. "Wait." Jason stared at them. "Wyatt, you rat." Jason punched his brother in the arm, just like when they were kids. "You two aren't going through this insanity. It's already a done deal."

Wyatt laughed and Emily blushed, her cheeks shadowed in the dim night light.

Jason was surprised at the hitch of some unusual emotion ripping through him as the two shared a look. "When?"

"A couple weeks ago," Emily whispered, not taking her gaze from Wyatt's. "My boss performed the ceremony one afternoon. Convenient working for a county judge." She shrugged and smiled.

Jason glanced over at his brother who looked totally smitten.

"Congratulations. But, why?"

Wyatt looked down at Emily. "It seemed like the right thing to do. We didn't want to interfere with DJ and Tammie's day. They needed the big to-do. We just needed—" Wyatt paused and his smile softened. Jason felt himself smile, too, pleased that this woman made his brother happy.

"Each other," Emily finished for him on a whisper, gazing up, just as besotted, at her new husband.

"I—uh—think I'll turn in." Jason headed into the house, fairly certain neither of them heard him leave.

Inside, Tara and Addie cleaned up the few dishes, their dresses rustling in tune as they moved, while Mandy fed the baby and Lane sat nearby. It was comfortable, safe. Home.

The day was winding down. Jason wouldn't tell anyone that Wyatt and Emily had eloped—that was their news. Though he was tempted to tell Tara she would need to buy one fewer bridesmaid's dress. She'd be relieved.

After saying his goodnights, he went upstairs to the guest room, his mind full of coffee and curiosity. What the hell was Pal Haymaker up to? And how would it affect the people downstairs? His family.

Jason didn't live here in Texas. He wasn't a provider like Wyatt, nor a soldier like DJ had been, but he had his own way of protecting the people he cared about. He'd studied the law and every one of his siblings had benefited from his advice at some point—Wyatt with the business of the ranch, Tara with her restaurant idea and Mandy with her son's future.

Jason knew he'd do just about anything, even work for an asshole like Pal Haymaker, if it kept those people downstairs, nearly all the people he loved, happy and safe.

According to Wyatt, Pal had been banned from the big house. Pal Jr. had paid the bail money and hired a high-profile attorney, but wasn't speaking to his father after he'd nearly burned up the entire county. As for Trey Haymaker, Pal's grandson and DJ's friend, he had disappeared. If anyone knew where he was, they weren't telling. Jason didn't blame him.

The old man had done a number on everyone.

The original hundred-year-old ranch house was still impressive, though. It dwarfed even Wyatt's place, and the trees had easily been around for an additional century. An older woman answered the door, nodding but not smiling as she let Jason in. He followed her as she slowly walked down the long hallway, her serviceable shoes squeaking against the polished wood floors.

She stopped at the wide entry of a room, waving him in before turning back and returning the way she'd come. Squeak. Squeak.

"Someone should buy that woman some decent shoes." Pal's voice came from the corner of the big room.

The old man sat there in a leather recliner, his scrawny legs lifted up, a newspaper spread over his lap. Clear green tubing from an oxygen tank beside the recliner snaked around the chair, finally wrapping around Pal's weathered face. He aimed a remote at the giant TV screen and turned it off.

"You wanted to see me?" Jason didn't hesitate.

"Have a seat." Pal leaned forward and lowered the footrest. "I ain't gonna get a crick in my neck for this, and I sure as hell can't get up."

Jason nodded and took the chair facing the man. He hadn't brought his briefcase, or anything to write on. He didn't intend to take this job. Curiosity had brought him here today—that, and the need to make sure this jerk was no longer a threat to his family.

"What did you want to talk about?" Jason leaned back, forcing himself to look casual, uncaring.

"I got business out in your neck of the woods." Pal slowly folded the newspaper. "I'm heading out there on Monday."

"I thought you were under house arrest."

The old man laughed—laughter that dissolved into a fit of coughing. "My attorney's taking care of that." He looked Jason in the eye. "I'll be dead long before they can lock me up. So, what's the point?"

He probably had a point, if the blue tinge to his skin was any indication. As a corporate attorney, Jason mainly worked on business deals, but oddly enough a lot of business deals resulted from deathbed promises.

"What kind of *business* are we discussing?"

"My demise. I'm adjusting parts of my will—"

"I'm not helping you screw your family more than you already have." Jason began to rise. He'd had enough of this man.

"Now sit your ass down, young man." Pal spat out. "I ain't gonna take anything away from either of my boys." Another coughing fit made Pal pause. "I'm talking about someone else." Oddly, Pal's eyes and voice grew faded and distant. "Somethin' I gotta make right 'fore I go."

Pal Haymaker had a smidgen of conscience? Not possible. "What are you talking about?"

The old man leaned back, spearing Jason with a glare. "I'll let you know when I get to LA."

"That's not much answer, old man." Jason sat on the edge of the chair, preparing to leave. He had a plane to catch.

"Not supposed to be." Pal leaned closer. "There's too many ears in this house."

Was Pal paranoid, or was there a grain of truth in what he was hinting at? He wouldn't put it past Pal Jr. to place a spy in his father's house.

"Here's the deal." Jason stood. "You get to town, get in touch with my assistant." He pulled a white utilitarian card out of his wallet, flicking it with a decisive snap onto the side table. "If you time it right, I'll meet with you." He headed to the door. "You've done enough damage to this world, so make this good."

He didn't wait for Pal to dismiss him. Walking out into the hot Texas morning, Jason took a deep breath, the fresh country air clearing his head of the stink of rotten old man.

"You learn anything?" Chet leaned against the truck's fender.

"No. He's as tight-lipped as usual. But Wyatt's right. He's up to something." They climbed into the sun-heated cab of the truck. "He's heading to LA next week. Wants to discuss the details then."

"How's he gonna do that? He can barely move." Chet drove toward Wyatt's place.

"I don't know."

"Wyatt won't like it that you're meeting him again."

"I don't recall being accountable to my brother, not since I turned eighteen." Jason met Chet's gaze, holding it until the older man looked away.

"It's your skin."

They turned into the yard of the ranch, which was a hive of activity. All the siblings were leaving today. Everyone was packing up their things, filling vehicles. Tara was taking Jason to the airport, so he hastily grabbed his bags and slung them in the back of her car.

"What did Pal want?" Wyatt asked, coming around the front of Addie's truck.

"He wasn't specific, unfortunately."

"So you're not going to work for him." It wasn't a question.

"Haven't decided yet. He said he's coming out to LA. We'll talk then."

"You cannot work for that man!" Addie's voice carried over the car's roof.

"Like hell," Wyatt barked in the same instant.

Jason's hackles rose. "Addie, Wyatt, back off." He slammed the trunk. "I'm not a child. He'll come to the office, I'll deal with him there. End of story."

"I don't trust him."

Jason laughed. "If you knew most of my clients, you wouldn't trust them, either." He thought of the business partners who inhabited the corner offices and the upper floors. Wasn't much trust there, either. They were as cold-blooded as Pal. He turned to face his older brother, purposefully changing the subject. "It's been a good visit. You tell the others your news?"

Wyatt shook his head. "Emily doesn't want to say anything yet. She's—"

"No problem." Jason smiled. "But you'd better tell them all at once. Word gets around in this family like wildfire."

"Yeah." Wyatt looked over at Emily, a smile tugging on his lips. Jason knew that look, that silent communication from when they'd been kids. "Hey, everyone."

Emily obviously knew her new husband, too. Her eyebrows lifted as she shrugged and smiled, walking toward Wyatt. "You want to? Now?" she whispered.

"Yeah." He wrapped an arm around her, pulling her against his side. "We have news." A gasp waved around the group gathered between the cars.

"We got married!" Emily practically burst with the words. Jason laughed. Neither one of them had really wanted to keep this secret. And he was relieved to find the attention focused elsewhere. Now he didn't have to explain his business with Pal.

This was a much better way to end this visit.

CHAPTER TWO

GROWING UP IN TEXAS, Jason's experience with dancing involved square dances, country bars and prom—oh, and those not-to-be-forgotten weddings. Since moving to LA, his horizons hadn't broadened much. Hours behind his desk, busting his ass to make partner, kept him busy.

Seated now in a private box at Glendale's Alex Theatre, watching the Los Angeles Ballet with Pal Haymaker, he felt strange. Jason glanced sideways at the old man. How the hell had they gotten here?

After he'd seen Pal that morning following DJ's wedding, Jason would have laid money down that the old guy wouldn't be able to make the trip. But that had been several days ago, and here he was. Cleaned up, in a custom-tailored suit, Pal looked every bit as out of place as Jason felt.

The lights dimmed, and the old guy pushed to the edge of his seat. The oxygen tubing rubbing against the arm of the wheelchair was loud in the silence that fell as the curtain rose. No one else seemed to notice, so Jason breathed a sigh of relief.

The music began, and a line of ballerinas came

on the stage. Jason leaned back in his seat, hoping to find something to enjoy about the event.

"There she is!" Haymaker said loudly and Jason cringed. The music, thankfully, mostly covered his voice.

"Who?" Jason asked.

"My daughter."

"Who?" It was a reaction more than a question. Jason stared at the man he'd known most of his life, a man who'd been Texas's biggest pain in the ass for years. He had a son, well into his fifties, and a grandson who'd run around with Jason's older brothers back in high school. Other than Mrs. Haymaker, there hadn't been any other women in that equation, unless you counted housekeepers.

"You didn't think I had it in me." Pal chuckled and dissolved into a fit of coughing. The nurse appeared out of the shadows with a cup of water and a little white pill. The old man waved her away and turned his rapt attention back to the performance.

"See her there?" He pointed toward the left side of the stage, his arm trembling. "The redhead, like her mama. Second from the end." More coughing. He took the pill.

Jason looked. All the women were dressed identically in white toe shoes, tights and leotards. White gauzy tutus circled each slim waistline. A white band of fabric scraped their hair away from their faces, and the only color difference between them was the thick coil of hair at the nape of their necks.

He saw a strawberry blonde. He'd never recognize her, or any of the other matching ballerinas, if they passed on the street.

"Next act," the old man wheezed. "Solo."

"Are you sure you're up to this?"

The old man didn't look good, but the glare Jason received was as strong as ever. Haymaker sat back, watching, waiting. For the woman he believed was his daughter.

As Pal struggled to breathe, Jason struggled with the ramifications. Pal had two heirs as far as anyone knew. His physical condition was quickly declining. The prognosis, according to the doctors, was not good.

The reason Jason was here with Pal tonight had apparently just appeared. On Monday, when Pal had shown up at Jason's office, he'd demanded Jason's attendance here tonight. Jason had agreed just to get the old man out of the office before he keeled over.

Pal wasn't one to leave anything undone. A carryover from all those years on the Texas prairie, building the Double Diamond Ranch into one of the biggest operations in the country. Out on the range, unfinished work could mean life or death.

Pal quieted and, for a minute, Jason thought he'd fallen asleep. He hadn't though. His eyes were as alert as ever, drinking in every instant the young woman was on stage.

Just as he'd said, in the second act, she came out

into the spotlight alone. This time, she wore a black leotard, tights and toe shoes. No tutu, just a wispy, diaphanous skirt that formed to her hips. Her hair, though, was what caught Jason's gaze. Long light copper curls hung down to around her hips, swaying with every move.

Jason couldn't tear his eyes away from the sight. He knew that if he saw her on the street, he'd definitely recognize her, and probably stop and stare. She was stunning. The dance beautiful—flawless as far as he could tell.

Time stopped. Haymaker faded into the distance. Nothing existed except her beauty and perfection. Music wafted around him, slipping inside somehow. He felt his heart echo its rhythm. Beating. Stopping. Pounding.

The emotions of the story came to life. Anger and pain ripped across the stage and tumbled into an anguished heap in the center of the floor. A single light remained. She didn't move. He barely breathed.

Arms, a multitude of bare arms, reached out of the darkness and lifted her limp body. Her limbs dangled lifelessly as the darkness swallowed her whole.

Jason's eyes stung, and he shook his head to clear his mind of the image and emotions. He looked over at the old man. Tears trickled down his pale cheeks.

The audience shot to their feet. Jason could see

the old man wanted to, his legs trembling as he tried to scoot forward. Jason reached out and put a hand on the bony shoulder. "I'll do it for us both."

Jason stood and applauded hard and strong. She deserved the acclaim.

The rest of the performance flew by, but there were no more signs of her, and Jason felt disappointed. The old man settled back, nearly dozing off, as if he knew the show he'd come for was over.

With the lights on and the curtains down, Jason rose to his feet once again.

"Call the driver," Haymaker barked to the nurse.

Jason frowned. "Aren't you going to go see her?"

Haymaker spun the chair around with surprising speed. "Hell, no. She doesn't know I exist." The anger was more mask than real. "I didn't just invite you here for a show."

Jason had known that, but he'd learned years ago not to question a client until they were good and ready.

"Then I'm charging for my time."

Pal grinned. "I expect you to. Here." He pulled out an envelope from his jacket pocket. "Take care of this. Make sure it's all California legal. Dallas will courier the rest of the file when the time is right."

There was no address, nothing written on the outside of the envelope. Jason turned it over and found it unsealed. He pulled out the pages. There were only a few. One handwritten. The scrawl was messy. It was Haymaker's own hand. There was a birth certificate, with no father listed, and a detailed report from a private investigator. And a neatly folded copy of a will.

Haymaker had been shrewd, as usual. He'd made sure every *T* was crossed and every *I* dotted. Jason skimmed the report, then the letter and will. The old man was changing everything. The "boys" as he referred to Pal Jr. and Trey, got to keep the ranch, but every investment vehicle, and every other blasted thing Pal owned was to be put on the auction block the instant he died, the money divided three—not two—ways.

Except for a property in Northern California that, according to a separate report, had sat vacant for over twenty years. That was to be hers. And hers alone.

"Back in Texas, you said you weren't going to screw the boys."

Pal laughed, or what served as a laugh. "I don't owe you or anyone an explanation, but I'll tell you something, boy. My kin don't have a clue what the hell I have. So dividing it up this way is more than they expect." He looked away. "More than they deserve," he whispered.

By the time Jason looked up again, the nurse had wheeled the old man down the ramp to the exit. Jason knew a limousine would be waiting just on the other side of that door. He wanted to run down that ramp and catch the old man, to demand an answer to the question of "Are you crazy?"

But he knew Haymaker. There was nothing crazy about the old man. Nothing.

Jason glanced back at the empty stage. That girl down there had been beautiful, pure. Clueless. She had no idea she was about to become a very rich young woman.

And damn it. He did not want to be the one to tell her. Not like this.

Later that night, at midnight exactly, Jason stood in the hospital room's doorway. The call from the nurse who'd gone to the ballet with them had surprised Jason. He'd thought Pal was on his way back to Texas already.

"Get in here," the eldest Haymaker barked when he saw Jason.

With a fortifying breath, Jason stepped into the room. In between gasps for air from the oxygen mask, Pal tried to look intimidating. But he was just a sick, broken old man now.

Pal struggled to sit up straighter. It was a waste of time. He only started coughing and had to outwait his own body. Jason fought the urge to remind the man that paybacks were a bitch. Law school and two years in private practice had taught him well how to hold his tongue.

"You check it?" Pal demanded.

"Business can wait."

"Like hell it can."

"Before we get to this." Jason waved the papers Pal had given him earlier—that he'd barely had time to glance at much less read thoroughly. "Tell me what you really have in mind for her."

There was no way Jason was going to put this young woman at risk. Heck, just being Pal's child put her in danger. Pal Jr. and Trey would want to kill her. If Pal even intended to tell them the truth.

"That's none of your damned business," he bit out between gasps.

"Like hell it isn't. You hired me. You made it my business." Jason turned to leave. "Guess we're finished here."

A wheeze of hard-won breath filled the air. "You're nothing like your brother." Another breath. "He's a good, fair man."

"Yeah, we're nothing alike." Jason wasn't talking about Wyatt, and he knew the old man caught his meaning. "I have very little respect for you, and you have even less for me. That's part of why you had me do this job instead of your attorney in Dallas."

Cough. "Just get on with it." Pal waved at the papers. "She's safe."

Jason stood there for a long minute, the papers tight in his hand. "I'll hold you to that. Everything has to protect *her*. Not *you*."

Oddly, the old man relaxed. His eyes grew distant, almost sad. That wasn't possible—Pal Haymaker didn't have emotions.

"I know you hate me, boy," he whispered. "But

thirty years ago, I was a different man." He paused, trying to catch his breath. "You might have even liked me." He cleared his throat. "But that man died—" Breath. "With Lauren's mother."

Lauren. The name held strength, and the pretty ballerina came to mind. It fit her.

Jason watched as the old man's gaze turned to the window. Emotions flitted across his weathered face. And something inside Jason shifted. He cursed. He didn't want to care about this man. Or his daughter.

GLOOMY, CLOUDY DAYS like today were perfect for staying home. Last night's performance had been the last of the run and Lauren needed the break.

A book, the soft aroma of candles—the day was set. She settled on the yoga mat, tuning her body before letting it loose for the day.

Her electronic bracelet that was programmed to her phone, the doorbell and a couple other devices, flashed as she settled into her first position. Damn. She looked at the bright light. The doorbell. Who the heck was here? She wasn't expecting anyone. It flashed again. They didn't seem to be going away.

Jumping up, Lauren padded to the front door and peered through the sidelight. She stared at the unfamiliar man on her doorstep. His hair was damp, looking dark yet blond. His expensive suit was getting ruined by the rain and the wing tips on his feet were buried in a puddle.

He didn't look like a serial killer…but who knew? She stared at him for a long moment, then pulled open the door as far as the chain allowed. Odds were, he wouldn't be able to communicate with her, but she'd give him the benefit of the doubt.

Slowly, she signed "Hello." Keep it simple. His frown told her way too much. Why was she disappointed? The usual loneliness she felt suddenly seemed more pronounced. She saw his lips moving, and while she was proficient at reading lips, he wasn't looking directly at her, his head turning as if to recheck the address. And she wasn't familiar enough with his patterns to read him from the side.

She cringed. Very few times did she need, or desire, to speak, but this was one. As a child, her older foster brother, Kenny, had told her often enough that she sounded like a "moron" when she talked. She'd refused to learn to speak after that, and now it was her normal.

"I'm sorry." She made the sign she knew he wouldn't understand. "I'm deaf," she continued, making the sign out of habit.

The man pulled a business card from his jacket pocket, just as the rain intensified. She took the card, and with the next gust of wind, she let him come in out of the downpour. Granted, it was just the vestibule, but still, he was a stranger stepping into her home.

Fear made her stomach clench, but she didn't have a choice. The white utilitarian card had clout.

He was from the law firm of Joseph and Brown. Big names here. What did he want with her? Was someone in trouble?

Times like this, she hated her deafness. She knew he wouldn't understand her, and it was doubtful he'd take the time to help her understand him.

He nodded and again his lips moved. She wished he knew sign.

Lauren waved toward the couch, hoping he'd take off his soaked coat. When he pulled it off and left it on the coat tree in the hall she sighed in relief.

While her home wasn't fancy, it was hers, each piece of furniture hard-won and loved. He sat carefully on the edge of the couch and gently settled a soaked briefcase on the floor beside her coffee table.

She hoped whatever he was here for was important enough to destroy such an expensive case. He unzipped a compartment and pulled out a pen and legal pad.

Taking her own seat across from him, Lauren smiled the smile her foster mother had diligently taught her. The one that was acceptably mellow to hearing people, the one that gave the impression she was "normal." She hated it, but knew it worked.

She wanted to get this over with. She waited patiently as he wrote. Shorter messages were always better. Straight and to the point.

I'm Jason Hawkins, he'd written. She glanced again at the business card, noting his name in the lower corner this time. She looked up at him. He looked like a Jason. Then he smiled at her. Oh God, he felt sorry for her. Her stomach churned around the earlier clench.

She looked back at Jason, frowning, wishing he were different.

He handed her the notepad where she wrote her single question. "Why are you here?"

He nodded, smiling like he'd uncovered the answer to some great puzzle. That gave her a drop of hope. At least he hadn't dismissed her. He seemed willing to try.

The man's handwriting was atrocious. She sighed again. He would be here for ages. Finally, he finished and turned the page to her. He'd written direct sentences. Easy and quick.

She looked back at the page. Then at him, confused. Estate? Her father's estate. She didn't even know she had a father...well, she'd known someone had to be her father, but that was it.

Again, Jason reached into the sodden briefcase and this time he pulled out an envelope. He opened it and extended a copy of a last will and testament toward her. She frowned and shook her head. What was she supposed to do with this?

He stood and came to stand over her. The damp scent of his cologne, light and warm, wrapped around her. Despite the fact that he was practically soaking wet from the rain, warmth flowed off him. He flipped the document's pages until he reached the third page, and pointed to a paragraph in the middle.

She stared at the printed words. Then looked up at him. Then back at the page. This wasn't possible. No.

Now? She shot to her feet. *Now? I have a father?* Her fingers flew. She knew the attorney didn't understand—confusion blanketed his face. She should stop and breathe. Stop waving and crumpling the pages he'd given her. But she couldn't stop herself. The twenty-three years since losing her mother was too much hurt to fight.

A father. Money. A house. All the things she'd dreamed of since the day her mother died. The day the social worker had shown up and packed her tiny pink princess suitcase and taken her to that first foster home. Five years old and alone. Without anyone to love her.

Where was he *then*? She signed the question, knowing this man couldn't answer her.

Why would a total stranger leave her anything? Especially when they'd stayed out of her life apparently on purpose.

Jason hadn't moved. He stood so close. Their eyes met and neither of them looked away. She dropped the papers to the coffee table.

She let her fingers form the words and concepts trapped in her mind. If only he understood. If only—

"I don't want it," she signed. Then, when Jason

shook his head, she wrote it on the page, the pen gouging the paper. He continued to frown.

"What? Why?" She could read that response.

"Don't need it." The very idea scared her, angered her. "Give it to someone else." Her fingers flew quickly, and his brow remained furrowed. After a long minute, he grabbed the notepad and dug in his briefcase again. He handed her the paper and another business card after he'd scribbled some more.

"Come to my office," he'd written. "I'll get an interpreter to help."

He looked expectant.

Her hopes died. He was just doing his job, so why had she even hoped he'd try to understand her himself? Slowly, she nodded, took the card, and led him to the door. She grabbed his coat and handed it to him. He waved and forced a smile as he stepped back out into the pouring rain.

With the door finally closed behind him, Lauren slammed the dead bolt, knowing she had no intention of going to any office or ever seeing him again.

She was happy in her little world. She didn't need him or anyone else—especially a hearing person— reminding her of what was missing in that world.

CHAPTER THREE

LAUREN MOUNTED THE wide stone stairs, her steps quick and lively. Determined. Not because that's how she felt, but because Maxine was watching, she was sure of it, judging her posture, her form, and the tilt of her head. Lauren didn't want to disappoint her mentor. Or hear the inevitable lecture.

The wide double doors opened and Maxine's longtime butler, Hudson, stood there, a smile on his weathered face. The old man didn't know much sign, but over the years he'd learned to make the correct gestures for hello, goodbye and a few simple niceties. Today he greeted Lauren with a warm smile and led the way to the studio.

Maxine was already there, her slim, perfectly upright frame poised at the barre. At seventy-two years old, Maxine Nightingale, once a world-renowned ballerina, looked young and lithe. Only the lines on her face gave any hint of her true age.

Mirrors surrounded them while polished wood floors reflected almost as clearly. Maxine's lips and hands moved to speak. "There you are," she signed. "Time to work."

Her smile told Lauren they were listening to

Maxine's favorite. Lauren smiled in response. She knew the expectations, the moves, without having to think twice. Maxine didn't have to instruct her or gesture the routine the way she used to in class all those years ago.

Lauren left her things by the door and joined Maxine at the barre. Like images in the mirror, they moved together. Going through all the steps, matching poses, all the way through the entire first movement of the song. By the midpoint, Maxine was dancing with her eyes closed, getting lost in the sound while Lauren let herself relax and settle deep into the rhythm and her own thoughts. It felt wonderful. So freeing.

Finally, Maxine bowed, and the soft thump of the music vibrating the air stopped. Lauren took a deep breath and walked over to the small table in the corner by the narrow floor-to-ceiling windows. The sweet-scented towel made quick work of the sweat from her face and shoulders.

Hudson came in then as if on cue. No doubt he'd heard this same music for the past fifty years as Maxine's employee. He carried a tray of afternoon tea. The porcelain pot and matching cups were old, brought here from Germany by one of Maxine's husbands. Lauren wasn't sure which one. The scent of the tea and the sweet cakes wafted in the air as Hudson walked to the table.

Maxine reached over and gave Lauren a long

hug. Her fingers moved quickly, and Lauren smiled. "I've missed you, too," she signed back.

They each settled in their seats, just as they always did, as if months hadn't passed since Lauren had last been here. Hudson poured; then with a wave of her hand, Maxine dismissed him. He vanished, without a word or a sign.

Lauren sat back, waiting for the inquisition regarding her absence. Maxine wasn't one to beat around any bushes, but they both busied themselves with preparing their drinks. Finally, Maxine looked up, a frown on her brow.

Her aged hands were as graceful in sign as her body was on the stage. Her perfectly groomed nails and be-ringed fingers flashed in the room's ambient light. It also helped that Lauren had been reading Maxine's face and lips since childhood.

"So, where have you been?"

Lauren took a sip of tea and pretended to focus on settling the cup back in the fragile saucer, not meeting Maxine's eyes, not giving her a chance to read her. "Working." She focused on selecting a cake. "Working with *D-y-l-a-n*." She avoided Maxine's glare.

"That boy will be your downfall."

"No." They'd had a similar conversation many times before. Dylan was part of the reason Lauren had come here today. "He's good. One of the best." She waited a beat, then forced herself to catch her teacher's eye. "You took me on, didn't give up on me." The intensity of Lauren pointing her finger at Maxine then back at herself wasn't lost on the older woman.

Maxine fought the smile. Finally, she nodded. "You think he's that good?"

Lauren nodded. "I do." Neither of them moved for several long minutes. No fingers moving or flashing. Lips doing nothing beyond sipping the cooling tea. Finally, Maxine reached over and curled her fingers around Lauren's hand to get her attention. Their eyes met.

"All right. Let me see this prodigy of yours."

Lauren stared. Maxine was willing to give Dylan a chance? Maxine couldn't work with Dylan the way she had with her. Fifteen years ago, Maxine had been well past her prime as a performing ballerina, but she'd been one of the best teachers in the world. Lauren had been the troubled deaf girl Maxine had taken in as a foster child, a poor replacement for the son she'd lost to death the year before.

Even now, Lauren felt the weight of that role. She'd been angry, lost, and this regal woman had demanded so much. Had found the talent buried inside Lauren's silent world.

Did Dylan really have that same spark? Lauren thought she saw it, but Maxine had a sharper eye. An eye and knowledge that came from much more time on this earth, and experience.

"Really?" she signed.

Maxine nodded. "You've got me curious."

Lauren knew not to let the opportunity pass. "When?"

"Next week. Tuesday. I'll come to your studio."

Maxine's composure returned and the predictability of it took Lauren back. It was comforting, and she realized how much she'd missed Maxine. She'd been so edgy lately, and Maxine's controlled manner eased that edginess.

She admitted to herself that that was truly why she'd come here today. She'd needed reassurance. And Maxine did exactly that.

Jason Hawkins, the lawyer, with his papers and startling announcements, had turned her world upside down. The security Maxine had always given her wrapped comfortingly around her now. In her mind's eye, she saw Jason as he'd left her place. Plunging into the pouring rain, he'd seemed unconcerned that he was soon soaked to the bone as he climbed into the dark car parked across the street.

"What's going on?" Maxine asked, only with her lips and a frown this time.

Maxine knew her better than anyone else. Too well, perhaps. She'd spent endless hours coaxing the shy foster girl out of her self-imposed shell. That same intensity and focus, which characterized Maxine overall, paid off in that there was no hiding anything from the woman's eagle eye.

Lauren glanced at her satchel propped beside the door. The papers Jason had given her were inside, badly wrinkled and creased from all the times she'd pulled them out and read them.

She wanted to share the information with someone, needed to discuss it. Needed to—

Maxine's hand settled on Lauren's forearm and Lauren looked up. "What's the matter?" Maxine prompted. The concern in her foster mother's eyes was so deep. Lauren started to tell her.

But she held back.

While Maxine could help her, she would take over. Was Lauren ready for that?

"Is it the show?"

Lauren nodded, taking the reprieve Maxine inadvertently offered.

Maxine smiled and leaned back in her chair. Pulling her hand away, she signed as she spoke. "You'll do magnificent, like always. Last year was a huge success."

Lauren nodded, though still anxious about how this year would go. The annual fundraiser brought in the biggest chunk of the studio's budget, after tuition. "There's so much to do."

Maxine tilted her head, an eyebrow lifted. "You don't have to do this—"

Lauren was already shaking her head. They'd had this conversation a dozen times since Lauren had opened the studio. "I know," Lauren signed. Looking around at the sumptuous surroundings of Maxine's home, Lauren knew what Maxine meant.

Maxine had been on the stage as a child prodigy of ballet by five years old. Her toes had graced every great stage in the world. She'd earned more money than she could ever begin to spend.

She had offered to fund the studio for Lauren. An offer that tempted Lauren frequently, especially when the bills came. She made good money, just not enough to support a business *and* herself.

But if she accepted Maxine's offer, her mentor would make a change here, a change there. She'd buy something new just because she felt it was necessary, something Lauren might not want. Lauren would lose control.

"Thanks, but I like doing the show." And she did. Last year it had raised enough money for them to order half the new costumes and replace the stage curtains. "I want to do a good job."

"The offer is always there."

"I know and I appreciate it."

The stillness stretched out. Maxine sat looking at her. "You're not telling me everything." She crossed her arms and met Lauren's gaze with the piercing glare Lauren knew well.

Getting slowly to her feet, Lauren walked over to her bag and pulled out the papers, giving in to her need to share this with someone. Handing them to Maxine, she watched her eyes widen. "Your father?"

Lauren nodded, still not used to the idea.

"In Texas?" Lauren nodded. "Why now?" Lauren shrugged and the motion caught Maxine's attention.

"Oh, honey." She stood, setting the papers down on the table.

As if sensing Lauren's mood, Maxine stood and took two steps to reach her. She pulled Lauren to her feet, and enveloped her in the motherly hug Lauren had fought against for so long, but which she now savored.

Finally, Lauren pulled away. "Why didn't he find me when he was alive?" she signed slowly, not really wanting to admit her thoughts.

"You may never know." Maxine tapped the papers with her finger. "But he owes you. This is what you deserve."

Lauren wasn't so sure. She wasn't even sure what *this* was.

"I don't want it!" She shook her head to emphasize her point. Maxine frowned but wisely didn't say anything more. One third of an estate could be anything—or nothing. No sense getting her hopes up for nothing.

An hour later, Lauren headed home. Coming out of Maxine's house, she paused at the top of the hill, waiting for the cab to wind its way up the long driveway, and looked out over the city.

Maxine's parents had built this place, back when LA was a much smaller city, when the town hadn't yet reached these hills. The other homes around were smaller, newer, not nearly as interesting as this place. Lauren remembered when social services had first brought her here. She'd been so scared.

This was so far beyond anything she'd experienced. While she'd never thought of it as home, she was comfortable here.

She'd always been safe here.

The headlights of the cab cut through the growing night. She'd learned long ago to carry business cards with her home address on them. If she wasn't going to drive, it wasn't fair to expect a total stranger to know sign language. The man smiled at her and as she handed him the card, she signed hello, knowing he'd realize she was deaf. He glanced at the card and nodded.

They drove down the hill, the lights of the house blazing in her wake, the lights of the city reaching out and flashing over them as they moved.

He stopped at her door and she paid him. Her little condo was dark. She hadn't left any lights on, not expecting to stay so long at Maxine's. She laughed. Who was she kidding? There was no such thing as a short visit with Maxine.

Still, when she entered the small foyer and flipped the light switch, she smiled. This was hers. *Her* place. *Her* home. She'd worked so hard to afford it.

Putting her bag down, she saw the corner of the envelope. Had she done the right thing in telling Maxine? The doubts still lingered—about everything.

She stared at the envelope, suddenly curious about the two people who were listed to split the estate with her. She hastily pulled the pages out again. Palace Haymaker Jr., Palace A. Haymaker III—or Trey, as he was called. Why hadn't it dawned on her before? A brother. A nephew.

Racing into the other room, she booted up her computer, wondering, hoping. Her fingers froze on the keys. Was this right? For so long she'd kept to herself. As a child, she couldn't communicate with others, so they'd never asked questions. And neither had she. But…she'd never wanted to know so badly before.

She opened the browser. And typed in Palace Haymaker. Her finger hovered over the enter button for a long time. Then with a deep breath, she stabbed it, and watched the little hourglass spin.

Several notations filled the screen. An obituary? She swallowed. She wasn't ready for that yet. She scrolled down. The Cattle Baron's Ball in Dallas? *Oh. Wow.* She clicked the link and watched as pages of images flashed on the screen. Cowboy hats and big hair characterized them all.

Hungrily, her eyes scanned the page, skimming the captions. None of the faces, none of the names familiar. And then she saw it. *Pal Haymaker and his son, Pal Jr. enjoy the music and drink.*

The two men looked so much alike. Two big men, gray Stetsons on their heads. Neither of them smiled, looking at the photographer as if they were doing him a favor. Her father. Her brother. She stared, hoping to find some resemblance to herself. The hats made it difficult to see what color their hair was, and she assumed the cut was short. She remembered her mother having bright copper hair, the same color Lauren'd had as a child. The color that had faded as she'd grown up.

Maybe in the eyes? Leaning closer to the screen, she couldn't tell what color they were. Her frustration grew. She needed something to prove this was real.

She typed Trey Haymaker into the search box. Another smattering of pictures appeared. Another reference to the Dallas ball. This time, a young man's face stared back at her, smiling under a too-long mop of bright blond hair. She gasped. He looked too much like the face she saw in the mirror each day.

His eyes shone bright, blue and light. He looked like the opposite of the other, austere faces. He looked happy.

Maybe…maybe…this was real.

She swallowed, and before she could stop herself, she saved both images to the hard drive.

They were the only pictures she had of anyone related to her by blood. Her only family photos.

She turned off the computer, not wanting to look anymore. A faded image filled her mind as she climbed the stairs to her room. Her mother's picture, the only one she'd had, captured in a cheap fake-brass frame, had vanished in one of the many moves between foster homes.

Her mother's image had faded in Lauren's mind with time. The wispy memories were vague now. She wished the internet could find her mother, but Rachel Ramsey had vanished long before there was an internet to capture pictures, words, lives.

She'd made it halfway up the stairs when her phone vibrated in her pocket. Who was calling so late? Her heart hammered in her chest as she pulled up the screen.

Dylan Bishop. His words appeared and she froze. I'm in jail. Help me. An address she recognized as the courthouse flashed on a second message.

Her heart sank and she turned back around, hurrying down the stairs. What had happened? Her mind filled with images of the boy, in a cell, no one understanding his sign, no one bothering to realize he was deaf. She took a deep breath and texted for a cab.

Please, please hurry. She had to purposefully stop her fingers from moving in the flow of the words.

The bright yellow cab pulled up, and she hastily ran to greet it, leaving her quiet home and newfound images behind. She had no time for herself. Dylan and his sister, Tina, needed her. That was more important.

JASON STARED AT the computer screen. For once, he understood what all of his clients meant when they referred to legal gobbledygook. The pages on the screen looked like that to him right now.

His concentration was off. It had been for days, ever since visiting Lauren Ramsey. Foolishly, he'd believed that Haymaker had given him full disclosure. Standing there in the rain, he'd felt like an idiot as she'd tried to explain her situation using sign language.

Vague memories of having to learn the finger alphabet in something like fourth grade nagged at him. Fat lot of good that had done him. He couldn't remember a damned thing.

In anticipation of her coming in to the office, he'd found a sign language interpreting service. Their number was on a sticky note on the frame of his monitor. He'd also gotten online and downloaded a copy of that long-forgotten alphabet.

He'd tried to make his fingers remember even simple letters. He had the skill level of a three-year-old, and for a lawyer who thought he had a fairly quick mind, who prided himself on his communication skills, that was very…daunting.

But she hadn't come in, called or emailed. Nothing. He'd wrestled with the decision of whether to contact her again. He wouldn't normally, but then he didn't normally go to people's homes, either. He'd done that at Pal's request.

He stared at the folder on his desk. He'd give it to his assistant, Susan. Have her send a follow-up note to Lauren and call the Dallas firm for the rest of the info. Decision made, he forced himself to turn back to the computer and the briefs he needed to finish.

"I don't understand you." He heard Susan's voice come from outside his office. "I still don't understand you," she said a bit louder this time. Her response was the closest thing he'd ever heard to a frustrated growl from her. What the heck?

He stepped to the office door and leaned out. Shocked, he stared at Lauren who stood in front of Susan's desk, a tall, African American kid standing behind her. The boy's anger practically singed the room, but he just stood there. Glaring.

Jason watched, enthralled once again as Lauren's fingers and hands flew. He didn't understand any of it. She was too agitated, too fast for his meager skills.

Susan's voice broke through the haze of his mind as she practically yelled "I don't understand you." He had to save her and Lauren from this mess.

"Susan, it's okay." He put a hand on Susan's shoulder and smiled at her. It wasn't her fault. She just didn't know sign language and didn't have the skills to automatically recognize a hearing-impaired person. He hadn't the first time he'd met Lauren, either. The yelling wasn't appropriate, though.

"But, Mr. Hawkins, she doesn't have an appointment," Susan argued.

Jason looked over at Lauren and held up his hand, hoping she'd understand his makeshift sign for wait a minute. He didn't want her to leave.

"I know," he soothed Susan. "But I don't have any appointments this afternoon. I'll take this. Why don't you head over to the coffee shop next door? I'll buy." He handed her a couple of bills and hustled her out of the office. She frowned, looking at the kid and Lauren as if she needed to protect Jason.

Once Susan was gone, he turned back to Lauren and the boy. He didn't want Susan there for several reasons, the least of which was her yelling. He was reluctant to step out of his comfort zone and show anyone at the firm that he was trying to figure out sign language.

Facing Lauren, he very slowly forced his fingers to form the letters of her name. He didn't know any full words, and his mind scrambled wondering how to communicate with her. He pointed at himself and formed the letters o-f-f-i-c-e. He didn't know the sign for follow me, but he used the polite bow and wave toward his door.

He met her gaze and saw her eyes widen. Her face was so incredibly expressive. Surprise and pleasure bloomed over her features. He was so damned pleased with himself, he had to shake himself out of it. She made a sign in response that could have been anything from thank you to go to hell, for all he knew. She turned to the boy and pointed him toward the office. Jason breathed a deep sigh of relief.

Her fingers said so many things Jason couldn't

understand, and Jason quickly realized the boy was deaf as well.

Lauren frowned and grimaced, then changed her features so quickly. He saw now that her features were a part of the signing. Like a bell going off in his mind, some things became very clear. What he was seeing now weren't her emotions. Her body language was a part of her signing—her communication. She was talking with everything she had to the boy. She extended her arm and pointed again to the office. The frown she gave the boy reflected her displeasure with him.

Jason kept staring at her, fascinated. His heart picked up pace. Maybe he could learn how to do this.

He wasn't stupid enough to think it would be easy, or quick. He had to get through this meeting, and he couldn't conduct it all spelling out each word. Billing by the hour, he'd be the most expensive lawyer in history. He'd also drive himself nuts.

He knew from his initial call to the interpreter that they needed a minimum of an hour's notice. So what the heck was he going to do? He started hunting for a legal pad.

The computer he'd been so frustrated with earlier seemed to glow as it sat there. He smiled. Then, hurrying behind the desk, he waved Lauren and the boy into the two chairs facing him.

Jason didn't have to know sign to read this kid.

He did not want to sit or even be here, but for some reason, Lauren had dragged him down here.

Jason cleared the screen and pulled up a blank word processing document. He turned the monitor toward them and typed his first question. Hello, Lauren. What can I do for you today? God, it sounded so formal, but he wasn't good on the fly. He was better if he could analyze every word a zillion times.

Lauren looked at the boy and after he nodded, she reached for the keyboard. She typed, This is Dylan. He needs a lawyer or he's going back to jail. Can you help us?

Whoa. That came out of left field. Jason took the keyboard back. Hello, Dylan. Nice to meet you. I don't think I can help. I'm not that kind of lawyer.

She read and frowned. We don't know any other lawyers. Please?

The look on her face, thick with pleading was his downfall.

I can try. That's all I can promise. Tell me what happened. Maybe if he got the info, he could point them in the right direction.

Did he really want to get involved? When Jason looked at Lauren, the worry on her face answered him. There was no turning back.

She didn't take the keyboard this time, but pushed it toward the boy and crossed her arms. Waiting. Glaring. The boy glared back. Lauren uncrossed her arms and started to sign. Jason caught only a letter here and there. But he read her emotions.

Anger. Pain. Worry.

The boy was nearly as stubborn. He didn't move. Until she slowly shook her head and spelled a word. Jason stared, concentrating on her fingers, catching only a few letters.

But whatever she'd said, it got through to the boy. His face fell and he reached for the keyboard. Reluctantly he started typing.

Jason leaned back in his chair, waiting, watching both the boy and Lauren.

There was no self-satisfied smirk on her face, but the look in her eyes was a whole different matter. She was good. She'd played the kid—and him—well.

CHAPTER FOUR

THE BOY KEPT typing and Jason sat back and let him. Even if Dylan was spewing anger, it would give Jason a sense of the situation.

It also gave Jason the opportunity to take a minute to study Lauren.

Now that he'd gotten over that initial shock of not being able to communicate with her, Jason was even more impressed and intrigued by her.

He didn't stare openly at her—he did it out of the corner of his eye. The ballerina he'd seen on that stage wasn't here today. And though the woman before him was equally as beautiful, she wasn't as intimidating and awe-inspiring. More human. Approachable.

Lauren had her hair pulled back into a high, flowing ponytail. The style accentuated her smooth features and the long curve of her neck. She was sitting back as well, waiting and watching the boy.

Finally, Dylan leaned back, pushing the monitor just enough to turn it toward Lauren, not Jason—sending quite the attitudinal message.

When Lauren went to turn the monitor toward Jason, he shook his head and stood, walking around the desk to stand behind her so they could read it together.

The boy had typed more than Jason had expected. Several paragraphs filled the screen. After moving the mouse over to where she could reach it and indicating she should take control, Jason started to read.

There was no opening. All the sentences were direct. Short. He'd followed someone named Tina. Jason pointed at the name and frowned. He wished he knew the sign to ask a question.

"Who?" he asked in reflex.

Lauren, who had been looking at him, moved her lips into a very pretty near pucker, a silent imitation of the actual word. She drew the shape of a question mark in the air with a long slender finger.

"My sister," Dylan said in very halted speech. His words surprised Jason. He'd assumed he didn't speak either, like Lauren. He wondered why he hadn't spoken earlier. Jason noticed Dylan's hands moved in unison with his words, as if the two were tied together.

Fascinated, Jason tore his gaze back to the screen. Lauren turned as well. The autocorrect had made several words not make sense. Jason leaned closer, hoping to decipher them without having to ask.

Something sweet and soft wafted around him. The scent of Lauren's shampoo or perfume. He liked it. Liked it a lot. He had to shake his head in order to clear it and concentrate on the information.

Tina had snuck out of the house, despite their foster parents' warnings that they'd consider moving her if she did that again. Dylan had followed her, hoping to get her back home before they found out.

Unfortunately, she didn't want to go back, and was hoping to get kicked out. Dylan wasn't sure they'd end up together if that happened. She'd said she didn't care and that had made him angry. He'd grabbed her and tried to drag her home.

Unfortunately, a tall male dragging a kicking and screaming young girl down the street was a bit obvious. The cops had hauled them both in, not sure what was happening.

Jason pointed at Tina's name again. "How old is Tina?" he asked Lauren, who watched his lips closely, as he spoke. She nodded, but didn't immediately look away. And when she did, her gaze met his, holding for an instant. An instant that shot heat through him. He swallowed and tried to focus on the boy.

"Two years younger than me. Thirteen," Dylan answered in sign and speech.

Lauren's hands moved quickly, making the boy laugh. "Lauren says, going on thirty."

"Ah." Jason got the gist. A young, probably just blossoming, pretty girl if she had the same smooth features as her brother, wanting to taste freedom. Wanting out of a foster home.

Jason had read the whole report and still had several questions. He reached for the keyboard, and typed. "Where are your parents?" He hated asking, but it was part of the whole equation.

"Mom's dead." The boy's eyes shone for an instant, but he quickly recovered as if he'd learned to shut it off fast. "Dad's got another five years. Armed robbery."

Lovely. Jason wondered which had happened first. Another whiff of perfume made him glance over at Lauren. What she was thinking? He was usually good at reading people, but she was tough. Partially because there was a bit of playacting in her signing, an emphasis for the words' sake. Right now, she was frowning. And since her hands weren't moving, he was pretty sure that was her true displeasure.

"How do you know Lauren?" he typed.

"She's my teacher."

"Teacher?" After pulling back, he looked back and forth from Dylan to Lauren. "Ballet?"

Dylan nodded, and his face, which was much easier to read, glowed with defensiveness. Jason understood that. The kid had probably had to defend himself many times, to many people.

"Is he any good?" He pointed at Lauren after the words appeared on the screen. "Like you?"

She fought the smile, but not before he saw it.

She nodded and signed something. Dylan grinned. "She says I'm better."

Whether that was true or not, Jason couldn't miss the fondness in her eyes and the pride she let shine on the boy.

Lauren signed as Dylan nodded. "She wants to know if you're a patron of ballet. Have you seen her perform?"

"Once." Jason's gaze met hers and the wonder of that night returned. Time stretched out.

Needing a bit of distance from Lauren and the feeling she stirred, Jason paced around his desk and went to the windows to stare out at the hustle and bustle of the city far below. What the hell must it be like to live in foster care in LA?

He'd lost his father when he was young, but he'd had his mother, and older siblings who were *definitely* stand-in parents.

He couldn't imagine being practically alone in the world as a kid. In the reflection in the window, he saw Lauren and Dylan signing back and forth. For a second he felt excluded, which made him wince. He wondered how many times they'd felt like that on a day-to-day basis.

"Okay." He faced Lauren so she could read his words. Watching closely, he hoped he could tell if she understood. "I don't do criminal law." When she frowned, he lifted a hand. "I have colleagues here who do. Let me do some research." He pulled out a card and grabbed a pen. He wrote on the back.

Bring your foster parents with you. Come back and I'll help. He added his signature so they'd know it was legit.

He handed the card to the boy, which brought a smile to his young face. He nodded and made a gesture cupping his hand from his jaw to his chest. "Thank you," he said in accompaniment.

Then Jason faced Lauren. She was making the same gesture and smiling at Dylan. She signed quickly and Dylan answered, then faced Jason again. "She thinks my foster parents will be glad."

Jason lifted his hand and, for one last question, he used his rough finger spelling. "Tina?" He made the question mark in the air as he'd seen Lauren do earlier.

The boy's face fell. "She's mad at me. But she came home. Should she come?"

Jason slowly nodded, a look of what he hoped was resoluteness on his face. Lauren signed. "We'll try," Dylan said.

That's all he could ask. As they stood and turned to leave, Jason took a step and reached out to touch Lauren's arm. She looked back with a questioning frown. Jason tapped her file on the desk and held it up. "We need to discuss your inheritance."

She stared at the file. She put her hands together, then moved one forward in front of the other an inch or two.

"She says later," Dylan explained.

Lauren's hands moved quickly again, and Jason's frustration returned.

"What?" Jason asked.

Dylan's movements in sign were fluid, perfectly in sync with his words. "She says if you keep me out of jail, she'll consider it."

That was it? Even he could read the message in her body language—she wasn't asking him. She was telling.

Reluctantly, Jason nodded and tried to imitate her gesture for later, then slowly created *O-K*. He must have been close, because she smiled and the boy laughed.

Jason walked with them to the elevator, feeling strange not speaking the normal, polite conversation his mother had beat into his thick skull, but they seemed comfortable.

The metal doors whooshed open to reveal a startled Susan, a cup of coffee in one hand and cardboard cup holder with three paper cups nestled tightly in the other. "Oh." She stared at them.

"For us?" Dylan asked, his eyes bright.

"Hot chocolate for you, young man," Susan said, not bothering to notice they couldn't hear her. She pulled one cup out, skillfully not spilling anything, and handed it to the boy. She turned to Lauren with a frightened look on her face, as if she knew she'd screwed up earlier, but didn't know how to not do it again. With a tentative smile, she offered the coffees.

Not to be outdone, Lauren peered at the cups and chose one, making that same scooping gesture Jason now knew meant "thank you." She took a sip of the sweet drink, and Jason found his gaze glued to her slim throat as she swallowed.

Susan cleared her throat.

"Uh, yes. Thanks, Susan," Jason said.

Lauren and Dylan stepped into the elevator and waved as the doors closed. Jason fought the urge to jump in behind them.

He didn't say a word, simply grabbed the last coffee and headed back to his desk. He did *not* want to know what Susan was thinking.

"New client?" She sipped her own drink as she stood in the doorway.

"Uh, sort of. She's not new. The boy is."

"Uh, what kind of business does he own?"

Jason looked up at her, not appreciating the speculation sparking in the woman's eyes. "It's a different type of case."

"Really?"

He wasn't explaining himself, certainly not until he understood what the hell he'd gotten himself into. "Check out sign language classes for me, would you?"

She actually looked surprised. He glared at her, not liking what was most likely going through her head, though it was probably fairly accurate.

"And sign us both up." Jason sat down at his desk and rearranged the computer setup, trying and failing to put his world back to the way it had been before Lauren Ramsey had walked in.

THE ELEVATOR'S MOVEMENT was smooth, and, before Lauren knew it, they were down on the main floor in the shiny marble and chrome lobby. Dozens of people passed, coming and going. The revolving door never stopped.

Outside, the day was warm, the sky clear. She sipped her coffee, walking with Dylan toward the bus stop.

There was something different about that man, Jason Hawkins. Lauren couldn't quite put her finger on it, and the fact that she couldn't peg it, bothered her.

Growing up as she had, in foster care, in rough neighborhoods early on, she'd had to learn to read people. Even once she'd gone to live with Maxine, she'd maintained and honed that skill.

The rich were no less predatory than the poor. They just looked prettier doing it.

But Jason Hawkins wasn't like anyone she'd ever met before.

His office was high-end, chrome and glass, with polish written all over it. But back on the credenza, she'd spied a photo frame of over a half dozen people, all smiling, looking like family. His family.

Between the frame and his law school diploma

had sat a belt buckle. One of those big, shiny Western ones.

She'd wondered if it was his, or someone else's. And what was it for? It had caught her eye, and her curiosity.

She'd had the "joy" of meeting an endless stream of lawyers, judges and social workers in her childhood. Maybe as a kid she'd had a skewed view. But the few lawyers she'd come across as an adult hadn't changed her harsh impressions.

Until today.

Jason had paid attention to both her and Dylan. The fact that he'd figured out how to communicate effectively with them both surprised and pleased her. Everyone else used an interpreter or dismissed her.

He'd made her feel like she was just like everyone else.

She stopped, and Dylan, who'd been following her, nearly ran into her.

"What's up?" he asked, trying to ask and balance his drink.

She shook her head, not really able to explain. She glanced back at the building they'd just left and frowned.

Dylan tapped her arm and pointed to the street. The bus was coming. They had to hurry the last block or wait another hour for the next one. Dylan broke into a run and while she didn't join him, she did hasten her steps, as much to get away from her own confusing thoughts as to catch the bus.

AFTER LAUREN AND Dylan left, Jason stood at the windows behind his desk, staring at the street below. He shouldn't be able to make out individuals from up here, but he saw Lauren clearly. Her copper-gold hair bounced in the sun as she hurried behind Dylan toward the bus stop.

Jason frowned. Why was she riding the bus? One of the world's prima ballerinas who surely rode in limos and private jets on a regular basis, was catching the bus in downtown Los Angeles?

He watched until she disappeared inside the bus, and then continued to watch until the bus turned around the corner and vanished between the next street's skyscrapers. Shaking his head, he turned back to his desk. He had work to do.

"I'm heading home, boss." Susan spoke from the doorway and Jason looked up to see her standing there, her purse over her shoulder, jacket over her arm and a scowl on her face. He really wished she'd smile more.

"See you tomorrow." He lifted a hand and pretended he was focusing on the screen.

"You can't fool me," she said. "You're signed up for the sign language classes, by the way. They start on Thursday. 7:00 p.m. At the Y." She spun around, and he listened as the even tone of her heels echoed through the empty office.

"You'll be there, too, right?" he called after her.

"Yes," was her begrudging reply. "I had both registrations put on *your* credit card."

He heard the elevator's ding and the whoosh of the doors. Maybe when she stepped off the elevator she'd be in a better mood, maybe when she got home, she wouldn't be so grumpy.

The ringing of the phone a few minutes later startled him out of his thoughts. "Hello."

"Hey, little brother." Wyatt's voice boomed through the line, as if he were in the next room instead of Texas.

"Hey, yourself. Is everything okay?"

"Why does something have to be wrong for me to call you?"

"Because that's the only time you call." Despite the ribbing, he knew Wyatt would be grinning on the other end of the line.

"Yeah, well. I've been thinking."

"That's dangerous."

"Funny. I was thinking about your offer. Emily and I've been talking. We think we'll take you up on it."

"Offer?" He racked his brain. What offer? Oh, yeah. "To come visit?"

"Don't sound so shocked." Wyatt's laughter sounded good, comforting. "And don't worry, we aren't going to crash at your place. This is technically our honeymoon, you know."

Jason wasn't touching that one. "Yeah? So when are you planning on coming?"

"In a couple of weeks. Emily's got to clear her docket, and we're moving the last herd upstream. After that, we should be able to manage."

"How long you planning to stay?"

"Remember what Mom used to say?"

"No." Wyatt, being the eldest child, had had more time with Mom, more chances to learn about her.

"When they start asking how long you're staying, it's time to leave." Wyatt's laugh came again. "Four, five days at most."

Jason found himself nodding, looking forward to time with his brother and new sister-in-law—to picking Emily's brain about family law and the situation with Pal's will and Lauren.

None of his family had come out to LA to see him. Not in the two years he'd been here.

Partially because Jason had made plenty of trips home. When DJ was hurt, then again when he was planning to take off to find Tammie. More recently when his sister Mandy had baby Lucas, and again for DJ and Tammie's wedding. He hadn't really been away from them long enough to miss them—and vice versa.

So, why did LA feel so empty and lonely sometimes?

"Sounds great." Jason smiled at his own reflection in the window. "Let me know when you finalize your plans."

"Will do."

The office seemed too silent after he hung up. As always, Jason had tons of work to do, but none of it appealed to him right now. Except for the research he still had to do. Opening the browser, he punched in names and pulled up facts and faces. Lauren's publicity photo stared at him from an old news story about a dance studio opening.

Studio? He followed the link and leaned back in his chair as he scrolled through the beautiful, professional photos of her dance studio. The obviously posed photos of dancers sold the value of the place, touted her skill as a dancer and teacher. One face was predominant among the models. A tall, young man.

Dylan.

Jason smiled. Looked like he had a field trip ahead of him. He reminded himself this was research. Research for the case.

Just research.

CHAPTER FIVE

MAXINE DIDN'T OFTEN come to Lauren's studio. Lauren's pride and joy was in a part of town her foster mother disapproved of. But Maxine knew why Lauren had built it here, in this once beautiful, iconic theatre that now sat on the fringes of one of the poorest neighborhoods in Los Angeles.

"It's the only way to reach them," she'd told Maxine. "Them" being kids like Dylan and Tina—kids on the streets with talent that might otherwise go undiscovered and lost.

Much like Lauren would have been had Maxine not taken her in.

After hitting the play button on the state-of-the-art sound system, Lauren returned to her position in front of center stage. Maxine stood right beside her as Lauren lifted her arms to signal the beginning. Dylan appeared in center stage, a bright light washing over him.

The last two weeks of relentless practice had been worth it. Dylan did every single move Lauren asked of him, perfectly. She couldn't have been more proud. But the frown on Maxine's face made her breath catch. Lauren always struggled to read her when they were in the studio.

At home, in public, even backstage before a performance, Maxine was an open book. But here, like this—nothing.

Lauren finally couldn't stand it, her fingers flying to ask the question. "What do you think?"

Maxine paced, her eyes intense, her posture perfect. "Good," she spoke, absently signing at the same time. "Very good." She turned to Lauren so she didn't have to sign and Lauren could read her lips. "Maybe too good."

"No." Lauren knew a dodge when she saw one. This whole audition, her hopes of getting Maxine to take on Dylan, was as much about Maxine as it was the boy.

Maxine was retired from the stage, and more recently from teaching. She spent her days alone, with only her butler as company. The garden had never looked better—Maxine's other passion besides ballet.

At seventy-two Maxine was slowing down, and Lauren was worried.

Lauren wasn't ready to lose even one drop of time with the only person who'd cared about her after her mother's death. Maxine needed to stay active and involved.

Dylan was part of that plan. The fact that he could benefit from Maxine's guidance was just as important. Done with the routine, he grabbed a towel from his gym bag and joined them, the towel hooked around his shoulders.

"How'd I do?" he asked Lauren.

She pointed to Maxine. "Ask her."

He turned hopeful eyes to the older woman, and Lauren cringed when she saw his expression fall.

"You really want to dance ballet?" The older woman signed as she pinned Dylan with that laser-beam stare. That gave Lauren hope. Maxine was interested.

"Yes, ma'am, I do." His earnest desire covered his features.

Maxine walked slowly around him, looking him up and down. Assessing. "You know how hard it is?" The drama of her sign only added to the question. Her well-manicured fingers pointed at him, pointed right in his face.

Dylan nodded.

"You realize the ribbings you'll take? Boys your age don't do ballet—they—" She paused a moment to get her elderly fingers to spell the word. "*R-A-P*."

"That's a stereotype. Ma'am." Dylan jutted his chin up defiantly and Lauren held her breath. She kept her thoughts to herself. If Dylan and Maxine were going to work together, they had to iron out the particulars on their own. The shadow of a smile in Maxine's eyes was a good sign.

"You like girls or boys?" she asked, pushing another taboo button. Lauren wanted to crawl under the wood floor.

Dylan didn't flinch. "As friends, both." His fingers were harsh as they hit together in the signs. "Not gay, if that's your question. But so what if I was? It's not your business." His finger point to her was nearly as accusing as hers had been.

Maxine laughed, her smile broad. "Oh, yes. He'll do." She looked at Lauren. She returned to sign. "Well done, my dear." She nodded at them both as she turned toward the chair in the corner.

Once she'd settled, she looked at Dylan again. "Get some rest." The sign of her laying her head on her hands looked almost too soft with her intense stare. "We—" Her jewelry sparkled as her hand moved back and forth between them. "We are going to work hard. Starting tomorrow."

"Tomorrow?" Dylan looked surprised, but he held back the excitement.

Maxine nodded. "Be here." She pointed at the floor. "Four." She signed the number. "Right after school."

Dylan glanced at Lauren, his brow furrowed in question. "Attorney?"

"At two." She held up her fingers to match. "You'll be done in time."

"Four." Dylan made the same gesture as Maxine had and smiled.

The older woman nodded, then waved him away. "Go. Change. Rest."

Now it was Lauren's turn to face the inquisition. She waved at Dylan just before he disappeared through the door.

Maxine barely let her sit down. "What attorney?"

There was no sense lying. Lauren had to tell her, and now. If she found out later, there would be hell to pay, and Dylan would be the one paying. "He has a sister—"

"Is she deaf?"

Lauren watched Maxine make the familiar sign, and for an instant, it flashed through her mind that it was an odd one. Deaf, and yet she pointed at her ear and then her mouth. "No." Lauren shook her head. "She hears." Her own gesture, a spiral from the lips seemed just as odd. Backward almost.

"She dance?"

Lauren shook her head. Tina had refused all offers of classes, though Dylan had said she'd been keen on it until she was about six, which would have been about the time their father had gone to prison.

"Attorney?" Maxine prompted.

She explained the situation to Maxine, and the older woman rolled her eyes. "Youth." She shook her head as her hand bounced in the air at the height of a child's head. "I don't tolerate troublemakers."

Lauren remembered learning that lesson the hard way. The one and only time she'd rebelled against Maxine's authority had been her junior year in high school. And as punishment, Maxine had taken the lead in *The Nutcracker* away from her.

Maxine taught her that you don't just work to earn something—you continue working to keep it. They both lived by that rule.

After a short pause, Maxine leaned forward and met Lauren's gaze. "The police didn't know he was deaf, did they?" Maxine knew all of Lauren's fears.

Lauren slowly shook her head. The fear of being misunderstood and mistaken for insane, or drunk or high had haunted Lauren since childhood. She shuddered.

"Who is the attorney? Did you call Wakefield?" Maxine's attorney was as much friend as lawyer, but he was retired now. To be honest, there'd only been one attorney who had come to mind when she'd needed one.

Jason Hawkins. She forced herself not to smile. She felt the heat rise in her cheeks.

"Ah." Maxine's eyebrow rose and she laid a hand on Lauren's arm. "Someone else." Keen interest shone on Maxine's face.

Another eyebrow lifted. Lauren was surprised Maxine didn't ask any more questions. Maxine surprised her even more by pulling her hand back and preparing to leave.

They were at the front door before Maxine said anything else. Hudson was at the curb, standing in the awful LA heat in that ugly black uniform. He'd already opened the back door of the Cadillac.

Maxine stopped and met Lauren's gaze. She

didn't sign. "You know I love you as if you were my own."

Lauren nodded.

"If you ever, *ever* need anything, you know you can always come to me."

Lauren's eyes misted. "I know." She pointed at her heart, then her forehead, slowly, making the first part longer than the second, to emphasize the strong love that beat in her chest for this woman.

Did Maxine actually think she wouldn't turn to her if she needed her? Her last, and best, foster mother had been there so many times, Lauren had lost count.

Maybe she should have called Wakefield... No. She'd have only been doing it to please Maxine, which would have given her the opportunity to interfere.

Jason was the best choice. She didn't stop to analyze why she'd come to that conclusion.

On impulse, Lauren hugged Maxine hoping that somehow that told the woman how much she meant to her.

THE CLASSROOM IN the basement of The Y had to be fifty years old. Long tables were set up classroom style. Susan was already there, still wearing her business suit and pumps. He'd have to tell her that while this was technically on the clock, she could dress down.

Several other people were also present. An older

man, two teens and a young woman who stared at her phone. A middle-aged woman was at the front of the class, pulling books and papers out of a satchel.

Old habits died hard, and Jason snagged a chair in the back. He'd just settled when the teacher turned around and counted heads. Then she turned to the old-fashioned chalk board and wrote Anne Sidel on it. She pulled out a notebook and faced them.

"That's me," she said, a slight accent to her words. He frowned, finally noticing the hearing aids nestled in her ears. "I'm your teacher for this class. Let's take care of a little business before we get started."

From the list in her hand, she read names, waiting for a raised hand instead of the spoken responses. He felt like he was back in fourth grade but abided by her rules. He lifted his hand and spoke. She nodded and check marked on the page.

"Okay, let's discuss how I'll conduct this class." She walked around and sat against the front of her desk. "Tonight is free. We talk. I'll answer your questions and we'll go over a few things. After tonight, the class is silent. No speaking."

She waited for that bit of information to sink in, looking around and meeting every eye with a solid stare. Everyone nodded to her unspoken query. "Questions?"

The girl with the phone tentatively lifted her hand. "No talking. At all?"

"Nope. None."

"But what if we don't understand?"

"Finger spell. You'll have this week to practice."

"But what if I have to leave unexpectedly?"

"Again, we'll sign to each other."

"What if there's an emergency? Like there's a fire or something?"

The teacher struggled not to laugh, and Jason realized he liked her.

"You can tell us that. But let me ask you—does the deaf person you're learning to sign for have that luxury?" The girl stared. "This is the sign for fire." Anne raised her hands, waving her fingers.

The girl mimicked her. "Oh!" She grinned. "I'm signing."

Anne turned away briefly, hiding her smile. "I have information and a book for each of you. By next week, practice the alphabet. Here." She passed the packets to each of them. Jason smiled. He already knew the alphabet. Well, part of it anyway. He just wasn't very good at it. Yet.

They talked, asking questions, and Anne showed them each the formation of the letters. He could do this.

After class Susan caught up with him. The speculative glint in her eyes was not good. "So, now are you going to explain to me who that woman in the office was?"

He wasn't escaping. "The Haymaker case? You filed it. That's the daughter."

"That's the daughter?" She stared. "Why didn't you give her the paperwork?"

He signed. "She doesn't want it." He headed toward the parking lot.

"She doesn't have a choice, does she?"

That's what Jason needed to figure out.

THE NEXT AFTERNOON, Lauren and Dylan were ushered into a conference room at Jason's office by the young woman who'd sat at the front desk. Dylan was obviously excited about his training later that day with Maxine, but Lauren could see the fatigue around his eyes. Had he slept at all last night? Was it anticipation, or chasing after Tina, again?

She almost asked him as they were led into the chrome-and-glass conference room, but held back when she saw a woman was already there. The middle-aged woman smiled at them as she introduced herself in sign. Anne Sidel. She was an interprcter and would help with the meeting.

Part of Lauren was disappointed that yet another person would be there to hear Dylan's story. But she also felt relieved that Jason considered it important enough to get it right. Even though Dylan could speak, his interpreting for her, and trying to get the details right, could be too much. And this was too important.

Jason came in just then, a smile for them both

as he held the door for someone behind him. His secretary, Susan, who'd brought the coffee on their first visit, led Will and Rhonda Hancock inside. They were Dylan's foster parents. Blue-collar and middle class, they were a harried couple. Lauren liked them, but hadn't quite figured out where Tina and Dylan fit in their busy lives. Both adults worked full-time jobs, often more than forty hours a week.

Where did their own three kids even fit in?

Tina shuffled along behind them. Lauren frowned. The young girl with her tight ponytails and demure white sweater was not the budding young woman Dylan had described in his story. In fact, Lauren had never seen her look like this before.

Lauren looked over at Jason with a puzzled frown. What were they trying to pull? Why the masquerade?

Before she could say anything, another woman came in. Lauren stared. She was everything Lauren was not. Tall, curvy and a brunette.

She wore a fashionable, close-cut business suit that conveyed a whole lot more than business. With her long legs and a cap of thick sable hair, she was a commanding presence.

Jason greeted her warmly, holding her arm after they'd greeted each other with a business handshake. He guided her around to face them.

Chloe Devries introduced herself, speaking

clearly, but not slowly or demeaningly. Anne provided the sign introduction.

Lauren had to look away to see the interpreter's hands, but Chloe's image was burned in her mind. Lauren was often around beautiful women in the ballet, but this one wasn't just beautiful—she was smart, too. Lauren fought the sense of inadequacy trying to settle over her.

Chloe was a partner in the firm. Her name was actually stenciled in gold on the massive glass doors. Lauren remembered seeing it the first time they'd come here. She was going to help Jason with this case?

Chloe stepped toward Lauren, causing Lauren to have to tilt her head back. She didn't often feel small. Petite yes, but this was different. The woman exuded intimidation.

"I've seen you perform. Magnificent. It's such a joy to meet you." Chloe smiled warmly as she shook Lauren's hand and Lauren relaxed a little.

"Thank you," she signed, hoping to diminish her celebrity status. This was about Dylan.

"Your work with underprivileged kids is almost as lovely."

Lauren blushed, not wanting that part of her life to be so public. That wasn't why she did it. It didn't help that Jason tilted his head in question, curious now.

Anne interpreted, but Lauren chose to focus on Chloe's face. She caught most of her words, and while she could tell the woman wasn't being fully open, something she doubted Chloe ever was, she was glad to have Chloe on their side.

Lauren took her seat and everyone settled around the massive glass table. Chloe took control at one end. Lauren and Dylan sat across from the interpreter, and the Hancocks sat at the other end, Tina close at Rhonda's elbow.

Jason settled next to Lauren. Though she'd caught a strong whiff of floral perfume when Chloe had walked in, Lauren was surprised when the subtle cologne Jason wore cut through it. Strong. Sharp.

Forcing herself to mentally step back, she focused instead on the rest of the room.

Both Jason and Chloe had legal pads in front of them. Lauren wished she'd thought to bring paper to make notes. It always helped her focus and remember questions she wanted to ask later. It also gave her the ability to communicate independently, if need be.

The question about Tina's appearance came to mind and she signed to ask to borrow some paper and a pen. Jason quickly complied, tearing off a couple of sheets and sliding them and a pen across the table to her.

She reached for it, her hand brushing his. She froze as the sensation of his skin touching hers seeped over her nerves. Warm. Solid. Her gaze couldn't move away any more than her hand could. His hands were big, and for an attorney, oddly scarred. Not damaged—just showing evidence of use beyond shuffling paperwork.

Looking up, she met his gaze, and for a long minute held it. His eyes were green, with flecks of brown scattered in the iris. A pretty combination, though she doubted he'd appreciate the compliment.

"Let's get started." The interpreter sat forward as Chloe's lips moved.

Dylan was just as focused as Lauren on the interpreter. Lauren answered in sign, with Anne speaking her responses as Chloe asked for introductions. Anne explained how Lauren was Dylan's ballet teacher, a good friend, and that he'd contacted her when he'd first gotten into trouble, knowing she'd understand the challenge of his deafness in the legal system.

Dylan spoke for himself, signing at the same time and confirming his wish to have Lauren present.

Body language was a part of sign language. Frowns for negative or intense words. Smiles for happy inviting words. Head tilts also had meaning. But with an interpreter, it was an artificial emotion.

Lauren found it too easy to lose the meaning of the speaker without the correct body language. She tried to glance at the others as they spoke, to read them, but then she missed words. Her frustration grew.

Dylan told his story, which thankfully she already knew. When he talked, he faced Lauren and signed to her so she could see his face and body as he spoke. The others could hear him.

When it was her turn, Tina made no attempt to sign at all, though she was fluent in ASL, having grown up with Dylan. Lauren could tell it disappointed Dylan, and she lifted a hand to ask her why she didn't.

"I'm not deaf." Tina lifted her chin.

Ah, there's the girl we all know and love.

"I don't have to," she spat out the words.

"It makes it easier for Dylan," Lauren signed and saw Anne's lips move to repeat.

Tina shrugged and continued to talk without sign. Luckily, Lauren knew Tina, so reading her lips was easier. Dylan's disappointment took up space in the room, and he chose to watch the interpreter instead of reading his sister's lips.

Lauren put a hand on Dylan's arm beneath the table. He nodded, nearly imperceptibly, thanking her before moving his arm away.

TINA WAS A BRAT. Jason watched the inhabitants of the room as she talked. He saw Lauren's indecision as her gaze flitted from the interpreter, then to the girl and finally to Dylan. The foster parents kept sharing glances of approval, then a flash of fear at Tina's defiance.

"I don't know why Dylan came and got me that night." Tina met Chloe's gaze with a glare. "You'll have to ask him."

Chloe didn't miss a beat. "I've already heard his story. Let's try this again." She pulled out a copy of the police report.

Jason watched her closely. This female shark in the beautiful suit homed in on the girl's attitude. He admired Chloe's skill, but she scared the crap out of him.

"Tell me where you were when Dylan showed up."

"At the park."

"Who were you with?"

"My friends."

"Which friends?"

This was like pulling teeth. Jason wanted to push Tina on her behavior, but he held his tongue, waiting for Chloe's next move. This was her case now, and she knew how to handle it.

"Just friends."

"Can you give us their names?"

The girl just glared.

"Okay. No problem." Chloe wrote on the notepad in front of her for a long minute. "We'll just have the court locate them." She met Tina's stare. "I'd probably be prepared if I were you."

"What for?"

"The backlash when your friends are picked up in a squad car at their homes. Their names are in this report. I'm simply confirming them. I'm not sure they'll be thrilled at having you for a friend after this."

Scare tactics worked great on kids. Jason remembered his mother being quite adept at wielding that particular tool. He almost laughed as Tina started naming names and Chloe checked them off the list. But she only gave the girls' names.

"And the boys?" Chloe sat with pen poised over the list.

"Boys?" Rhonda Hancock gasped.

Tina swallowed. She reluctantly gave the boys' names, too. They'd get a statement from each one of them. Hopefully they would confirm Dylan's version of the truth.

Now that the battle was nearly over, Jason turned his attention to Lauren. She was tense, her shoulders tight.

He'd scooted over next to her after handing her the paper. This way he was directly across from Anne, hoping to learn more about reading sign, as well as see things from Lauren's view.

It was nuts trying to focus on the woman's hands *and* the person talking. At least he could hear the words. What the hell did Lauren do?

He tried and finally gave up. He'd need to learn a lot more sign. He'd missed half the conversation.

An hour later, they wound things up. Anne breathed a sigh as she flexed her fingers in an absent-minded exercise.

"Thank you," he said to her and smiled.

"You're welcome." She continued to sign, though he couldn't tell if it was to be polite to Dylan and

Lauren, or habit. She and Lauren headed to the door, their hands engaged in what he assumed was the small talk that Jason normally exchanged as he escorted clients out. It was strange to watch, and not participate.

The room quickly cleared. The Hancocks ushered both Dylan and Tina out, as if they couldn't leave fast enough. Jason's radar went up. Something wasn't right there, but he couldn't tell if it was just their unhappiness with the trouble both kids were in, or if there was something deeper. He'd talk to Chloe about it later.

Or maybe he should ask Lauren now. Hastily, he moved to catch the women before they climbed into the elevator.

"Lauren." He called her name as he slowly spelled it. Anne tapped her on the shoulder and pointed at him. Lauren turned around. Her hair swung against her shoulders, and the smile that brightened her face was stronger than anyone else's. He didn't understand, but let himself enjoy it.

"Can I ask you a few questions?"

Lauren nodded.

"Do you want me to stay?" Anne asked him, signing for Lauren.

"No." Jason waved her offer away. "If Lauren will come to my office, we can use the computer. It'll only take a couple of minutes."

Lauren nodded, obviously remembering how they'd communicated before. Then she signed to

Dylan, "Meet you at the studio." The boy left with a thumbs-up sign.

"She says that's fine. She doesn't have to be back at the studio just yet."

The elevator arrived, and Anne disappeared inside. Jason extended his hand to indicate Lauren precede him. She'd been to his office before, so he didn't have to lead the way.

Once she sat down, Jason hesitated in the doorway. He always closed the office door for a meeting, but the room suddenly felt small, close... intimate. Slowly, he shut the door.

Shaking his head, Jason gathered his thoughts and settled beside her. He turned the monitor, pulled the keyboard forward then typed a simple question. How well do you know the Hancock family?

Lauren sat for a minute, a frown between her eyes. She began typing. They've been Dylan's foster family for about six months. I didn't know them before that.

He sat back and thought before typing. Do you think the kids are in a good place?

She didn't immediately respond. He liked that she gave it some thought. I think so. She hesitated in between typing. They live very busy lives. Tina is a handful.

He laughed. "I got that," he said aloud. Then went to type it.

She touched his arm and smiled. She typed, I read your lips.

"Can you do that?" He faced her. Of course, she could read lips. He should at least try to make it easier for her.

With her hand, she made the nodding gesture, then typed. Yes, if you face me, it's easier. Once I get to know you and your speech patterns better, I'm pretty good at understanding.

He nodded. "I am still lousy at understanding you," he admitted.

She smiled. Keep practicing. She typed it, then made the sign, rubbing her fist back and forth along the side of her index finger on her flattened hand.

Jason copied her gesture. "That means practice, right?"

She nodded, and for the first time, he realized he understood her. Without writing it down on paper or typing it or having someone else interpret. He understood her. It was a beginning.

Their eyes met. And held. So much was going on behind those pretty eyes, in her bright mind. Suddenly, he wanted to ask her a million questions and get to know the woman sitting beside him.

He turned back to the screen. Typing was still easier for them both. I got some strange vibes where Tina was concerned. Is she normally that reserved and quiet?

Lauren barely paused. No. She rummaged around in her purse for her phone, sliding her fingers quickly over the screen. Finally, she turned the bright blue phone to face him. The image of a young girl, her shirt open well past appropriate, wearing a very short skirt, with another group of kids, filled the screen.

He cursed. That's what he was afraid of. "Can you send that picture to me?" If that was who Dylan had been dragging home, versus the prim and proper girl in the meeting, that could make a huge difference in his case.

Lauren nodded. He typed his phone number and heard his phone beep, indicating he'd received the text. He confirmed it and smiled at her. "Thank you." He said it and made the gesture.

She smiled back, and once again their gazes locked. He couldn't look away. She was amazing and beautiful and... A client. Of sorts.

Clearing his throat, he turned back to the screen. It was a safer, less intimate means of communication. If there's something— Bad? Abusive? He settled for odd going on, would Dylan tell you?

She paused to think, slowly reaching over to type. Their fingers bumped.

I think so.
Could you let me know if he does?

She didn't nod as quickly this time.

It could make a difference in his case.
Okay.

She was so close, her fingers still poised over the keys. The scent of her, soft and sweet, wrapped around him and he leaned closer, aching to be a part of her inner circle.

Hastily, Lauren shot to her feet. She fumbled to catch her purse, shoving the strap up on to her shoulder. She spelled *g-o* and pointed at the door. She walked quickly, pulling it open before he could even reach for it. She hurried to the elevator, waving vaguely, before stepping inside.

There was something in her eyes that confused him.

And concerned him.

CHAPTER SIX

LAUREN'S HEART POUNDED hard against her ribs. Sweat drenched her skin, and she leaned against the wall of the elevator. The cool metal felt blessedly good as the car descended. She had to catch her breath before she reached the lobby, had to get control of herself. She had to meet Dylan and Maxine in—she glanced at her watch—just over an hour.

She needed to get it together.

Jason was probably shaking his head, thinking she'd lost her mind. He'd been kind, and he was working so hard to understand her. The conversation they'd had was simple, mainly because it took too long to write anything complex.

The dawning comprehension in Jason's eyes when he'd understood her sign, the broad smile that transformed his face, had triggered too many memories. Her heart had hitched as he'd met her gaze. She'd nearly gotten lost in the hazel brightness.

But ugly memories obliterated his image, reminding her of the pain that came with letting people in too close.

The last time she'd let herself believe that she was someone to be interested in...

Kenny had been in foster care with her. She'd thought of him as a friend, hoped for that anyway. She'd been about the same age as Tina was now. Kids didn't need to talk as much as adults did. She'd hoped he was different, right up until he'd pushed her against the school yard fence.

She'd run then, too. Run for everything she was worth. Escaped his painful grip. She hadn't heard any of the foul things he'd suggested they do, but she'd seen them form on his lips. The lips that had come too close to hers.

She'd run until she couldn't run anymore. Blocks and blocks away from the school, in the opposite direction of her foster home. She didn't stop until the sharp, painful stitch in her side made her. She hadn't even known where she was. Darkness was falling, much like the afternoon shadows now. She shivered, remembering how she'd kept walking until she found an open grocery store. She'd gone inside and the manager had called the police.

One of the few pluses of being a kid in foster care was that she was in the system. She already had a file.

They'd taken her back to her foster home, and she'd tried to pretend nothing had happened, but Kenny's behavior had turned awful. Teasing. Tormenting. Demeaning. "Sound like a dummy... you're a moron who can't talk right..."

Her caseworker finally picked up on the bullying and had her moved. Any place was better than that place.

Almost. That's when she'd stopped trying to talk, refused speech therapy. Ultimately, she'd been placed with Maxine. But the damage was done and the half dozen in-betweens still hurt too much to think about.

Jason's suspicions about the Hancocks couldn't be correct, could they? If there was something wrong, Dylan would have said something, wouldn't he? She was positive of it. She wouldn't let another foster kid suffer, especially one who couldn't necessarily spcak up for himself. No one was going to go through what she had. No one.

This time, as she left Jason's office, instead of waiting for the bus, she went over to the doorman and wrote a note asking him to help her get a taxi.

She couldn't wait a half hour for the bus. Not when the memories lurked, waiting to pounce. She stood at the lobby's glass wall, in the bright light, watching for the yellow cab the doorman's note had told her was on its way.

JASON WANTED TO kick himself. What was it about Lauren that made him do things he wouldn't normally do? Going to her house. Taking a criminal case. Feeling an attraction to a client—amend that, *potential* client. He thought at first that he'd understood why she'd moved away from him just now, but her reaction was too strong. She really was upset. And while he couldn't be positive, he was pretty sure he'd seen fear in her eyes.

The idea that she had to be afraid of anything made his blood boil.

He was a Hawkins. He took pride in that. His younger brother, DJ, was a marine who'd been injured in Afghanistan. His older brother, Wyatt, had stepped up when Dad died, and still took care of them all, including DJ's son when DJ was hurt. His three sisters were no slackers, either, and were probably even more protective than he and his brothers combined.

Jason was no different—he just chose other means to protect people. Legally. But right now, he wasn't thinking very legal thoughts.

Someone had hurt Lauren. That type of reaction didn't come from anything else. The person who'd put that fear in Lauren's eyes needed a good old-fashioned taste of the Western justice he'd grown up with.

Except that would probably scare her just as much, if not more.

He reached the lobby in time to see Lauren climb into a cab that quickly pulled away. "Nick?" he asked the doorman who was behind the valet stand. "Did you call that cab for her?"

"Yes, sir."

At the other man's nod, Jason continued. "Did

she give an address of where she wanted the taxi to take her?"

Nick frowned. He pulled a small trash can out from under the desk. He plucked several pieces of crumpled paper out, opening the balls, tossing those he didn't want. Finally, he handed Jason a semiflattened piece of paper.

"Can I keep this?" Jason asked.

"I'm just gonna toss it back in here."

"Uh, yeah."

This wasn't a residential address.

Jason vaguely knew the neighborhood, and he wasn't pleased when he realized this was her studio. What had Chloe said about her working with underprivileged kids? Right, she had planned to meet Dylan here.

Jason headed back to his office. He finished up a few things as quickly as he could. An hour later, he shut everything down and headed to his car.

He needed to apologize. Jason hadn't meant to scare Lauren. He couldn't call her and texting seemed so…impersonal.

He drove through the streets, the streetlights flashing intermittently across the car. It didn't take long to reach the address.

The old theater, built with classic Art Deco styling, was beautiful. Elegantly restored, and lit, the facade looked as if a world premier were happening tonight. Too bad the rest of the street wasn't as bright. Shadows and broken streetlights were more the norm.

Jason parked across the street from the studio. The marquee splashed a white glow clear across the street, over him and his car. Where there would have been a show title on the white background in the old days, the black plastic letters announced Lauren Ramsey's Dance Studio.

The old ticket booth was shuttered, but the front doors, newly painted a bright red, were open when he turned the handle. He shook his head at the shoddy security as he stepped inside. The lobby was shadowed, the only light coming from the marquee outside. Farther down the wide hallway, squares of white light spilled out onto the carpeting. He headed that way.

THE STUDIO WAS EMPTY, the last student had been picked up, and Lauren had the place to herself. Peace slipped over her. She so needed this after today.

She went back to the locker room. Opening hers, she pulled out her toe shoes. These were her old practice ones. She stared at them a minute. Not tonight. She put them back—she needed something more. Lauren quickly changed into her favorite leotard, then headed to the booth that housed the sound system.

The components were old, and one of the next things she hoped to replace. But for now, this was familiar and she quickly found the music she wanted. As the song title scrolled on the display, she laughed. Yeah. This was perfect.

Somewhere in her early teens, she'd discovered that she could feel music if it were loud enough. She'd gone to a concert with hearing friends— not wanting to be the outsider, but knowing she wouldn't enjoy it. Until then, music hadn't been a part of her silent world.

Maxine would have killed her if she'd played this on her sound system at the mansion. But headphones and earbuds were worthless. Lauren needed the music to rattle her bones. So now, she cranked the volume. Through trial and error, she'd learned where the limit was to not blow the speakers. Counting, she knew exactly how much time she had to get out on the floor to be in sync with the music. She prided herself on that exactness.

She felt the beat inside. It throbbed in the air, through her feet, up along her spine, wrapping around her limbs, dragging her onto the dance floor. This was not ballet. It was wild and free, beat-driven. Rock. Hard and loud.

In the middle of the wood floor, she moved with the magic, letting her body follow the music's lead. This was heaven.

She watched herself in the mirrors that lined the walls. She spun, letting the lights morph in her eyes.

She couldn't remember the last time she'd felt

this free, felt this in tune with her body. So much of her time was spent in rehearsal, learning, re-learning routines and rhythms. Or in class with the kids where precision and discipline were required.

But this? This was something she'd never shared with anyone.

JASON STOOD IN the doorway of what looked like a rehearsal hall. He'd hoped to simply slip in and watch the tail end of a class, or catch Lauren as she left.

Halfway down the hall, he'd felt the beat of the music through the soles of his feet. He recognized it as something he'd blasted from his car stereo as he drove across the Texas hills back in high school.

She had the music up loud, probably as loud as the system would allow. Not like there was anyone in the old abandoned neighborhood to complain.

The smooth polished wood floor seemed to stretch endlessly from the doorway where he stood. One wall was all mirrors, with a wooden bar run-ning the entire length. Nothing else filled the room.

Nothing except Lauren.

Her eyes were closed, her head thrown back. Her wild copper tresses that she normally kept bound in the braid down her back had fallen loose. She wore a bright blue form-fitting leotard that clung to her every curve. Her legs and feet were bare.

Jason swallowed as he stood there and watched, enthralled with the magic before him.

The music hurt his ears, but it pounded in his chest in time with his accelerated heartbeat. She turned and ran across the room, leaping and landing, gyrating and bouncing on the balls of her feet. She was the human interpretation of the music he felt.

Her arms waved and cast about in the air…imploring what? The gods to come to her? The music to envelop her?

How did she do that? How did she let herself go and take that leap, landing so perfectly? He'd never admired anyone. He wasn't easily impressed. Today, just like the night Pal had taken him to Lauren's performance, Jason was speechless.

She turned then, her eyes meeting his. Her squeal of surprise startled him. She stumbled, and instead of catching herself, she let her body continue into a roll. Finally, momentum slowing, she settled, cross-legged on the floor. And glared at him.

Words formed in his mind, but none matched any of the signs he knew. Slowly, he made the gesture for "I'm sorry."

Lithe and limber, she rose to her feet and stalked to the back of the room. She grabbed a towel and wiped the sheen from her face and neck as she snapped off the stereo system. The ensuing silence fell thick and heavy. At least for him. He realized it was the norm for her and that bothered him.

She spun on her heel, signing quickly and heading into what looked like a locker room. He had no idea what she'd said.

For once, ignorance was bliss. He hung around. Slowly, he checked out the studio. On closer inspection, the polished floor showed signs of age and wear. The stereo system was imbedded in a back wall, and it, too, was old.

The mirrors lining the wall made the room appear twice its actual size. The wooden bar had nicks and scratches from years of use.

Lauren stepped out of the locker room and froze in the doorway. She was back in her jeans and blouse from earlier and had pulled her hair back in the familiar braid. With a frown on her face, Lauren looked him straight in the eye and lifted her chin.

Now what? They'd have to rely on her lip reading. How the hell was he going to understand her? He didn't know.

"I wanted to talk to you."

She frowned, then grabbed her phone from her purse. Seconds later, his phone vibrated and he took it out of his pocket.

What about? her text asked.

Earlier, he texted back.

About Dylan?

No. You. Me. I'm sorry for upsetting you.

She looked confused. With a sigh, she reached around the corner and turned off the locker room lights. She headed toward him, passing him and pausing at the studio's door. She focused on her phone. Don't worry about it. She waved him off and headed toward the door. I have a bus to catch.

She flipped the studio's light switch, leaving him in the dark. He hurried after her. The rest of the theater was dark, with only the light of the marquee falling in through the front windows to illuminate anything.

Did she normally stay this late? And always alone? Without locking the front door? The only way to know was to talk with her. And he couldn't type and chase after her. Damn it. How did people do this?

Jason watched her lock up the studio and walk down the shadowed street. She walked down this street—alone—at night?

"Laur—" He cursed. She couldn't hear him. She couldn't hear anything. Couldn't hear someone sneaking up on her... Any given psycho could just...

Worrying like this was so unlike him. He watched her walk away. She didn't have a clue how much she put herself at risk.

WHAT WAS JASON doing here? Lauren fought the trembling shock she'd felt when he'd still been there when she'd exited the locker room. She'd signed a very clear "goodbye." Surely he knew that sign.

She'd known it was rude, but she was used to being thought of that way. Maybe this time it would work in her favor.

He unnerved her. He didn't owe her any apology. Earlier in his office, for a brief instant, she'd thought he was going to lean in and kiss her. And she'd wanted him to. She was the one with the problems, not him.

She was so stupid. Why would he do something like that? Why would she even think he would… and why couldn't she stop thinking about it? All through the lesson with Maxine and into her class tonight, her painful memories, mingling with the desire to know Jason better, had become too much.

Finally, she'd let the kids work on their own, which had degenerated into utter chaos. They'd had fun, but they'd accomplished nothing. And she hadn't been able to find any peace in her own mind.

That's why she'd stayed to dance tonight. But now she had to hustle if she was going to make the last bus.

Sensing someone behind her, she spun around. Seeing him still here, she glared. Her fingers flew and she could tell by the confusion on his face that he couldn't keep up. She slowed down. "Stop" and "go away" were simple enough.

He shook his head, stopping barely a foot away from her. The shadows cloaked his lips, making reading them harder. He was slowly finger spelling. Carefully forming each letter, waiting for her to respond.

Frustrated, she reached out and grabbed his arm

and pulled him out into the light. Then rubbed her lips telling him to speak.

At the corner, she saw the lights of the bus slow, but not stop at the bench. She started to hurry, knowing the driver had no intention of stopping for her, even though he knew she rode the bus every Thursday. He stopped for no one. If you weren't right at the stop, he didn't even slow.

As the bus pulled away, she stamped her foot and spun around to glare at Jason again.

JASON DIDN'T NEED to know sign to read that look. He was not leaving her here, at night, to wait for the next bus. He couldn't say, much less sign his arguments. "No bus," he simply said and shook his head.

She pointed at the now empty street where the bus had disappeared. "*L-a-s-t* one," she spelled. Before Jason could begin to spell anything in answer, she continued. "You." She pointed at him. "Drive." Easy to understand as her hands were at the traditional ten-and-two position, moving back and forth. "Me." She pointed at herself, then made the shape of a house. "Home."

Relieved there wouldn't be an argument, he nodded and gestured toward the Lexus sitting across the street.

"You remember?" She pointed at her forehead.

"Your house?" He formed the shape of a house as she had. She nodded, but he couldn't tell if it was because she knew what he was trying to say, or if she'd read his lips. This was so confusing.

He nodded and once again pointed at his car.

Lauren paused, and with a deep breath, she surprised him when she gave a simple nod. He wished it was his company, but he knew she needed the ride and he saw the way she sent a furtive glance at the car. He wasn't the first guy in the world to use a car to get a girl.

He led the way across the street, hurriedly yanking open the passenger door for her.

When he climbed in his side, she was holding up a book, looking at it in the dim interior light that hadn't yet turned off. He'd forgotten that the book from his sign language class was on the passenger seat.

She pointed at him. "You?" She tilted her head to the side and tapped the book.

He hadn't told anyone, except Susan, about the classes, not that he was embarrassed—not about taking the classes anyway. But his abilities...that was another matter completely.

She flipped through the book. She nodded. "Good." He knew that sign. "*E-a-s-y?*" she spelled—twice before he got it.

It was hard enough making the signs, reading them from the other side, nearly impossible. He laughed and shook his head. "Not easy at all."

She handed him the book and settled back in the seat as he tossed it in back, taking her time buckling the seat belt. "Keep practicing." She made that same sign she'd used earlier in his office.

Jason started the car and pulled away from the curb. The streetlights flashed over her features, and he let his gaze bounce back and forth to look at her in between focusing on the road. She looked amazing in the streetlight's glow. Wisps of her hair danced in the gentle blow of the air conditioning. Her eyes weren't looking at the road, or the sights outside, but at the dashboard.

He wanted to ask her so many things, but his frustration grew. How the hell did deaf people hold a conversation in a car? He took one hand off the wheel and made the question mark in the air— asking her, "What?" She smiled and pointed at the radio.

He frowned and with a shrug, nodded. He had no clue what she wanted, but he'd let her do just about anything to keep her engaged. Her long slim fingers, with their carefully trimmed nails, reached for the knobs, turning the dial until she reached a specific number. He'd half expected the rock music he'd heard before to fill the car. Instead, classical music floated around him. He liked it but he'd never bothered to learn anything about it. Her eyes lit up as the name of the song scrolled across the readout. She lifted a thumb and pointed to the roof of the car. Was she asking him to turn it up? He nodded.

She turned the volume up. Not too loud, not really, but louder than he was pretty sure those speakers had ever gone. Her smile grew. He looked at her and pointed at her. Then at his ear. "You hear it?"

She shook her head, scattering more of her curls. Slowly, she ran a finger down her breastbone. He recognized that sign and had to force his gaze back to the road. "Feel it," she told him.

She could obviously feel the sound in the close confines of the car, probably better than in the big open studio, he realized.

That possibility would have never occurred to him. Her smile spoke volumes. Her fingers moved, but the shadows and his simple lessons didn't allow him to understand. Still, he was glad she was trying to communicate with him, something she'd avoided up until now except when she'd wanted his legal skills.

He smiled, making note of the song, of the radio station. For the first time, he felt as if he might find a connection with her.

CHAPTER SEVEN

OVER THE NEXT few weeks, time stretched out in a busy mess for Lauren. Dylan came to the studio three times a week to work with Maxine, and Lauren loved having the people she cared most about together and around her. The studio became a warm, creative place.

Only twice did she feel the need to crank up the music and dance away the stress.

Jason had picked her up after her late class two Thursdays in a row, now. Tonight, as the kids all headed home, her anticipation built. He'd told her his concerns about the neighborhood, the security issues with her walking alone at night. He'd tried to convince her to change her class schedule, sounding too much like Maxine. Unnecessary, his concern irritated her but she was getting used to seeing him each week.

And liking it.

An hour later, however, as Lauren left the studio and locked up, her spirits dipped. Jason hadn't come. He hadn't texted, which was their normal method of communication, either. He didn't owe her any explanations, so she tried not to feel disappointed. Or worried.

Then she turned around.

Across the street, Jason leaned against his beautiful, shiny Lexus. The streetlight's glow cast his face in shadow and accented the breadth of his shoulders. He'd crossed his arms over his broad chest and his legs at the ankles.

Normally, he came straight from the office, so he wore suit pants and a dress shirt. The only concession he made to the fact that he was off work was to roll up the sleeves to expose his tanned forearms.

But tonight, he looked different. He wore a dark T-shirt and a faded pair of jeans. And were those cowboy boots? He looked casual and relaxed standing there, waiting for her.

Her breath caught as she stared at him. He was one of the handsomest men she'd ever met, and while she kept reminding herself they weren't in any way "that way" with each other, she couldn't help but wonder.

What would it be like—

No. Stop that.

He hadn't given any indication since that first day in his office when he'd leaned toward her, that he was attracted to her. She'd thought then that maybe—but she'd been stupid and run away. Even if he'd had any ideas, she'd certainly killed them.

"What's going on?" Lauren signed slowly. He

was getting better with sign but still had a lot of work to do.

"With what?" As he opened the passenger door for her, Jason faced the light so she could read his lips.

She waited until he'd climbed in on his side of the car. "You work today?"

"Yes." He started the car, but didn't pull away from the curb. The half smile on his face told her he was up to something. Finally, he turned to face her. "You eaten?" he signed.

Last week as they'd sat in front of her town house, they'd had another simple conversation. It was good practice for him and she'd enjoyed the company.

It had taken five minutes to explain that on Thursdays she went home, threw a sandwich together and went to bed. In response to this question, Lauren shook her head.

Jason grinned at her. "Trust me?"

Her heart flipped and panic threatened. She had to take a couple of breaths to focus on her heartbeat. Trust? Did she trust him? Did she trust anyone—really?

Slowly, she met his eyes and nodded. Jason hadn't done or said anything to make her *not* trust him. She was the one with the issues. It was her baggage from the past—and this was the perfect opportunity to work on it.

He winked at her as a reward, and she forced herself to relax as he pulled away from the curb.

They moved through the city streets, mingling with the traffic. He turned the radio on and waved at it to let her know she could choose the music and volume. Lauren shook her head, turning it off.

She wasn't in the mood. She'd never liked surprises.

Jason headed toward Glendale. Not too far away, but an unfamiliar part of town. The sights intrigued her, and she felt a sense of anticipation.

Finally, Jason pulled into a large parking lot filled with pickup trucks. The neon sign on the roof shone bright orange, casting a glow over everything.

Lauren had never been to any place like this, and her anticipation tried to morph into anxiety. Jason squeezed her hand and gave her another of those smiles that kept the emotional shift at bay.

"Come on," he said, climbing out and coming around to her side of the car. As they walked across the parking lot, he took her hand again, and she let him. It seemed…right.

His hand was strong, warm and calloused, and any uncertainties she'd had fled. She let herself smile back at him.

The building's facade was decorated with old barn wood and Western shapes cut out of iron. Hay bales lined the front entrance to complete the cliché. Jason opened a big wooden barn door and the thump of country music washed over her.

The sharp, sweet scent of barbecue and mesquite filled the air, making Lauren's mouth water. Her tummy rumbled.

A hostess in a short gingham dress and cowboy boots led them to a table, then set large plastic menus in front of them.

The cute young waitress was talking to Jason, leaning close. Lauren half expected her to bat her eyelashes right in his face. And all Jason did was nod and focus on the menu. He didn't even watch her walk away, despite the girl's sashay.

"Hungry?" Jason signed. "I am." He studied the menu where a large picture of a mega steak covered the top quarter of the page. Apparently if you ate the whole thing, it was free. She tapped her fingernail on the picture and saw him laugh.

He paused and slowly signed. "My brother in Texas would try."

Lauren remembered seeing the legal diploma from Texas in his office, as well as the family picture and belt buckle.

"Texas? Home?"

He nodded. "Grew up there."

She made the sign for a belt. "Yours?" and when he frowned, she spelled and added, "In your office."

He smiled, but it wasn't that happy smile she was used to seeing. It was more melancholy. "My dad's," he answered.

Jason returned his focus to the menu, and Lauren

didn't push, despite her curiosity. Instead, she pondered her own menu choices. Once she'd made up her mind, she turned her gaze to the room around them.

Much like the outside, wood was the main decor. A mirror-lined bar ran the length of one long wall and in the center of it all was a dance floor. It was empty right now, but there were lots of people sitting just as they were, eating dinner, around it.

The waitress came back, and when he ordered, Jason pointed to a steak on the menu. He ordered just as Lauren had, with gestures. What was he doing? Why not order normally? Then as the waitress questioned him about something, he cupped his ear and leaned toward her. He held up two fingers and nodded.

He wasn't patronizing or making fun of her—it was just loud in here. Lauren wanted to kick herself for her initial thought.

What was wrong with her? Why couldn't she trust?

Once they'd ordered, Lauren rummaged in her purse for a pen, then grabbed a napkin from the steel bucket in the center of the table. She wrote, "Why are we here?"

"To eat." He chose to answer her in sign. "And—" He extended his arm. "*D-a-n-c-e*." He paused, and with a laugh, tapped his chest. "My dance."

"You?" She pointed. "Dance?" She waved two fingers over her forearm.

He just shrugged. Their meal arrived and the conversation naturally faded. It was comfortable sharing the meal with him. Watching him.

Just as they finished, a band took the stage in a far corner. Live music gave off a different vibration than recorded music from a speaker. Especially like here, where the speakers were hung from the rafters rather than on the ground. With a live band the whole building would shake.

As the band warmed up, Lauren watched. The drum beat vibrated in her chest, and she smiled. When the bass player hit a couple of notes, she felt their resonance move across the air and through her. She looked at Jason and couldn't resist smiling. This was going to be fun.

JASON COULDN'T KEEP his eyes off Lauren. She'd been so reluctant to trust him. He'd seen it in her face in the car, but she'd gone along with him anyway.

She'd still been skeptical when they'd gotten here, but she'd followed him inside and seemed to enjoy dinner.

Now, the music was alive in the air and he felt it, understanding how performances must work for her with the orchestra right there in the pit at the edge of the stage.

The first hour was for dance lessons. He knew all the steps from when he was a kid, but a refresher was certainly in order.

"You know?" he asked her. From his ASL teacher, he knew the sign for class. He made it and pointed at the sign by the bar giving the times. She shook her head, but her smile didn't dim.

He waved at the dance floor and opened his arms in invitation. She moved so quickly, he'd barely gotten to his feet before she stood in the middle of the floor. He joined her, as did several other couples.

Couple? Why did just thinking that word make him pause? He forced himself to focus on the forming lines and the instructor who was setting up at the front with the band.

His heart sank when the woman started to talk into the microphone. He looked at Lauren, then relaxed as she nodded.

She reached out and took his hand, pulling him to the front, forcing her way to stand right at the stage's edge. She was reading the woman's lips. And probably understood better than he did as she was actually paying attention. He was distracted.

Way too distracted.

And nothing changed as the lesson went on. Lauren moved, smooth and even. He was the one stumbling over his feet. Feet that seemed to have forgotten how to move.

Suddenly, she looked over at him and spelled, "*F-u-n.*" Then the dance steps spun her away from him.

An hour later the lesson ended and they both collapsed in their seats. He signaled the waitress.

"*B-e-e-r*?" he spelled to Lauren. The look on her face of indecision was adorable and cute. He almost didn't want her to decide.

She nodded and the waitress delivered two long-necks with a fast slam to the tabletop and quick two-step away.

Lauren took a deep swallow and once again, his gaze caught hers. This had to stop. He reminded himself they were just friends. Heck, she could be viewed as a client, which technically, she wasn't. Not really. Pal was. Not Lauren.

Way to rationalize.

She set her beer down and turned to watch the dancers. This group was nothing like the class had been. This bunch definitely knew what they were doing.

Still she was eager to join the fun. Over the next couple of hours he wasn't her only partner, and many of the dances didn't require a partner at all. And Lauren tried them all, barely taking a break.

When she finally slumped back into her seat and finished the last of her most-likely warm beer, he left the rest of his beer untouched. He needed to stay clearheaded since he was the driver. But there was another reason to remain sober—the realization of how much more he wanted from tonight beyond dancing.

Lauren looked over at him and made the sign for dance. Then put her fingertips against her palm. It took him a second to remember that meant "again."

She was asking him to go back out *again*? Already? This song was slower. Did she realize that? It'd be easier for a beginner, but it was a waltz.

He stood and let her take his hand. She led him to a miniscule spot in the center of the dancers and lifted her arms.

Slowly, she looked up at him, and for the first time, he felt the difference in their height. He was right at six feet, shorter than his brothers, but taller tonight as he was wearing boots.

She couldn't be much over five feet. She seemed small beside him, something he hadn't noticed before. Hadn't felt before.

He swallowed. She might dance on a daily basis, coming into close physical contact with the other dancers, her students and the like. But he was an attorney. The closest he came to physical contact was when his assistant handed him files.

Lauren smiled at him, ready to dance, and he pushed his discomfort aside to slide his arms around her slim waist. She didn't lean into him, but balanced carefully in the circle of his embrace.

He nodded, silently signaling that they were beginning. And they moved around the floor with all the others. He marveled at the beat of the drum and the bass, but was also suddenly aware of the boot-stomping accompaniment in the soles of his feet.

Lauren didn't need to hear the music, and for the first time, neither did he. He could feel it, sense it vibrating around him. Was this what she experienced whenever she danced? The look on her face told him that yes, this was her norm. Her sweet norm.

Jason watched her move. The grace she wore was like a mask. Was there something behind it? She let herself fall into the music, let the dance take control. He marveled at her.

He'd been foolish to think that the ballet dancer wouldn't be as graceful in a field of rowdy, boot-stomping cowboys. Yet he had. And she'd proven him wrong.

Images of the first night he'd seen her on the stage came back. The beauty of her performance had amazed him then, but this eclipsed even that. Unfortunately, that memory also brought back the reason why he'd been there. Pal. Her father. The file.

He stumbled and Lauren followed his lead, falling against his chest. He caught her, and while the others moved around them, they stopped. Frozen.

Her face shone in the dancing lights. Her lips turned up into a smile, her eyes bright. She was in love with the moment. He hated to see it end.

But her unspoken invitation had to go unanswered. Too public, he rationalized.

He stepped back, then headed to their table.

"Time to go?" She pointed at her wrist, then the door, silently asking the question he didn't want to answer. He nodded and waved the harried waitress over to settle their tab.

Once outside, the air felt muggy and at least a dozen degrees cooler. He could still hear the band's blaring music, but he could no longer feel it. Did music stop suddenly like that for her? His sense of unfairness reared its ugly head but he tamped it down.

At the car, Lauren waited for him to unlock the door and let him open it for her—let him take care of her.

Once he'd climbed behind the wheel and started the car, he reached for the radio dial, but froze when her hand covered his. She pulled his hand back and shook her head.

"Can we talk?" she signed.

"*A-b-o-u-t*?" The glow of the streetlights washed over them from outside. He could see her, so he knew she could see enough to read his lips.

"Was this a...*d-a-t-e*?"

He stared at her, understanding her words but not sure how to answer. "I think so." He paused, shook his head as he looked out the windshield, before turning back to her. "Do you want it to be?"

She nodded. "You?"

"Yes." He couldn't lie. He'd never met anyone like her, and he wanted more. Words filled his mind, few that he knew sign for. Long seconds of silence filled the car as his frustration grew. She frowned, as if expecting him to say—or do—something more.

He could talk and she'd read his lips, but he couldn't even begin to understand her. He felt so inadequate.

Frustrated, he reached for the wheel and pulled away from the curb. He didn't look at her, didn't encourage her to sign. Didn't let her read his lips.

He hoped that by the time they reached her place he'd figure out what to say—and how to say it.

Jason knew the way to her townhouse well. He knew that in less than half an hour, they'd reach her home and she'd disappear inside. Again.

The car flew through the darkened night, even with the thick traffic. She leaned back against the leather seat, her eyes closed, a hint of a smile lingering.

This time as he drove, he took the opportunity to study her. The sense of awe inspired by tonight reminded him of how he'd felt that night with Pal.

His gaze flicked back and forth between her face and the streets. Her hair had come loose again and he liked it that way, falling in ruffled curls past her shoulder, pooling on her forearm that rested on the console. Her eyes were closed, the lids shining with a color he recalled was a smoky gray. The contrast to her pale skin was dramatic enough to catch his attention.

At the bottom of the exit ramp, the sound of a car horn startled him. He refocused on the road, disappointed to see the dull concrete and asphalt of the city in front of him.

Another couple of blocks, temptation beckoned and he let his eyes turn to the side again, hoping to find her still relaxed. Instead, he found her eyes wide, watching him with that smoky gaze. Heat rose on the back of his neck and he nearly jerked the wheel too far to the left as he yanked his gaze back to the road. He forced himself to not envision her staring at him, her eyes saying more than any words could...

Her hand, slim and pale, startled him as she touched his arm.

No ONE HAD ever tried to understand her like Jason did. Lauren stared at him as the streetlights flashed in even intervals over his face as he drove through the city.

It was a handsome, strong face—the face of a man who didn't bother looking down at the hurdles. He just strode on over them, headed for the finish line.

She'd thought for an instant there on the dance floor that he was going to kiss her. She'd anticipated it. Why hadn't he? She'd seen her desire reflected in his eyes.

Jason was essentially a stranger to her—and yet she felt as if she knew him.

When he'd first come to the studio looking for her, Jason had given her a ride home because he'd caused her to miss the bus. The next week when he'd shown up, she'd only been slightly surprised.

He'd driven her home, not speaking or pretending to sign some inane conversation neither of them would understand. He'd given her control of the stereo with a wave of his big hand, just as he had tonight.

She'd turned the dial and found the station she knew so well. The volume had been at five, she'd turned it to eight. At eight she felt the thump and vibration of the music. It was as if her heart grew and encompassed everything and everyone around her.

He had looked over at her then and smiled, and she'd nearly stopped breathing. He'd nodded as if the song was to his liking. She'd smiled back, not so much in response to him, but to the warmth spreading through her. The same warmth she felt now.

His approval meant too much to her, but she didn't know how to change that.

Music was her escape, her sanctuary. She'd never actually heard a single note. Yet she felt each melody. And tonight?

She'd felt more than the music. The undercurrents were thick, especially when she and Jason had waltzed. Had she imagined it? Was the music influencing her? She shook her head, tearing her gaze away from Jason, staring out at the city flying by as the euphoria from the dance faded.

Except he was reflected in the window. Her gaze focused on him, and she couldn't pull her eyes away from him. An ache grew inside her. Once again, she was on the outside, looking at a world that wasn't hers. Wishing for something she couldn't have…

All too soon, they were winding through the darkened streets of her neighborhood. She wanted to drive on forever, watching him; wanted to go back to the dance floor where they'd laughed and had fun together. She didn't want it—whatever "it" was—to end.

When Jason parked by the curb, he turned off the engine. He stared straight ahead for a long moment. Lauren felt the night settle over them, as the pounding became the one in her heart.

THE STREETLIGHT ACROSS from Lauren's door spilled a circle of white that almost reached the curb he parked against.

Jason had barely turned off the engine when Lauren hastily shoved the passenger door open and stepped out. He got out to follow her. She didn't look back, didn't even pause, until he gently grabbed her arm.

She froze. He had to step in front of her to catch her gaze. "What's the matter?" he asked, hoping she could see through the shadows.

She rubbed her chest in the sign for sorry.

"What for?" He felt like a heel. She'd misinterpreted his silence. He was a fool.

"For *d-i-s-a-p-p-o-i-n-t-i-n-g* you." Her fingers shook as she pointed to him.

Oh God, no! "I." He shoved his fingers through his hair, pacing in front of her door. How did he explain? He had to hope she'd understand him. "You never do that." He didn't want to spell. He wanted to use words. Full words. "You." He pointed at her, letting his finger linger in the air. He had to spell. "*A-m-a-z-e* me." He slowly touched the center of his chest. He swallowed hard, then reached out to run that same finger down the edge of her chin. "So—" He made the swish around his face that said, beautiful. "Beautiful," he whispered, wishing she could hear how much he meant it.

He paused, nearly hauling her into his arms. He made sure he faced the streetlight, so she could see his face. "We need to talk. About your father's will." He needed to put something, some distance between them. He wasn't ready for where this was headed. "About so much before—Lauren," he sighed her name, loving the sound of it.

LAUREN TILTED HER head to the side, focusing on Jason's lips, reading his words, but not understanding. Her brain was beyond words.

She read her name on his lips. Saw him lean closer. Felt her breath and heart rush forward to meet him.

Her eyes drifted closed, as his lips, warm and firm, finally found hers. The spicy warm scent of him wrapped around her, pulling her to him. His chest, solid and safe beneath her palms, eased the trembling in her limbs. He made her feel so safe. His arms were a gentle welcome.

Then suddenly, he was gone. He'd pulled back, a frown erasing the smile she'd so enjoyed. "What?" she signed. "Something wrong?"

He didn't look at her until the Lexus stood between them, the moonlight glinting off its polished frame. Time stretched out. Their eyes caught, and she gasped at the heat staring back at her. Slowly, she shook her head. "Don't go." Her fingers made the request as she deepened her frown, needing to deepen the intensity of her words.

Loose curls tumbled over her eyes, and she impatiently shoved them back. "I—" She jabbed a finger hard into her own chest. "Want." Her hands weren't enough. She pointed at him then the space before her. "You here."

He swallowed hard enough for her to see his throat work even in the shadows. He closed his eyes. Instead of reaching for the door handle and climbing into the car, he slowly walked back around the car.

As if something had given way, some resolve or excuse, he was pulling her almost roughly to him, burying his fingers in the curls beside her face. Holding her to kiss her.

He tasted of the night, sweet and cool with an edge. An edge that felt entirely too much like restraint.

Lauren lifted her arms, slipping her fingers into

the soft hair at the nape of his neck. Gently, she
urged him closer. His sigh rumbled through her.
She trembled, drinking in everything he gave her.

Wanting nothing but more.

CHAPTER EIGHT

EVERYTHING VANISHED. THE NIGHT. His worry. Her hesitancy. Everything except the taste of her lips and the feel of her against him. Jason pulled her tighter.

Lauren's arms slid around his neck, and he realized she stood on her tiptoes. She weighed next to nothing, and he could lift her into his arms, but that would move them into a whole new level of intimacy. He ached for it, but not yet.

He stepped back, leaning against the still-warm car, and let her lean into him, resting his chin on the top of her head. He enjoyed the feel of her snuggled against his chest.

There was no way to communicate right now, and he wasn't sure there were even words made for this. It felt damned near perfect.

Lauren pulled away first, tilting her head to look up at him. The night and shadows caressed her face just as his fingers itched to do. Her gaze never left his as she stepped back, smiling when she took another step, and then another. Still facing him, she backed to her front door.

She waved before she closed it and disappeared

inside. Jason stood there, watching the lights come on, imagining what she was doing. Getting ready to go to bed…

"Hell." He had to get out of there before he did something really stupid.

Like follow her.

FIRST KISSES ALWAYS scared Lauren. But this one was different. Not forced, like her true first. Not stolen like a few in high school. Definitely not awkward. But right.

Lauren climbed the stairs to her room, intent on going to sleep. She had an early meeting with the ballet company at the theater in regard to the next production. She should be exhausted after a long day and dancing half the night with Jason. But while her body was exhausted, her brain wouldn't shut off.

What was *he* thinking? Anything? Had he gone home, falling asleep without a further thought about her? Or was he lying awake, too?

After half an hour of tossing and turning, she threw back the blankets. She had to derail this train of thought.

She powered up her laptop and settled against the pillows. She'd check her email, then if she still couldn't sleep, maybe play a game or download a new book.

She couldn't let Jason take over her mind. It had

been a date, that's all, she reminded herself as she clicked the icon for her inbox.

Her email box quickly filled with unread messages. Communications about tomorrow's meeting. Notes from students—and want-to-be students.

Maxine's name popped up. Lauren smiled. Her note would be less like a message and more like an old-fashioned letter. Lauren opened it, anticipating a nice read.

Oh darling, please text me when you get this. I am so upset. I need to talk.

Lauren hadn't checked her phone all evening. She reached for it on the nightstand. She'd missed two messages. They said essentially the same thing as the email.

Her heart pounding, Lauren checked the time. Surely Maxine was asleep. Still, if she was upset… Lauren texted Sorry. Missed your calls. Are you awake?

Time stretched out painfully. Had something happened to Maxine? Was she ill? Was Dylan? Or Hudson?

Finally, her phone flashed. Oh, dear. Yes. I may never sleep again.

What happened?

Another friend has passed away. I keep losing people.

Oh, no. Maxine had reached an age where her long-time friends were dying. Illness was more common than not. Already this year, Maxine had lost three friends. "Who?"

"Wakefield."

Her attorney? Yes, he'd been around a long time, and they did socialize, but this seemed like too strong a reaction, even for Maxine. The last time Lauren had seen him, he hadn't looked well. This couldn't be a surprise. What happened?

He's been sick. Went peacefully in his sleep. I'm devastated.

The drama came to the surface whenever Maxine needed a little extra attention. That wasn't new, either. Lauren sighed. Want me to come over tomorrow?

Oh, I'd love that. Thank you!

Lunch? Early meeting at the theater, sorry.

Yes. Lunch. Love you.

Love you, too.

The texts ended and Lauren plugged her phone back in. She shut down everything, finally yawning, and slid beneath the covers. Maxine had gotten what she wanted, and now all would be right with the world again. Until the next catastrophe.

While Lauren empathized with Maxine, she had long ago stopped letting herself get too attached to people. Losing her mother so young, losing foster family after foster family, and friend after friend growing up, she'd stopped letting herself care enough to experience that level of loss.

As she drifted off to sleep, faces floated through her mind. Maxine. Dylan. Jason. An hour before her alarm was set to go off, she awoke, cringing at the cool damp of the pillow against her cheek.

She rose to start her day, ignoring the proof from her dreams that she wasn't so immune after all.

HUDSON ANSWERED THE door in his usual, distant manner, but Lauren knew he was disturbed. That one tiny line denting his brow was, in Hudson's existence, a big deal.

He led the way to the front room, not Maxine's usual place. It was a room primarily for show. He paused at the doorway, gently touching Lauren's arm and waving her a few steps into the hall.

He shocked her by signing, quite proficiently. "She and Wakefield were lovers a long time ago." He paused, a bright blush on his cheeks. "Bad of me to tell you."

Lauren wasn't sure which shocked her more. Hudson's signing or Maxine's history with her attorney. "You sign?"

The older man looked chagrined. "How do you think I kept up with you two all these years?"

"Why didn't you tell me?"

"My secret weapon." He looked entirely too pleased with himself. They stared at each other for a minute, the world shifting around them. "She's very hurt." He pointed to the open doorway. "Help her."

"I'll try," she signed and turned to join her foster mother, still feeling a bit off-kilter.

Maxine looked up as soon as Lauren's heels hit the wooden floor. "Oh, there you are, dear," she said so Lauren could read her lips. The older woman's eyes were red and her normally perfect makeup was badly disturbed. A large hat box sat on the sofa beside her, the lid open, showing a stack of papers. Moving closer, Lauren saw cards, letters, photographs and other memorabilia. One of the photos was of Maxine and Wakefield, both of them much younger.

It looked like an innocent photo, and Lauren remembered seeing it somewhere before. But now, after what Hudson had said, she saw it differently. It wasn't just a candid cocktail party shot. There was a glint in their eyes, a secret wafting between them.

Lauren settled on the other end of the couch and waited. Maxine's tears began anew, and she grabbed for another tissue. A pile of the white fluffy things already lay scattered across the tabletop.

"I'll miss him," was all Maxine said, as tears flowed down her cheeks.

Lauren moved the hat box and scooted next to Maxine, slipping her arms around the woman's thin shoulders. Maxine laid her head on Lauren and let herself cry.

How many times had Maxine been the one to comfort Lauren, when kids made fun of her, when her heart was broken, when she lost a part in a ballet production? She couldn't remember Maxine ever crying or being this upset. Angry, yes, but never this.

"Thank you," Maxine signed. She sat there a moment, then pulled away, but not ready to let go of the comfort yet, she curled her fingers around Lauren's.

Maxine picked up another photo and showed it to Lauren. This one she'd never seen before. Someone had managed to take a photo of Maxine and Wakefield in a very hot and heavy embrace. Shocked, she tried to look away, but couldn't help staring. That was here. In this room. Was that why Maxine was in this room now?

"My graduation party."

Lauren recognized the decorations in the background. Maxine blushed. "He was good to you."

Maxine nodded and wiped at her tears again.

When she looked at Lauren, hurt filled her eyes. "I miss him. I don't want to do this."

"I know." Putting her fingertips to her forehead, slowly tapping the sign, Lauren was reminded of Hudson's furrowed brow. Once again, she felt the world shift. She wasn't the kid, hurt and crying— she was the comforter now.

Just then, Hudson came in and announced that lunch was ready, speaking and in sign. Then he did something else totally out of character. He came over to the couch and offered his hand to Maxine, assisting her up and escorting her to the dining room.

Lauren sat there and stared. Everything around her was changing. And she wasn't sure she was ready for that.

"Uh, boss?" Susan poked her head around the door frame.

When Jason looked up, she started to speak. "There's a—"

An elderly woman swept into his office just then, cutting off Susan's words and filling the room with her personality.

Petite, with perfectly coiffed hair, and nails the color of blood, the woman strolled right up to the edge of his desk as if she owned the world. She extended one of those claw-tipped hands. "I'm Maxine Nightingale."

Jason shot to his feet, his mama's manners

drilled in too deep to deny. "Hello, ma'am." He had no idea who she was, but the look she gave him said he should.

Susan shuffled across the office, coming up beside him. She cupped her hand along her face and whispered loudly, "The ballerina. You know. She's famous." The last word came out so loud, even he winced.

"Ah," he took the woman's hand and gently shook it. "Another ballerina." The other one had haunted his waking and sleeping hours ever since that sweet kiss. He was tired today, having tossed and turned every night since.

He nodded toward the door, indicating to Susan that she could leave. His normally obtuse assistant stepped toward the door, but didn't leave, just stared at the older woman with wide, awe-filled eyes.

"Susan, you can get back to work now."

"Uh, yeah, I…" Susan turned to go then hastily went back to the woman. "Can I, uh, get an autograph?"

"Susan." Jason was fairly certain he would have to shove her bodily out of the room.

"No problem, dear. I'll stop at your desk on the way out." Maxine's smile could only be described as benevolent.

"Thank you." To him Susan said, "I'm leaving." She even remembered to close the door behind her. Miracle, that.

"What can I do for you, Ms. Nightingale?"

"Call me Maxine." She settled in one of the chairs facing his desk, gracefully crossing her legs and meeting his stare.

He didn't have time for a meeting right now. "I only have ten minutes, then I must leave for court."

"Oh, this won't take long." She looked up at him. "You see, my attorney has—" She faltered and had to clear her throat. "Recently passed away, and I find myself in need of your services."

"I'd be glad to set up another meeting—"

"Oh, we'll do that, my dear, in due time. I needed to meet you before we get to business. And—" She looked around. "I never discuss such things in offices. Too sterile." She actually shuddered.

Jason took a long look at the woman seated before him. He was definitely missing something here. He just wasn't sure what.

"Why did you choose me?" Maybe her answer would tell him something.

"Lauren has mentioned your name. A couple of times actually." The silence was thick. He got the impression she wasn't telling him everything.

"Lauren Ramsey? Do you work with her?" Though Susan had identified Maxine as a ballerina, that didn't mean it was the only way she knew Lauren.

"Oh, no." Maxine laughed and fidgeted with her purse handle, not because she was nervous, but as an obvious ploy to make him wait. "Not for years anyway. She hasn't needed me for some time."

Her voice suddenly sounded wistful. Jason settled in the desk chair, not relaxed, but on the edge of the seat. He waited. She had more to say.

"Lauren is my daughter." She fidgeted more. "Excuse me, foster daughter. I'm here to make sure she's not making any mistakes, if nothing else."

He leaned back in the chair, watching Maxine with a less than trusting eye.

"She said you handled her father's estate, and helped with Dylan." Maxine smiled. "Surely, she has told you about me?" Her hope was obvious.

Lauren hadn't mentioned a thing, but that didn't mean much. They'd merely had one "official" date and he'd only been taking ASL classes for a few weeks. "We haven't had that many in-depth conversations," was all he told Maxine.

Her eyes dimmed a bit. "I see. Do you know sign language?"

"I'm learning. Slowly." He wouldn't lie.

She nodded, her expression brightening. "Do you have any idea of who I am?"

He wasn't sure what this was about, and he didn't have time to find out. He stood and gathered the files he'd been working on when Maxine had barged in. "I'm afraid the ballet world is as new to me as sign language. But I'm learning. And I really do need to leave."

"I understand." She stood as well, waiting until he led the way to the door. "I'll be at the Scarlett Tea House tomorrow afternoon at four." She walked out into the lobby. "I'd like to invite you to join me. They have the best high tea. We can discuss details then."

Despite her lack of stature, the woman intimidated him. "I— Details? Of what?"

"Why, your representing me, of course. Now that Wakefield has made the unfortunate journey to the great beyond I need someone to handle my estate."

"Oh, what good timing," Susan piped up from her desk. "You don't have any appointments tomorrow after two. I'll put that in your calendar," she offered and started typing.

"Why, thank you." He choked out the words and wondered what they'd really discuss if he went to that meeting. He headed toward the elevator, indicating that Maxine could precede him.

"Oh, thank you, dear." Maxine smiled too brightly. "But I did promise this lovely young lady an autograph. I'll see you tomorrow."

Jason took the opportunity to escape, sending up a silent prayer that he'd have a practice left when he got back. He fully intended to have a chat with Susan.

He sighed. He needed to focus. He had a hearing to get through, and then he hoped to talk with Lauren tonight. He didn't have time to worry about what this woman really had in mind.

But Lauren didn't answer any of his texts that evening and he felt like a stalker when he drove by the darkened studio on his way home.

Despite his reluctance to go to the meeting, he found himself driving to the Scarlett Tea House the next afternoon. If nothing else, he was curious about Maxine and her relationship with Lauren.

New experiences were becoming the norm in Jason's life. First the ballet. And now? High tea? He seriously needed to book a flight home soon and schedule some beer and ranch time with his brothers.

The front doors of the Scarlett Tea House were as frivolous as he expected. According to the internet the Victorian house had never actually been a home. It had been built in this style specifically to be a tea house a hundred years ago.

He strode inside, purpose in his step and as much swagger as he could muster.

The Scarlett Tea House had been a well-known celebrity hangout a decade ago. It was still an elegant place where wheeling and dealing happened, but not with the younger set.

Lacy curtains, white tablecloths and dainty furniture made him wince. It was one thing to envision himself as the bull in a china shop—it was totally different to be one.

Maxine sat near the largest picture window, clearly showcased in the afternoon light. The elderly woman sat regally in one of those tiny chairs, wearing a bright red suit, as if she were part of the decor, with a floral-decorated teapot at her elbow. He made his way—carefully—through the maze of tables until finally reaching her side. "Maxine. Hello."

"Oh, Jason. Please, have a seat." She waved across the table toward a chair that didn't look big enough for his nephew, Tyler, to perch on, much less him. He carefully sat.

"Can I pour you some tea?"

He nodded, dreading the idea of trying to drink from one of the dainty cups and not fall off the chair he was so precariously perched on. But he couldn't think of any way to politely decline. They probably didn't serve whiskey here.

He sipped the brew from the paper-thin china cup, and once he'd done his due diligence, he carefully put the cup back on the saucer.

He had only met Maxine the one other time, yet he liked her. Liked the fact that she cared enough about Lauren to be curious about him. But while he liked her, trust had to be earned.

Movement at the doorway suddenly caught Jason's eye. He glanced over, surprised to see Lauren standing there, her gaze intense. She strode through the delicate tables without any evidence of the trepidation he'd felt.

"What are you doing?" She faced Maxine, signing with broad angry movements, which made it easier for him to read her sign.

Maxine wasn't fazed. "Interviewing my new attorney," she said. "How did you know where we were?"

"*H-u-d-s-o-n*. He has no secrets now."

Maxine sighed and carefully set the fragile teapot down. "Join us."

Lauren waved at the waiter as she pulled a chair from the next table. She picked up a place setting and made room for herself. She sat down with a thump.

If he hadn't been stuck in the middle of what looked like two very headstrong women, Jason might have sat back and enjoyed the show. Growing up with three sisters, he knew better than to say a word right now.

The waiter brought a second teapot and settled a dainty cup and saucer in front of Lauren.

Lauren signed quickly to Maxine. The older woman looked over at Jason then spoke as she signed. "I know it's only been three days. But if Wakefield taught me nothing else, it was that business comes before pleasure." Pain flashed across the woman's features, but was quickly masked.

"Unless there's something urgent, we can wait—" Jason began, pausing when Maxine glared at him.

Lauren faced him, and while her frown was less angry, she was struggling. "She may *h-i-r-e* you. She'd be stupid not to." Lauren glared at Maxine. "But she's really checking up on me."

"I am not," Maxine said. "But since you brought it up, is there anything I should know?"

"No," Jason said and Lauren signed at the same

time. Maxine's knowing smile made the color rise in Lauren's cheeks.

To ease Lauren's discomfort, Jason reached out and covered her hand with his. He squeezed Lauren's hand gently, then withdrew it so he could sign and speak to Maxine. "We only recently met. I enjoy her company. I'm not going to do anything to hurt her."

Maxine took her time sipping her tea. She glanced at them both before setting her cup down to speak and sign. "I *am* worried. Lauren is as close to a daughter as I have."

"I'm a grown woman."

"Who takes unnecessary risks. Building a studio in the ghetto. Staying out late with strange men. No offense." She nodded to Jason.

Maxine's tone was lost on Lauren, but Jason heard the disapproval mixed with motherly caring in it. It sounded a lot like his mom, and a stab of grief caught him off guard. He missed her.

"I'm sure she knows you're capable," Jason spoke, facing Lauren. "It's normal to worry." He wouldn't say anything against the studio—he knew how much she loved it.

Lauren sat for a minute, then took more time pouring her tea. It reminded Jason of Maxine playing with her purse yesterday to stall. Interesting.

"The studio is doing well." He understood her sign this time.

"And I'm proud of that, dear." Maxine reached

out to pat Lauren's hand. "But that doesn't stop the worry."

"Why did you bring Jason here?" Lauren signed quickly.

Maxine smiled. "To check him out." When she got the knee-jerk reaction she must have known Lauren would make, she laughed. "And honestly, to hire him. I'm serious. I need to get this taken care of." Jason wondered if they even remembered he was there. He didn't remind them.

"Why?" Concern hastened Lauren's fingers. "Is something wrong?"

Maxine shook her head. "Nothing new. You know how many people I've lost lately. What if—" Her voice broke and her fingers paused. "What if I go like Wakefield? Just go to sleep…"

"That won't happen." Lauren shook her head.

"It could."

The silence and stillness stretched out. As if on cue, the waiter came over with a tray of tiny sandwiches and cakes. Jason just stared. They weren't even big enough for a full bite. The man took his time explaining the selection with practiced hand waves toward each. Both women sat waiting, neither signing nor asking for an interpretation. The way Lauren selected specific ones told him she was familiar with them.

Jason stared at the food. Lauren's hand on his arm made him look at her. She pointed at a couple.

"Try these." Using the dainty server, she put several on the plate and handed it to him.

He had to admit they were tasty, but the entire serving tray wouldn't even fill him up.

Once they finished and the empty tray was whisked away, Lauren faced her foster mother. Maxine tried to pretend she hadn't noticed, but she couldn't ignore Lauren tapping her arm.

Jason sat to the side, so reading her sign was a challenge, but he'd done better today.

"You can't keep interfering. I'm a grown woman. I know what I'm doing."

"I know that, but—"

"No buts." Lauren wasn't budging. "Trust me."

Maxine fidgeted with the remaining silverware on the table, straightening the mess. The bluster and strong facade wavered for an instant, then she took a deep breath and looked up. The world-class ballerina was back. "Very well." Maxine slowly stood, gathering her purse. She looked at him, then said. "I'll be in touch."

Jason was surprised to see an elderly gentleman appear. After handing Maxine a receipt, he signed a greeting to Lauren, then took Maxine's arm and led her out of the room.

"That's *H-u-d-s-o-n*," Lauren explained. "Her *b-u-t-l-e-r*."

Who had a butler in this day and age?

"I'm worried about her," Lauren signed. "I can't give in to her need to *m-e-d-d-l-e*. Took too long to get this far." She stared after the couple until they were gone out the front door. Then she stood to go.

"Need a ride?" he asked as he stood as well.

"No. Thank you. Just a couple of blocks." She pointed in the direction up the street.

He wasn't about to step on that independence. So he nodded. She turned to go, then hastily turned back. Stretching on her tiptoes, she reached up and kissed him, hesitantly, on the cheek. Then hustled away, leaving him standing there in the middle of all that finery, not sure what the hell had just happened.

He hightailed it outside, taking in deep breaths of the hot city air. Women were strange creatures. He'd never understand them. That had been the most civilized cat fight he'd ever witnessed, and he'd seen plenty growing up. Maxine and Lauren had argued—in the midst of tea sandwiches and lace. And not a single plate had been broken.

His sisters would never believe him.

CHAPTER NINE

THE DANCE STUDIO teemed with life. Lauren was teaching in the back, and another of the teachers, Linda, had a group up front—a dozen little girls using performance tutus for the first time—and Maxine was actually upstairs on the stage with the main performers. Maxine wasn't speaking to her, and had bypassed the usual staff meeting for practice.

Friday night would be a great performance—if they managed to get through the next couple of days.

Lauren took a deep breath, stepping back, and lowering her arms. This group meant the most to her. These were "hers." They were all hearing impaired, and a big reason she'd wanted to start the studio in the first place.

Everyone was here, except Dylan, who'd landed the male lead. For the last week, Maxine had run him through the toughest paces he'd ever faced, and he was ecstatic. He still had moments where he worried about the legal case and Tina. But he was learning to separate the two worlds, not an easy task at fifteen. Heck, not an easy task at twenty-eight.

Lauren waved her arms, to get the kids' attention and pull her own scattered attention back on track. As soon as they were all looking at her, she signed the next set of instructions, and they eagerly went to work. She clapped in time with their steps, guiding them the way Maxine had done for her as a kid. She enjoyed their performance, as much as their accomplishment. They'd come so far.

Ah, to be so young and innocent.

Simply wanting to dance and please. Not have to make a living with all this, not being responsible for the success—or failure.

The kids completed the final movement with perfection. Beautiful perfection. It almost eased her concerns. Almost.

"Okay, everyone." She signed to her group and waved at Linda. The other group came over, giggling as they tried to sit in the stiff tutus. Finally, all the children settled on the floor, looking up expectantly. They knew the drill. Lauren would sign, and Linda would interpret for those who were hearing.

"Friday's the big night. Are you all ready?"

Heads nodded and ponytails bobbed. "Ms. Ramsey?" Sarah Wilson asked, lifting her hand at the same time. "Is there really gonna be people there b'sides Mom and Dad?"

Linda laughed, as Lauren smiled at her. She'd read the girl's eager words. Still, Lauren signed for the others. Christy piped up before either of the adults could answer. "Well, of course, silly. My mom and grandma are comin'."

Lauren signaled for silence again. "There will be a full audience." *She hoped.* The studio needed the money, and they'd sold most of the tickets. "You are all ready for this." She didn't ask them. She told them. Every head nodded in agreement.

Maxine and her group, the older kids, came in then, not sitting on the floor with the little ones, but leaning against the walls or standing behind the group. Dylan stayed a bit back, his arms crossed over his chest. Maxine's brow was furrowed. Now what?

She sighed and gave the signal for everyone to finish up. Only Dylan and Maxine remained behind. The vibration of all those little feet on the floor as they headed to the locker rooms felt like a wave.

"Dylan is out of sync today." Maxine didn't hold back. Her signing was harsh and angry. Dylan recrossed his arms.

Yesterday he'd missed cues and lost track of where they were in the routine. Lauren hadn't called him on it then, hoping today would be better.

"What's wrong?" she signed, trying not to come across as angry. She needed him to relax and open up. She looked pointedly at her foster mother, wanting time alone with Dylan.

"Fine." The older woman threw up her hands in her typical dramatic way. Lauren tried not to smile.

"Hudson is outside. I'll see you both tomorrow." She did the whole air-kiss thing with Lauren, and though her hands shook, telling Lauren she wasn't as calm as she wanted them to believe, she signed goodbye to Dylan.

"She cares about you," Lauren signed. "Don't be so stubborn with her." They both watched Maxine walk slowly away, and Lauren wondered who that bit of advice was really meant for. She turned back to finish her conversation with Dylan.

He looked sheepish, clenching and unclenching his hands in a familiar nervous habit as he watched Maxine leave. "Tina didn't come home again last night." His fingers flew. He didn't bother to speak. They never did when it was just the two of them.

"Oh, no." Lauren squeezed his arm. "Did your foster parents do anything?"

He shook his head. "They didn't know. I'm worried. I texted her. No answer."

Lauren felt herself tense, her protective instincts going into high gear. Dylan was one of her best students, and one of the kindest people she knew. And a friend. She didn't like to see him hurting.

"Have you texted Rhonda?"

He vehemently shook his head. "That will get Tina into more trouble."

Lauren tapped her chin. How could she make Dylan feel better? She didn't like what Tina was doing—but in many ways she understood. Hadn't she done something similar as a teen? Pacing away, Lauren tried to think.

She had to do something. The performance was in two days.

"You have to focus." Lauren went back to Dylan. "How can I help?"

"You can't do anything." Dylan's face filled with defeat, and he slumped onto one of the chairs near the wall. "No one can."

JASON LEFT THE COURTROOM. He glanced at the grand old-fashioned clock mounted in the middle of the rotunda. An hour to spare.

It figured that the week Wyatt and Emily were finally able to visit him was one of Jason's busiest weeks, and one during which he couldn't rearrange much of anything.

Getting out early today was the best Jason could hope for.

His phone buzzed, and he pulled it out as he descended the wide stone steps. Lauren. He smiled.

Do you have a minute? she'd texted.

For you, of course. Then it dawned on him that maybe there was a problem. Everything okay?

No. Tina didn't come home last night. Dylan's upset.

Jason cursed. What was wrong with that girl? Nothing that wasn't typical teen behavior—except

Los Angeles wasn't the best place to experiment with spreading your wings at thirteen. And foster care didn't leave much room for mistakes.

How can I help? He shouldn't do this. He had to pick up Wyatt and Emily in an hour and a half. Did you text her?

No answer.

That could mean so many things. None of them good.

What's her number? Let me try.

A number appeared on his screen. He hurried to his car but grumbled when he found no service inside the concrete bunker-like parking garage. He hustled to drive outside, and stopping at the top of the ramp, he dialed.

It went straight to voice mail. He texted Lauren, and she sent back a frowning emoticon.

What's Dylan's address? I can drive by and see if she's at the house. He had it in a file, but getting it this way was much faster.

He's afraid Rhonda will get mad at Tina if she finds out she didn't come home.

Those concerns Jason had about the family returned with a vengeance. He didn't give a damn if anyone got upset. The girl's safety, and that Dylan was okay, was all that mattered at this point. What's the address? he typed again. I'll say it's for the case.

When the address appeared on the screen, he glanced at his watch. The house was about halfway between the airport and the studio. If everything worked out, he'd make it. Maybe.

I'll let you know. Tell Dylan not to worry. Jason tossed his phone onto the passenger seat then headed out into traffic.

A short while later he was in front of a small craftsman-style house. The yard was thin, patches of dirt showing through the pale green grass. Ancient metal fencing surrounded the yard in a neat little square. Heat shimmered off the broken pavement of the street and, as he climbed out of his car, Jason heard the hum of a window air conditioner.

Disrepair had a hold on the neighborhood and was creeping deeper. Like the neighborhood around Lauren's studio, time and neglect had left its mark. The house itself still looked in good repair and fairly well kept for a home with half a dozen kids living in it.

He was halfway up the walk before he heard the voices. The loud, angry voices.

"You try that again, young lady, and I'll lock you in all night." The woman's voice was harsh and familiar. Rhonda Hancock. Was this the anger Dylan had feared?

"No!" Tina cried.

"Then get that cleanin' done, now. Or tonight will be the same."

Same as what? Jason hurried up the walk. The hair on the back of his neck was at full attention now.

"But I have to—" The sound of skin hitting skin cut off Tina's words.

"You don't have to do anything but get to work." A phone rang, interrupting the conversation. "And give me that," the woman yelled.

"Not my phone!"

Something shattered and Tina sobbed. Jason took the steps two at a time.

"That's Dylan's only way—"

"Dylan has more important things to do than worry about you. He'll at least amount to something."

Jason reached the door and knocked hard. The voices fell silent. He pulled open the screen and rapped again, harder, rattling the wooden door. "Mrs. Hancock. Tina?"

The door flew open. Jason expected to see Tina, either at the door, or behind the woman. She was nowhere in sight. Only Rhonda Hancock. He wasn't ready to confront the woman yet, not until he knew where Tina was and who else was inside.

"I've been trying to reach Tina." He wasn't in

the mood for pleasantries. This woman knew full well who he was. "I have more questions for her."

"Oh, well, we can bring her to your office to-morrow."

"No." He took a step closer. "No, I need to see Tina. Now."

The woman's eyes widened, and Jason knew he was intimidating her. Good.

"Tina!" the woman yelled over her shoulder.

Shuffling steps came from the darkened interior. Slowly, Tina stepped into the light. Jason held back his reaction. Her deep, dark eyes were wide and sparkled with unshed tears. Behind those tears, he saw a strong shadow of fear, and on her left cheek was the clear imprint of a hand.

"Hello, Tina. Remember me?" For her he'd be pleasant.

All her attitude was gone, and Jason actually mourned its loss. It wasn't something she'd have easily given up. Tina nodded, hugging the edge of the doorway.

Jason pinned Rhonda with his best courtroom glare. "I need to speak with her. In private." He emphasized the last as much to see her reaction as anything.

The woman's glare matched his. "I don't think that's a good idea. She's my responsibility. You know that. You're a lawyer."

He knew crooks, too. "Why not? Afraid of what she'll tell me?"

That got her attention, and his stomach churned as he waited for an answer. Rhonda turned around and looked at Tina, who hastily shook her head, moving as if she might melt into the wall.

"I'm not leaving until I talk with you, Tina." He wanted to reassure her, but Rhonda was so unpredictable. For that matter, so was Tina. So he leaned back on his heels, affecting a less threatening stance.

The woman stepped away and cleared the path. "Be quick about it."

"Come on outside." Jason waved for Tina to come toward him and tried to smile at her. As she passed her foster mother, he saw the way she flinched.

"I'll be watching you both." Rhonda moved back into the doorway once Tina had passed. Jason held the screen open until Tina had stepped outside, then he let it close.

"Go all the way out to the gate," Jason instructed. He wanted to make sure Rhonda couldn't overhear anything.

Tina stopped right at the gate, looping her long thin fingers around the top row of metal.

"You don't have to answer anything for me." He spoke softly. "But I *hope* you will. First, is there anyone else in that house?"

Tina shook her head, still not looking at him.

"Where were you last night?" They didn't have much time, and he needed to know what he was getting into. Tina's shoulders hunched, and she stared at the sidewalk. She didn't answer.

"Dylan's worried. He's why I'm here. I don't really have any more questions for his case."

She looked up at him then. Her eyes once again flooded with damp.

"Does your foster mother know sign language?" Tina shook her head.

"Good. You can answer in sign. I'm not real good at it, but you can spell your answer if I don't get it."

Was that relief he saw wash over her face? "You came home last night, didn't you?"

She nodded.

Curses filled his mind. "I heard her say something about locking you in. Did she?" He knew this girl had caused trouble in the past, but he saw true fear in her eyes right now. "Tell me the truth," he urged.

Tina's nod was slower this time, and her nervous gaze kept darting toward the house.

"Where did she lock you in?"

"*B-a-s-e-m-e-n-t c-l-o-s-e-t.*" Her hands shook as she finger spelled.

Jason saw red and cursed. The only thing that kept him from heading back into the house and giving the woman a taste of her own medicine was the girl cowering in front of him. He reached into his pocket and handed her his phone. "Tina? Take this. Text Dylan that you're okay." Then he hit the button on his key fob and unlocked the car. "Get in my car, and I'll take you over to Lauren. Is there anything important in that house that you or Dylan need right now?"

Tina shook her head and hugged the phone like it was a lifeline. "She ruined it all," she whispered.

As soon as Tina opened the gate, Rhonda came flying out of the house.

"Get in the car, Tina. Lock the door behind you." He turned and faced Rhonda. "Stay right there," he ordered.

The woman froze, her eyes wide, likely not as much from fear as shock. He doubted many people stood up to her. She recovered fast. "Tina, you get in the house."

"No. *You* get back in the house, Mrs. Hancock." Jason stood his ground, his shoulders wide, his arms loose. Ready for anything. He took a step toward her as he heard the car door slam and the locks thunk into place.

"I'm callin' her caseworker right now." She tried to sound threatening. But if she was so concerned, why hadn't she already called the police?

"You do that. If you don't, I will. I'll expect a call soon." He took another step toward her. "Call every official you can think of. I'm sure they'd love to hear where Tina spent last night."

She stepped back, seeming to realize he was someone to be reckoned with.

"Pack all their things. Carefully, and if anything's missing or damaged, I'll hold you personally, legally and financially responsible." He figured that last bit got her attention. "I'll send a courier to pick it up."

His anger grew as scenarios of all the things she'd probably done to Tina flashed in his mind. And maybe Dylan. And how many other kids? He needed to get out of here before he lost control. He stalked over to the driver's door, and watched the woman scurry into the house. He had to consciously uncurl his fisted hands before climbing in and facing Tina again.

The girl had put on her seat belt, but simply sat there staring at the phone.

"What's the matter?" Jason started the car and carefully pulled away from the curb, wishing he could floor the accelerator and peel away to expend some of his anger.

"I— She destroyed my phone." Tina hiccuped a sob that cracked through the last of his anger. "I only know Dylan's number from my speed dial."

Poor kid. "He's with Lauren. Text her. She's in my contacts."

The bright, tear-soaked smile that blossomed on her face shot straight through him. Made him feel as if he'd done something good. Her fingers flew over the keys.

His phone dinged a few seconds later indicating a text had come in. "She gave him her phone. He's glad I'm okay."

Jason drove out of the neighborhood and breathed a sigh of relief.

"I don't know how to explain to him," she whispered.

Jason stopped at the light and faced her. "Don't text. I'll bring you to the studio. You can talk then."

"Okay."

Then the phone rang and they both jumped. The phone landed with a thud on the floor. It rang again and she reached down to pick it up. After she handed it to him, he saw Wyatt's number on the screen and groaned. He'd half expected it to be the caseworker. "Hello."

"Hey, little brother. We've landed."

"Great." Jason tried to sound enthusiastic. "I'm on my way." How long would it take them to get their luggage? Did he have time to stop by the studio first? He glanced at the dash clock. Hell no. "Still good for me to pick you up at arrivals?"

"Sounds great to us. Looking forward to this, Jason." Wyatt hung up, and Jason handed the phone back to Tina.

"I have to pick up my brother and sister-in-law at the airport. Are you up for a ride out to LAX before we head to the studio?"

She smiled. "That'd be fun. I ain't never been there. What do I tell Dylan?"

"Just let them know we'll be there as soon as possible." He had no idea how long this would take.

They drove in silence for a while, there being

no quick way to get to the airport. Jason wouldn't push, but he needed to know more from Tina. "Do you want to tell me what happened last night?"

She shrugged, her grip tightening on the phone.

"I won't get upset with you, if that's what you're worried about."

"That's what Rhonda says."

"What do you mean?"

"That if I tell her the truth, she won't be mad. But then when I do, she…"

"Locks you in the closet?"

Tina nodded, slowly, sadly. Dear God. Talk about a violation of trust. "You do know that's wrong, very wrong of her, right? Nothing you could do justifies that kind of treatment. Nothing." His anger rose again, and he had to take a deep breath. Last thing he wanted to do was scare her.

Trust was one of the things Jason valued most. "You don't have to tell me anything if you don't want to."

They left it at that and the silence grew. He thought of Lauren, wondering how she'd react to this. He suddenly missed her blaring his stereo. He occasionally glanced at Tina, who stared out the side window. He had no idea how he would explain all this. To anyone, not just to Wyatt and Emily. But he knew he'd done the right thing getting the girl out of there.

He felt for her, and Dylan. The boy wasn't going to take this well. Jason had seen Dylan's devotion to his sister, and he understood it. If something like this had happened to any of his sisters… Hell, his brother DJ had decked Lane after learning Lane was the father of Mandy's child. And Lane had been loving to Mandy.

"I… I only snuck out that one time," Tina whispered. "I didn't do it again after Dylan got in trouble. I swear."

"I believe you." And he did. "Does Dylan know that?"

Again the silence stretched out. "Dylan couldn't hear any of it." Tina continued to stare outside. "Even when I cried, he couldn't hear me."

Damn. "Did you try to tell anyone else?" he asked softly. Was there someone who could have helped before? The idea of her so alone did not sit well with him.

Tina shook her head. "Rhonda said if I ever told anyone, she'd make it so Dylan couldn't dance anymore. He loves to dance." And she loved her brother—that came through loud and clear.

Hell. What was he supposed to say to that? Words were his best tool, and he found himself at a total loss.

They reached the airport turnoff, and he was thankful he was forced to concentrate on the heavy traffic.

Only Wyatt would wear his best Stetson in the heat of LA. But there he was. Emily stood close to him, a stack of luggage behind them.

Emily was a judge back home in the family court. He'd thought to pick her legal brain this visit, but it looked like he would have to do more than that now.

"Should I get in back?" Tina looked so uncertain, so small.

"Nah, stay there. They're newlyweds. They like being close to each other."

Jason climbed out and hurried around to greet them. Emily hugged him, and Wyatt did that usual handshake shoulder-bump. Jason was glad to see them both.

Jason loved his big gregarious family, and glancing at Tina's small face staring at them through the passenger window, he appreciated them more than ever before.

"Who's with you?" Emily looked back and forth between Jason and Tina.

"Climb in and I'll make the introductions."

This ought to be interesting.

CHAPTER TEN

LAUREN STOOD IN the studio doorway, watching, fascinated, proud, as Dylan went through his routine yet again. His movements were fluid, and Lauren knew she'd done the right thing asking Maxine to coach him. The master needed to be the one to help him master his gift.

How she envied him. At fifteen, he still had ten, maybe fifteen, prime years on the stage. The possibilities he had ahead of him... Oh, she was still in demand, but that time was growing short. Her feet were the only part of her that looked forward to the day she'd hang up her toe shoes. Her heart hurt just thinking about it.

Shaking her head to dismiss her dismal thoughts, she turned away from watching him. Jason would be here soon with Tina. Why did her heart skip at the thought of seeing him? She didn't let that train of thought continue, either.

Once they got here, Dylan would have to stop dancing, stop hiding in the movement. She wasn't sure what they were facing. Tina was too volatile and unpredictable.

The siblings' devotion to each other interfered

with his training…and yet Lauren would never ask him to give it up. They were all each other had.

Which was more than she'd ever had. Still, being that alone had forced her to stand on her own two feet. She had never depended on anyone, and she intended to keep it that way.

That's part of why Maxine was barely speaking to her after tea the other day. She'd *had* to draw the line. So, why did it bother Lauren that the older woman had pulled back? Why did it hurt? Lauren didn't need her.

Did she? *No.* She couldn't.

What had Jason thought about their interaction? He hadn't intervened, but she'd seen the speculative spark in his eye. What was he thinking now? How could she explain? She looked at her phone. Maybe she could text something. Or write an email. No, too impersonal.

But he didn't know sign well enough for them to have a real conversation. He tried so hard, but she couldn't make him learn any faster. If he'd been born deaf, like her and Dylan, they could have a conversation, no problem. But he hadn't.

For the first time, the barriers between them seemed insurmountable. Her eyes burned, and she refused to acknowledge why.

Her phone flashed, and she thumbed the screen on. Maxine's complete, proper sentences, with perfect grammar and punctuation, appeared in the little bubble. Maxine would never give in and use emoticons or shorthand speech. Lauren fought the smile, and breathed a sigh of relief, pleased that her foster mother had finally reached out. Even if it was about Dylan.

Is Dylan still there? He's not answering my texts, and he needs to rest tonight. Only one more day of rehearsals.

As if Lauren didn't know when the show was? He's here. Still practicing. She didn't dare tell Maxine they were waiting for Jason and Tina. The woman would lose it.

Send him home.

As soon as he finishes this. She didn't explain what *this* was.

Thank you.

Dylan came over then, peering at her phone. "Was that Jason and Tina?" he signed.

Lauren shook her head. "Maxine. She says you need to go home and rest."

The boy smiled. Dylan liked Maxine, respected her—he'd told Lauren that earlier. He gathered his things and was halfway to the locker room before he turned around and walked back, a puzzled look on his face. "Can I ask you a question?" he surprised Lauren by asking.

"Of course."

"How do you—" He paused. "How do you make yourself not care?"

"I don't think that's possible."

"You do it."

Lauren stared at him. "I care. About you. Maxine. Even Tina." Where did Jason fit into that equation?

Dylan shook his head. "You." He pointed at her almost harshly. "You turn off your emotions. How do you do that? I want to learn."

No, he didn't. She thought of the love between him and his sister that she'd been analyzing earlier. And envying.

The thing he was asking to learn was the same thing she was most afraid of in herself. It was what stood between her and Maxine. It would stand between her and any relationship.

Was that why she couldn't write the email or the text to Jason? Not because it was so impersonal, or she couldn't put it into words he could understand, but because she was afraid to show him her greatest flaw? Afraid he'd do what so many others had done—leave?

She looked at Dylan for a long minute. He still wore his practice clothes, as did she. "I care," she signed slowly. "But you're right. It hurts too much sometimes. Let me show you a trick." She waved for him to follow her. "This helps lower my stress. How I turn off."

She pointed to the center of the now-empty studio. "Stand there." He frowned, obviously confused. She simply grinned as she headed toward the stereo.

When she found what she wanted, she cranked up the volume and hit play, then hurried to the center of the floor to face Dylan. "Don't you dare tell Maxine I do this," she teased.

When the hard rocking beat vibrated the floor, Dylan physically jumped. His eyes became wide, but as he watched Lauren move, his smile grew.

Everything shook with the rhythm of the music—the walls, floor, and every inch of her body. She couldn't help but move, swaying and jumping to the hard beat. She hadn't realized how tense she was.

"This helps you?" Dylan signed.

She nodded and kept moving. She laughed at Dylan as he tried to do some of his ballet moves. Shaking her head, she faced him. "Relax," she signed. "Move to the beat. Do not try to match movements or steps to it."

She snapped her fingers to the rhythm, waved her arms. Closing her eyes, she gave herself up to it, hoping he'd watch and learn. Hoping he'd understand that sometimes escape was how she "turned it off."

When she opened her eyes a few minutes later,

she saw him, several feet away, his eyes closed as well, his movement loose and abandoned. Yeah, he was getting it.

Lauren had never heard music. Born deaf, she'd never understood her friends' obsession with singers and musicians. Oh, they were good-looking all right. But not being able to hear them sing took away some of their allure.

She remembered sitting on Becky Harold's bed at one of their sleepovers. Becky and Lisa Davis had jumped up on the bed, holding their hairbrushes like microphones, singing, while Lauren read their lips.

Both girls were hearing impaired, not fully deaf, so hearing aids gave them sound. Gave them the ability to speak normally. Gave them a world Lauren couldn't even imagine.

And then, two weeks later, Becky had gotten tickets to a rock concert for her birthday. Lauren hadn't known a thing about the band, and even now she couldn't remember their name, but Becky had been in heaven.

Lauren hadn't really wanted to go, but she'd yearned to be a part of the group, to fit in with her friends. By the end of that night, she'd been in awe, but for very different reasons than the other girls.

The live music had vibrated the entire arena, under her feet, everything.

The amplifiers sat right on the edge of the stage, flinging all that amazing vibration over them. For the first time, she'd understood. And she'd danced. Her feet couldn't resist moving. She didn't sleep a wink that night. She'd ached to experience this new world of feeling sound again.

Two days later, walking home from school, she stopped at a dance studio she'd seen, and until then, ignored.

She'd had no idea what she was doing, what she wanted.

Maxine had been so much younger then. So beautiful. Lauren had snuck in through a side door and watched. Staring as the girls, some of them years younger than she, others her age, moved in sync with each other, and apparently, with the music. She'd been fascinated and yet disappointed. She knew the music was there, but she couldn't hear it—or feel it.

She hadn't thought about talking to anyone or letting them know she was there. She'd just wanted to "feel" the sound, and had expected it here. But eagle-eyed Maxine had seen her and confronted her. Or tried to. She'd been talking, and while Lauren read lips well, no one before or since had talked that fast to her.

Thank heavens one of the dancers went to Lauren's school and knew she was deaf. She'd rushed over to explain to Maxine. Lauren had left as soon as she could, slinking home, disappointed. Not only had she not gotten to feel the music, but her foster mother had grounded her—again—for getting home late.

When she'd been summoned to the principal's office the next day, she gulped back her fears, lifted her chin and marched down the empty hall. Her heart sank when she saw the woman from the dance studio—Maxine—sitting with the principal.

Life had never been the same since. Two weeks later, Hudson had parked in front of her foster home and climbed out of the big Crown Victoria to put her measly two suitcases in the giant trunk. They looked smaller than the spare tire.

Her then foster mother hadn't even bothered to help. She stood there on the porch, leaning against the rail. "Be good for them, kid," she'd signed. "This is your chance." Lauren knew she was leaving out the usual "don't screw it up."

The backseat of the Crown Victoria had seemed huge. Lauren hadn't felt that alone, that lost, in a long time. She'd been through a lot of moves. What was this one? Her sixth? Seventh move to a new foster home? She didn't count that first one. That hadn't been going *to* anything. That had been leaving herself, her life, her mother's loss, behind. That was a tearful journey *away* from her life and nothing more.

Fifteen years had passed since she'd gone to live with Maxine. Maxine had given her so much. Music. Dance. A career. A home. Structure in a life of constant change.

Was she a bad person for not appreciating Maxine enough? Was there something wrong with her that she craved her independence so much? Too much?

She shoved her thoughts aside, letting the music take over. Doing exactly what she was teaching Dylan. Escaping.

JASON NEARLY DROPPED his phone when he reached the doorway of the practice studio. The caseworker's voicemail told him to leave a message, but for the life of him he didn't know if what he said was coherent as he hung up.

Because Lauren was dancing. Dancing in the way that made Jason's blood burn. Dear God, she was beautiful, so fluid, alive.

If Tina hadn't been standing beside him, and Dylan there on the dance floor with Lauren, Jason wasn't sure what he'd have done.

Dylan stopped first. Seeing his sister, he rushed over. Lauren stopped and Jason smiled, wishing she would keep dancing forever. She went to the stereo, and the sudden silence wrapped around them.

The siblings hugged, and Dylan bent down to peer closer at Tina's face. As he touched her cheek, her tears began anew. Dylan looked up at Jason, his face wreathed in confusion and growing anger. "What happened?" he asked them both.

"Let me tell him." Tina stepped back from her

brother, lifting her chin, making Jason proud of her. This wasn't going to be easy. For any of them.

"Do you want to talk with Lauren now or later?" Jason asked.

"I don't know." Tina shrugged.

Lauren came to stand with them. "What's going on?" she signed.

"Maybe one telling is enough," Jason said, encouraging Tina. "Let's find someplace private." Although there wasn't anyone around, Jason didn't want to be inadvertently interrupted.

Lauren nodded and led them to a cozy office. The desk had a chair and there were two smaller chairs facing it. Jason perched on the corner of the desk, making sure the others were seated.

"You're in charge," he told Tina. "But I'm here if you need help, okay?"

Tina nodded, clasping and unclasping her hands. Finally, she told everything, in words and once she got started, she seemed to recall to sign. Luckily, both Lauren and Dylan were proficient at lip reading.

"I only snuck out a couple of times," she reiterated.

"Where were you the other times?" Dylan asked.

Tina looked up at Jason and he nodded, reassuring and encouraging her. Tears filled her eyes. "Rhonda." She hiccuped. "She locked me in the basement closet." Tina looked down, her head bowed.

Dylan jumped to his feet, hands fisted at his sides before he signed and spoke. "What?" He looked over at Jason, who nodded in confirmation. "Why didn't you tell me?" He stared at Tina, hurt, angry.

Lauren stood, too, though she instead moved to pull Tina into her arms. Tina let her, but soon pulled away just enough to look at her brother.

Jason stood and took a step to stand between the siblings. Dylan looked ready to kill someone, and while Jason understood the urge, the anger wouldn't help any of them. "Rhonda threatened to take all this away from you." He gestured around at the studio.

That took most of the wind out of Dylan's sails. He sank back into his seat. Lauren signed one-handed, keeping Tina close with the other. Jason couldn't even begin to read it.

"She says, now what? We can't go back there," Dylan translated.

Jason wasn't sure if the last was Dylan's or Lauren's words. "No, you definitely are not," he said, his own anger bubbling to the surface again.

Tina pulled away from Lauren slightly. "Jason told her off good," she said, smiling through the tears.

Thank heaven she hadn't heard what he'd really wanted to say to the woman. "I made it clear I'll hold her responsible. For everything. I told her to pack up your stuff. We'll have everything picked up and taken to my office." He looked at Lauren. "But I—"

Lauren did the one-handed thing, and Jason's frustration returned. He wanted to understand.

"Lauren says we can stay with her until our caseworker figures things out."

Jason nodded, relieved Lauren understood. "I left her a message. I haven't heard back yet. Rhonda threatened to call her. Either way she's been contacted."

"She won't contact the caseworker," Tina said. "Rhonda doesn't like her."

"You should have told me that sooner, and I could have sent her after Rhonda before."

Tina giggled, and the mood broke. Everyone tried to smile. A disaster had been averted, but there was still a long road ahead. Dylan went to change, and Tina followed him in search of the restroom.

Jason settled back on the edge of the desk, not really sure what to do next. Tomorrow he'd talk with Chloe about how this would affect the case, and hopefully by then the caseworker would have called back.

Lauren's hand on his arm stopped his thoughts. She closed the door and leaned against it. "Thank you," she signed.

Jason scrubbed a hand down his face, appreciating her thanks but knowing she needed to know more of the details than Tina had shared.

He looked at her and shook his head as if that could clear his mind.

"That woman." He slowly signed, having to think of each sign before making it. "She said some *a-w-f-u-l* things to *T-i-n-a*."

Lauren took a step toward him. There wasn't anywhere for either of them to go in the small office. "You're a good man, Jason," she signed. She reached out and took his hands in hers.

Her fingers spelling his name surprised and pleased him. He'd never seen her do it before. His instructor had explained that names were unique signs, not just generic gestures for a person's name, but key to the person. They were created. He rather liked it spelled—especially with Lauren's slim fingers doing it.

"No need to sign." She smiled at him. "I can read your lips…" She touched his lips. "Just fine."

Seated as he was, he no longer towered over her. They were close. Slowly, she put her hand on his chest, right there in the center where his heart thumped. She was so attuned to vibration, she had to feel it.

"I've never known anyone to be so mean to a kid." He knew he was enunciating too much, but he needed her to understand.

She tilted her head and lifted her hands. "Tina is a hard kid, but no one deserves *a-b-u-s-e*." The last she thankfully spelled. There were so many words he didn't know. He pushed back his frustration.

"No. They don't. I told Tina that." He paused. Lauren had been in foster care most of her childhood. Had she been abused? His gut twisted and anger rose up. "Were you ever—?"

She interrupted him by shaking her head vehemently. "Not that way. Just...*i-g-n-o-r-e-d* or left out." She pointed at her ears, then her lips—the sign for deaf—explaining the obvious of why.

He reached for her, enfolding her in his arms. She felt so small and soft and warm. So right.

Lauren slid her arms up his chest, a caress that led to those same, soft, warm arms around his neck. She leaned into him, and he dipped his head to claim her lips.

She returned his kiss with the same enthusiasm she did everything, setting him on fire. He realized she understood him, his frustration with the signing, with Rhonda, and that she sensed the pain he felt.

She tasted of everything he'd gotten a hint of before. Strength, sweetness and energy. His mind filled with the images of her dancing, and he gently moved his hands up and down her back, needing to feel all that grace and magic. She molded so perfectly against him.

The sound of voices startled him. Tina and Dylan were on the other side of that door—the only thing that kept him from taking more of what she offered.

"The kids," he signed as he pulled back and pointed at the door. "I'll take you home," he said.

"This—" He brushed his finger gently over her lips before pointing back and forth between them. "*L-a-t-e-r.*"

She gasped, in a sweet, soft way, and slowly nodded before pulling away and opening the door.

CHAPTER ELEVEN

DROPPING LAUREN AND the kids off at her town house felt right. It also left Jason feeling lonely as he drove back to his place.

Wyatt and Emily were at their hotel, but there'd been plenty of questions on both their faces when he'd dropped them off earlier. Emily had some type of sixth sense. She'd had the perfect touch with Tina. Talking with her, not about why she was with Jason, or what had happened to put those tearstains on her face, but on who she, Tina, was.

Emily made the girl feel important, and he'd seen Tina bloom right there in the car. Then when she'd had to tell Dylan and Lauren about their foster mother's actions, he'd seen the strength Emily had nurtured come to the surface.

He owed his sister-in-law a big one, *and* some explanations. But not tonight.

Traffic grew thinner, at least by LA standards, and he pulled into the parking garage the same instant his phone went off. He didn't recognize the number. He answered once he'd pulled into his spot. "Hawkins."

"Is that you, Jason?"

Maxine's voice surprised him. How had she gotten his private number? Probably from Lauren or Susan.

"Yes, it's me. What can I do for you?"

"Is Lauren with you?"

"I just dropped her off." He'd almost said *and the kids*, but he wasn't sure how much Lauren would fill Maxine in on.

"Oh. She's not answering my texts. I wanted to make sure she sent Dylan home. He needs his rest before the show."

"Show? What show?"

"The fundraiser. Didn't Lauren tell you?"

"Uh, no."

Lauren hadn't said anything, but then they'd had a whole lot of other things to discuss. He sighed. Communicating anything took twice as long when he and sign language were involved. He needed to get better at it before they could reach a level of normal.

The feel of her in his arms returned and he took a deep breath to clear his mind and focus on Maxine's next comment.

"You really must attend," Maxine said. "Most of the profits go to support the foundation Lauren runs to help hearing-impaired children access the arts."

Lauren had a foundation? Chloe's comments in the conference room came to mind about Lauren's work with kids. He had so much to learn about her.

"When is the show?" He'd like to support it. And any excuse to see Lauren worked for him.

"Day after tomorrow. You should come. I can get you great tickets." She laughed. "I have an in."

He joined her laughter as much out of courtesy as the fact that he liked the older woman. An idea half formed in his brain. "My brother and sister-in-law are in town. Think I could bring them?"

"Oh, yes. That would be wonderful." Had he heard the sound of her hands clapping together? Probably. The dramatic action fit her perfectly.

"Sounds good. Make it four tickets and you've got a deal." He'd see if Tina wanted to go.

"You're not bringing a date, are you?" Maxine's accusation surprised and pleased him.

"No." He laughed. "Just family."

"Well, then. I'll take care of it."

"Thank you." The quiet that came through the line was full of unanswered questions. "Is there something else, Maxine?"

"Have you talked to Lauren lately about her inheritance?"

How did she know about that? Again, Lauren had most likely shared the info. "Not yet. I agreed to leave it alone until Dylan's case is settled."

"You won't forget, will you?"

"No, ma'am." He fought the smile. "I won't forget."

"She works too hard on these things, and for a

pittance. Seems silly not to take advantage of her windfall, don't you think?"

Maxine was anything but subtle. "Is that what you want me to tell her?" he asked.

She laughed. "You have a good night, Jason. My phone just beeped. Lauren is texting. I'll get those tickets. And Jason?"

"Yes, ma'am?"

"Thank you." Her voice faded off just before she disconnected.

Once again silence settled around him. Why didn't Maxine talk to Lauren about the inheritance money herself? Lauren loved her foster mother, he could tell that, but their encounter at the tea house the other day came to mind. Two strong-minded women had to make for some interesting days. He smiled—like when his sisters were all under the same roof.

He grabbed his things and climbed out of the car. Soon he was opening the door to his apartment, stepping into more silence.

For a long minute he stood in the foyer. It wasn't a big apartment, but it had plenty of room for him. The kitchen, a narrow galley, went to the right. Another short hall led to the second bedroom and small bath. The master bedroom was on the other side of the main room—the reason he'd taken this place.

The living room, dining room, great room all in one space lay straight ahead. The wall of glass filled with the city lights, their glow reflecting on the windows. He tossed his keys on the small table and set his briefcase beside it. He yanked off his already loosened tie and draped it over the chair.

The view drew him as it always did. He didn't turn on any lights, didn't need to. The openness of it reminded him of the view from Wyatt's ranch house. From the wraparound porch, you could see most of the whole valley. The rolling fields, the river that glistened in the distance when the moon was high.

Before Wyatt had taken over the ranch, their grandfather had owned the land, and his father before him. Wyatt belonged there, he'd spent more time there than he had in Austin where they'd all grown up. And while Jason loved the ranch, he couldn't take the slow pace, the too-much quiet of each day.

He laughed mirthlessly. So what was different about an empty apartment and a beautiful view his only company?

With a curse, he headed to bed, forcing himself not to turn around and head back to Lauren's place.

THE FINAL NIGHT of rehearsal was done. Nothing more to practice. All she could do was believe they were ready.

And they were. Every one of the kids had given 110 percent tonight. She'd never been so proud of them.

Closing up the studio, she wished it weren't so late. She could have used another hour to dance off her frustration. Hudson and Maxine had taken Dylan and Tina to dinner and would bring them to her place after. She'd been so relieved the day before when she'd told Maxine everything. Maxine hadn't even hesitated to volunteer to help.

Lauren had too many last-minute details to take care of, and the solitude after they'd left had helped her focus.

All day, Jason's promise of later hung over her, wafting by on every breeze, whispering over her thoughts. He'd dropped her and the kids off at her place last night, but she'd needed to get Dylan and Tina settled. That left no time, no privacy. Nothing but the promise that hung between them.

His goodbye kiss had been necessarily short… and searing.

Tonight, she stepped outside the empty studio. Traffic was light, cars whizzing by the studio only occasionally. Soon it would be dark, but Lauren wasn't paying attention. She was too exhausted, having tossed and turned most of last night.

And now the damn door wasn't cooperating. She needed to find someone to look at it.

Half afraid she'd break the key off, she turned it slowly, trying to lift the heavy door just the micro amount to align the bar with the—*bam*—it finally slammed home. She leaned back against the door frame, and took a deep breath. This was getting old.

Something brushed her shoulder and she jumped, knocking her purse from her shoulder. Its contents tumbled, but she didn't dare lean down to see how badly, not at first.

The dark fur ball sitting at the edge of the curb, staring at her with big green eyes, didn't look nearly as perturbed as she felt.

She pointed at him. That was the third time this week he'd done this. She didn't normally dislike animals. But this cat—

Her overreaction was all Jason's fault. He'd been the one to point out that it wasn't safe for her to be out alone after dark.

She didn't have time for this. Hastily, she crouched down to gather the belongings that had fallen out. Hitching her gym bag onto her shoulder, her purse following, she glanced up the street.

The bus was just turning the corner. She had to hurry. She could see from here that it was the younger guy, the one who barely stopped long enough for her to climb on, much less get settled before flooring the gas pedal. She did not want to wait another hour for the next bus.

Thanks, Jason, she thought. She'd never minded before. She always carried a book or her e-reader just so she could relax and wait for the bus.

She reached the sheltered bench, just as the bus's brakes squealed. The whoosh sent her hair flying and the sliding door flew open. She grimaced and climbed on.

The driver lifted a hand, smiling broadly at her, as always. With a nod, he turned the wheel away from the curb. There were only three other people on the bus, all at the back, so at least she didn't have to fear falling on anyone as she battled gravity and centrifugal force to hand-walk to the first seat. She settled with a thump that jarred her bones.

Leaning her head back against the metal bar along the seat back, she let her eyes drift closed as she took several calming breaths.

A couple of stops later, she was the last one on the bus. The others had jumped off at the risk of their lives, as the driver barely slowed at each stop. The last one, an older gentleman, had stood at the curb yelling at the bus. Lauren watched the bus driver brush off his anger, a chuckle shaking his thin sweater-clad shoulders.

She shivered. He really didn't care. Would he just run over someone if they were too slow?

Her stop was directly across from her town house, which was part of why she'd chosen it. It was beautiful and home, of course, but the freedom she had with a bus stop right across the street was huge.

He slowed, which shocked her. Maybe since she was his last stop, he was in less of a hurry? He actually paused, and opened the door fully. Turning in his seat, he grinned at her again.

He'd always smiled and been friendly to her. Why was she suspicious? Damn Jason. Shaking her head, she waved at the man and hopped down onto the sidewalk. He didn't even pull away from the curb until she was nearly to her front door, and then he moved away slowly.

Was he watching over her? What was he waiting for? Hastily, she unlocked the front door, thankful that the lock turned smoothly. Home felt good.

The house was shadowed, leaning more toward dark now. Hudson would bring the kids by in another half hour. She breathed a sigh of relief, enjoying the peace.

Lauren turned on the lamp on the hall table, then moved through the main level, turning on lights, closing curtains. She hated this new consciousness of the world. She had liked living in oblivion.

Her bracelet flashed an instant before her phone vibrated in her pocket. She pulled it out and saw a text.

You home? Jason had texted.

The part of her that struggled with independence wanted to text him back that no, she wasn't home, she was walking through the streets toward home, and she'd be there in another hour. A thrill ran up her spine as she wondered how fast he would get here. Might be worth watching. And she'd get to see him. Without anyone around—

She texted back a simple Yes.

Could he read between the lines of a one word text? She leaned back against the wall, waiting for his response. He'd want more. He was a man who wanted words, explanations, always more.

Just using sign to communicate, while it came naturally to her, it was difficult for him still.

Bus or cab?

Should she lie? It would be for his own good, really. She thought of the bus driver, with his creepy grin. She let herself relax, glad she was home, secretly glad Jason was concerned. Friend dropped me off. That was just a little lie.

Good. His word came almost too quickly. Flashing dots on the screen told her he was writing more. Who?

Shoot. No one you know. Was her response too quick? She waited.

Glad you're home. Safe.

Thanks. She ended by keying a happy face, signaling the conversation was over. He'd keep probing and while she was okay fibbing to him, letting the lie grow was not okay. She slid her phone back into her pocket and headed to the kitchen.

Time for dinner. She'd never enjoyed eating alone and definitely not during performance prep, but she did enjoy cooking. She'd just make a big meal, eat as she cooked, and be full before she ever sat down. Then there'd be leftovers for the next few days. Until the kids found them.

SHE'D TAKEN THE damned bus. Jason stared out the windows, willing himself to suddenly develop X-ray vision so he could see through the buildings and the city to her place. Was she having dinner? Going upstairs to change? To shower...

Emily's voice cut through his thoughts. "Jason? Where do you keep the garlic powder?"

Garlic powder? He didn't cook. "Uh, in the spice drawer. Left of the stove." If he had any. Tara, his sister the chef, was the one who'd sent him everything for the kitchen.

"Got it."

He sighed. Having Wyatt and Emily in town was great. They'd spent the afternoon at the zoo while he'd worked, then he'd met them here for dinner. He'd suggested they go out, but Emily had insisted on cooking.

The smells coming from his seldom-used kitchen were making him glad she'd been so determined.

"So—" Wyatt's footsteps were loud on the wood floor. "What would you normally do tonight?"

Jason turned around and watched his big brother settle on the leather couch. "I'd probably still be working," Jason admitted. "So this is a nice break."

Wyatt nodded. Uh, oh. Here it came. The "do you think you're doing the right thing with your life?" discussion.

"You've done well for yourself, little brother." Wyatt leaned back. "Mom would be pleased."

Whoa. Who was this guy?

Wyatt laughed. "Not what you were expecting?"

"No," Jason admitted. "Not even close."

Emily came into the room, a glass of wine in each hand. "Here you go, gentlemen. It's not a long neck, but tonight, let's pretend we're civilized and go with long-stemmed instead." She set the glasses on the chrome-and-glass coffee table and returned to the kitchen for her own glass.

"To family," she proposed her toast and smiled at Wyatt. Then at Jason.

"To long, happy marriages," Jason offered, and glasses clinked. Lauren's image filled his mind, and he almost shook his head to dispel it.

He wanted to curse. Wanted to—

Leave now, speed across town and make sure she was eating dinner, or relaxing, safe inside the town house, not riding some damned bus through LA's streets.

"Dinner's ready." Emily thankfully interrupted his wandering mind. Jason didn't miss the way Emily and Wyatt linked hands beneath the table. If he hadn't thought it would get him clocked, he'd have laughed at his brother. The rough cowboy was in so deep. Did he even have a clue?

Probably.

"I see your mom's chair is here." Emily pointed

to the wooden chair that really didn't fit in with the rest of his place.

"Yeah. I wasn't sure where to put it. The kitchen seemed like the right place."

Wyatt nodded. "I think most of us put them there." His face grew distant. "It's too bad they have to be separated."

Jason nodded. His phone chirped then, and despite his personal philosophy that phones didn't belong at the table, he glanced at the screen.

Thank you. Lauren had written, with about half a dozen smiley faces of varying levels of joy.

He frowned. For what? he sent back.

His phone chirped again. A photo appeared on the screen. A picture of a bouquet of roses, sweet baby pinks mixed with a darker red center bloom.

"I didn't send that," he said aloud, eliciting a look from Wyatt.

"Send what?"

"Flowers to—" They didn't know about Lauren. He was hoping to introduce them tomorrow night at the fundraiser. "A…friend."

He wished he could call her. But that wouldn't do any good. He stood, excusing himself. He'd explain to them later. He texted as he walked out of the room. They are lovely, but I didn't send them.

Oh. Came her answer. A long pause before she typed back. I thought maybe. Another pause before the next bubble of conversation appeared on the screen. If you didn't, who did? Must be a fan.

How did you text a shrug? Maxine? They weren't the kind of flowers an elderly foster mother would send.

Doubtful. Sorry to bother you.

No bother. Not ever. He waited for a long time, waiting for her to answer back.

"Problems?" Wyatt stood in the doorway.

"No. Just, uh, a client." It was as close to reality as he could come up with. "She's, just got a couple questions."

"A client has your personal number?" Emily joined them, kicking her feet up as she held her still half-full wineglass.

"It's complicated."

"Uh-oh. First you're giving wayward kids rides home. Now a client has your private number?"

He laughed, realizing she was giving him the same look he'd given her all those months ago, when they'd been at the hospital when DJ was hurt. Jason called her on her BS then and she was doing that to him now. "Okay, we've become...friends. She's deaf and texting is the easiest way to communicate." He shrugged.

Wyatt wasn't saying anything, but Jason saw the wheels turning in his brother's head. Jason was glad Emily was here, though her lifted eyebrow over the rim of her glass told him what they'd be talking about later.

CHAPTER TWELVE

"THIS IS IT." Jason had managed to score a parking spot across from the studio, surprising even himself with the parallel parking job. He had to fight back the gloat as he glanced at his older brother, the one who'd taught him to drive. Back in the day, he remembered Wyatt cursing as he tried to teach Jason how to parallel park.

"It's beautiful," Emily said as she got out of the car. Standing on the sidewalk, she stared up at the art deco exterior of Lauren's studio. The street in both directions was lined with cars and the small parking lot was full. Jason hoped tonight was a success.

This time, the ticket booth was lit up, looking like it came out of an old-fashioned movie. A young girl, dressed in the costume of a flapper from the 1920s, handed out the prepurchased tickets. The sign above her head read the event was sold out.

"Jason Hawkins. There should be four tickets?"

The girl nodded and smiled, sliding them through the half circle in the glass. "Enjoy the show," she said before turning to the next people in line.

"Your friend owns this place?" Wyatt stared up at the glaring marquee. "Lauren Ramsey, right?"

"That's what he said." Emily punched his arm. "Weren't you paying attention?"

"Were you there?" He grinned at her. "Then, no. I was not."

Jason groaned and led the way into the lobby. He'd texted Lauren earlier, and told her Tina was welcome to join them. Tina had been pleased with the invitation, especially after learning that Emily was coming along.

"There she is." Emily pointed and headed toward the girl. Tina smiled. He'd done the right thing taking her out of that foster home.

"Hi." Tina grinned, her painful tears long gone. "Thanks for inviting me to sit with you guys."

"You're welcome." Jason moved closer, wanting to ask a couple of questions without anyone overhearing. "Did the caseworker come over today?" He'd talked with the woman this morning, offering to be present, if needed.

Tina nodded. "She met with all of us."

"All of you?" Emily asked.

"Lauren, Dylan and me. Even Maxine was there. She said she'd help."

Jason's hopes rose. Maxine was a powerful force, having taken Lauren in years ago. He had a sneaking suspicion the woman knew at least one judge a little too well, but he'd never voice it as a concern. "That's good. Really good."

Emily put an arm around Tina's shoulders and hugged her. "That's great, hon. You'll have to keep me posted on how it all goes after I head back home."

Tina's expression faded for an instant, but Emily evidently noticed and quickly changed the subject, commenting on her apparently new shoes. Heels? Who let a thirteen-year-old wear heels?

"Don't say a word," Wyatt said softly at his side. "Don't act like you even notice." To the whole group, he said, "Shall we find our seats?" He led the way into the auditorium.

Their seats were toward the front, nearly center. Green velvet curtains were illuminated with spotlights situated on the edge of the stage.

Jason's previous conversation with Maxine came to mind. This was a fundraising event for the studio, for Lauren's foundation. Maxine had said that Dylan was dancing, but Jason hadn't even asked about Lauren. "Is Lauren performing?" he asked Tina before thinking.

The girl grinned, then shrugged. *Little stinker.* She'd seen them kiss good-night and knew there was something between them.

"I hope so," Emily said. "I'd love to see her in person. The performance videos on the internet were amazing."

Jason looked at his sister-in-law, surprised, much the same way her husband did.

"Since when do you watch ballet?" Wyatt asked.

"Since Jason told us about Lauren." She smirked, much like Tina had. The two females looked at each other and laughed.

Again, Wyatt leaned over. "Give up, brother. Just give up."

Jason shook his head, and turned to stare at the stage, wondering what Lauren was doing now. He didn't have long to wait.

The lights fell, plunging everything but the stage itself into darkness. Music rose, and slowly, the curtains slid apart. A wide, wooden floor glowed with spots of bright light, the back wall of the stage painted in a blue glow.

A dozen little girls, wearing stiff tutus, moved onto the stage in a line. They looked like the ballerinas that first night he'd seen Lauren dance. Was this a typical ballet move? Another reminder of all he didn't comprehend about her world.

Would he ever know and understand it all? Would he ever—

Lauren appeared then. Where the little girls wore a white outfit, Lauren was dressed in black. Her hair was in a braid that fell in a red-gold rope down her back. The starkness of the colors was beautiful, as were her movements. So smooth and fluid.

The little girls all wore toe shoes, but even he could tell they weren't quite ready for that move. Lauren, on the other hand, was at the top of her game. Magnificent.

She twirled on her toes until Jason was dizzy

watching her. At least, that's what he attributed the heat in his blood to. It had nothing at all to do with the memory of how those twirling curves felt in his arms.

BACKSTAGE WAS NOTHING like one of Lauren's professional performances where she went to the dressing room, took off her makeup and costume, and headed home. The chaos there actually had an order to it.

Not this. This was two dozen pint-size ballerinas running and screaming, burning off all that nervous energy they'd been so good about holding in while on stage. It was insanity and Lauren loved every second of it.

This was a family event, so soon the parents would be picking up their children. But until then, she and Lisa were in charge. Sort of.

Someone tapped her on the shoulder and she turned around, expecting a parent looking for a wayward child.

Jason grinned at her and signed hello. Her heart skipped. He looked so good, and her excitement at the success of everything bubbled over.

A man and woman stood with him, and she knew immediately that this was his brother. The men looked so much alike—and yet, the city boy and cowboy were a definite contrast.

"This is *W-y-a-t-t*, my brother. His wife, *E-m-i-l-y*." Jason finger-spelled the names, but the rest he signed clearly. He'd been practicing, and another thrill went through her at his efforts.

"Hello," she signed, extending her hand to shake theirs. The greeting felt stiff, and yet she liked their warm smiles and how they seemed to enjoy being with Jason.

Tina stepped over just then and spoke as she signed. "This is the lady I was telling you about." Tina had filled Lauren in about the trip from the airport, and how Emily had been so friendly. It was nice to meet someone who understood the world of foster kids. She told Tina that, and she saw Tina turn to Emily and speak.

"You're welcome," Emily said, facing Lauren so she could read her lips. Tina had apparently explained that, too.

"Lauren is letting us stay with her until our caseworker can get things straightened out," Tina signed and spoke.

Emily nodded and smiled.

"I wish we could stay with Lauren forever."

Lauren stared at the girl, surprised by the sincerity in Tina's face. Did Dylan feel the same? Lauren had no intention of letting either of these kids out of her life—but live with her? Like a...family?

Why did that send a cold shiver through her? She wasn't the parenting type. None of her foster mothers had taught her how to be a real mom. Maxine was the only one who'd come close, and she seemed more of a mothering coach than what Lauren thought a mom should be.

Lauren measured everyone against the faded memories of hugs, love and bedtime stories from her own mom. But that was all she had. She didn't have the skills—

She'd never considered the possibility of ever being a mom. Staring at Tina, Lauren couldn't even focus. Her brain shut down. Tina wanted to stay with her? The girl who'd hated every foster home she'd been in? The kid who wanted no one? Something Lauren understood too well.

Jason touched her arm, a frown on his face. "You okay?" he signed.

She nodded, knowing it was a lie. But surrounded by dozens of dancers, visitors, and families, she couldn't say otherwise.

"I need to work," she hastily signed, then turned away, hustling two miniature ballerinas back to the locker room. Their parents would be here soon. They needed to be out of costume.

"See you later?" Jason signed when she glanced back over her shoulder. He waited expectantly for her to respond. She did the one thing she hated others doing. She ignored him, using her deafness as a shield. She couldn't talk to him, or anyone. She concentrated instead on herding kids.

For the next half hour, she gathered tutus, tights and shoes. It was all she wanted to focus on right now.

At last, the locker room was empty. The costumes were gathered on one table. Rita was coming in tomorrow to double-check them, repair any that were damaged and clean everything. Lauren stared at the mound of tulle and sank onto the wooden bench that ran the length of the locker room.

What if—

What if Tina and Dylan actually did move in with her permanently? What if she totally screwed it up? What if? Panic clenched in her stomach. She couldn't do this. What was she supposed to do? She couldn't hurt them by refusing to take them in. She remembered too clearly the disappointment of not being wanted. Of having to leave a place she'd come to consider home. She'd only made that mistake a couple of times before she'd toughened up and shut off her emotions.

A shadow fell over her. If it hadn't been the girls' locker room, she might have thought Jason had come after her. She looked up to see Tina. The girl's face was covered in hurt. "Did I say something wrong?"

"Oh, no!" Lauren shot to her feet and pulled the girl into a hug. She leaned back after an instant. She knew she had to explain "You just surprised me."

"Don't you want us?"

This was just proving Lauren's fears true. She was messing this up. "Oh, sweetie. I love both you and Dylan. I just don't think I'd be a very good mom."

Tina's face lit up. "You are the best."

Lauren shook her head. "I don't know how."

Tina turned around then, and Lauren saw the woman who'd been with Jason earlier, his sister-in-law. Emily?

She said something Lauren didn't catch. "You can learn," Tina translated in sign.

Emily slowly walked over to them. She faced Lauren. "No one knows how to parent. They learn."

"I don't know." Lauren cringed. She didn't shrink from responsibility, and hated that she was considering it now. Fear was not something she allowed herself to feel. With a deep breath, she faced Emily and Tina. "How about we see what the court thinks, and go from there?"

Tina's enthusiastic hug nearly knocked Lauren off her feet. She laughed and Tina joined her. Emily smiled, too.

For the first time in ages, Lauren actually felt like one of the girls. Something inside her shifted. She chose to ignore it. For now.

STANDING IN THE lobby of Lauren's studio, with no one but his brother Wyatt for company, felt odd. If they were together, they were usually at the ranch, not the ballet. The crowds were gone, and other than the women in the locker room, the place was empty.

Which only made Wyatt's pacing all the more

obvious. Finally he stopped and glared at Jason. "Tell me how she's related to Haymaker. 'Cause she sure as hell looks like one of them."

Damn. He really didn't want to get into it with Wyatt now. Okay, he never wanted to get into it with Wyatt.

"Is she part of the business he hired you to do?"

"Yeah, she's the reason."

"Damn it, Jason." Wyatt paced away. "What are they up to?"

"Nothing. Wyatt, just relax. She's Pal's daughter—"

"What?" Wyatt paced. "That old bastard." He turned to face Jason again. "You're kidding, right? I thought you were gonna say she was a niece or even Pal Junior's kid. She looks the same age as Trey."

"About." Jason couldn't share her personal info, and didn't want to. But he had to explain to Wyatt. "She never knew Pal."

Jason explained about the meeting after DJ's wedding, and how he'd gone to the ballet with Pal and first seen Lauren. He stopped short of telling his brother how attracted he'd been to her.

"Do Pal Junior and Trey know about her?"

Jason shrugged. "I assume so, since they received copies of Pal's will, just like Lauren did."

"Trey might not know. He was still missing when we came out here." Wyatt resumed pacing. "When they find out, there's gonna to be hell to pay."

"Don't worry, Wyatt—"

"Don't worry? Have you ever dealt with that family? I know DJ thinks a lot of Trey, but he's lost his mind since Pal tried to frame him for murder. And Pal Junior's a chip off the old block. Not near as mean, but greedy."

Jason cursed. "I'm sorry to drag you into this."

"What?" Wyatt faced him. "Me? No. Me and the boys can handle anything Haymakers can come up with. Chet's probably chomping at the bit for a tussle since it's been so quiet lately. No, I'm more worried about her." Wyatt tilted his head toward the locker room where Tina and Emily had disappeared. "If you're right, and she never knew Pal, she doesn't have a clue what kind of men she's related to."

A movement in the doorway made both men turn. Lauren stepped from the shadows just then, followed by Emily and Tina. Lauren faced Wyatt. Had she seen what Wyatt said?

She harshly signed, "*You* tell me about them."

Jason translated. Yep, she'd seen.

Putting her hands on her hips, she didn't look or move away when Wyatt's glare turned to her.

"She can read your lips," Jason supplied. "She wants to know what you mean."

Wyatt stood there, considering her for a long minute, then nodded. Jason wasn't sure if he was agreeing with her or himself. "Meanest bunch I've ever dealt with. Your father was the worst." Looked like Wyatt wasn't going to hold back.

"Not a surprise," Lauren signed and Jason translated.

Jason surprised himself that he was reading her sign pretty easily.

"He did *a-b-a-n-d-o-n* me to foster care after my mom died." Jason had to pause as she spelled then repeated the whole sentence again.

"You were better off," Wyatt said.

Even Emily gasped at that.

"I won't sugarcoat it," Wyatt explained to them all. "She needs to know what she's up against." Wyatt looked at Jason then, and Jason recognized that expression—worry. Emily must have recognized it, too, as she moved to stand beside him and put her hand on his arm.

"Tell me. All of it." Jason spoke for Lauren's sign.

Wyatt shoved his fingers through his hair in a familiar gesture of frustration. "Last I knew, Pal was under arrest. If he'd lived, he'd be facing trial for theft, accessory to arson and probably murder."

Lauren stood tall, and while her gaze darted to Jason, she faced Wyatt. She circled her pursed lips with her finger and her hands gracefully turned over in the sign for death. "Who died?"

"One of my guys. A young man whose dad Pal had swindled out of his property."

Lauren frowned, confused. She turned to Jason. "He what?"

"*S-t-o-l-e* his ranch." Jason wondered if there was even a sign for *swindle*.

"Go on," she indicated.

"The wildfire they set destroyed nearly half our county. They tried to frame Trey, your nephew, for it."

Lauren had gone pale, but she didn't turn away. She stared at Wyatt. Finally, she slowly signed to Jason. "Are the others—*T-r-e-y*—like that?" She looked so stricken.

Jason hated this. "Your nephew has a good heart. But he's hurt. Pal Junior—" He looked over at Wyatt and Emily, who shared a glance. They knew Pal Jr. better.

Emily was the one who spoke. "He's not as mean. But they won't like that you got something they think is theirs. Greed makes people mean."

The silence stretched out, and Jason waited for Lauren to respond. She finally signed. "Good thing I'm a *R-a-m-s-e-y*." And she smiled, hesitantly, as if it might actually hurt, as if not sure how they'd react to her comment.

Jason wanted to take her in his arms and block out the world. But he knew she wouldn't want that.

Wyatt was the one to move. He walked toward Lauren. He towered over her, but the concerned frown on his brow seemed to shorten the distance. "I told Jason not to work for Pal. I don't trust him, even now that he's dead." He paused. "I don't want to see either of you hurt."

Lauren smiled. Jason saw the way it only lifted the edges of her lips and didn't light up her face. She looked so defeated, but the lift of her chin made him proud. She turned to gather her things. She shouldered her bag and headed to the entrance. Exhaustion and something he couldn't identify put a frown on her face. They all followed and waited as she locked up.

Maxine had taken Dylan earlier, but Tina had asked to stay to talk with Lauren. She was quiet now, her eyes wide. She'd heard everything. They all climbed into Jason's car for the silent ride home.

EVEN SPENDING THE next day in her office, sorting through and counting last night's receipts, didn't erase Lauren's unease. The success of the fundraiser should have filled her with joy and relief. Instead, the images Wyatt Hawkins had put in her mind overwhelmed her.

Dancing was the only thing that could take her mind off all of it. She turned the music up loud this time.

"Why are you dancing like that now?" Dylan had come through the studio door and stood with his arms crossed over his chest, waiting for Lauren to respond.

She stopped dancing, but didn't turn off the music. Maybe she shouldn't have shared her secret with him. "Show's over. It was a success. I can take a break." She felt the vibration of the song stop.

"Tina told me." Dylan didn't elaborate.

The next song's beat came in, and while Lauren didn't return to her dancing, she wanted to. Escape was why she was still even here on a Saturday evening. Everyone else had gone home.

"It sucks to have a lousy dad."

She met Dylan's gaze. His father was in prison and Dylan would be a grown man before he was released. Both he and Tina understood.

But... At least they'd known him as something other than a criminal. Dylan and Tina both remembered their dad fondly and on occasion were able to visit him.

She had nothing to counterbalance the hurt. And she did hurt. But why? Why did she hurt for a stranger? A stranger who left and never came back.

She nodded, not knowing what, or if, there was anything else to say.

Suddenly, the floor beneath them shook, and not from the music. Dylan stumbled as if someone had shoved him. His eyes were wider than before. There were no further vibrations, just eerie stillness.

Lauren pointed at the door that was oddly closed. It had been open when Dylan had come in. They always left it open, what with the old building's bad circulation. Dylan ran to it and pushed it open. Black acrid smoke poured in. He hastily backed up.

Panic and smoke clogged Lauren's throat, and

she saw it reflected in Dylan's eyes. More smoke came in from under the locker room doors. Thicker. Darker.

They had to get out of here.

The only way out was the door. There weren't even windows in the locker rooms. She yanked Dylan's gym bag off his shoulder and pulled out clothes. "Cover your face," she signed and pushed him toward the door.

It only took an instant before she felt the burning sting in her eyes from the smoke. It was strong and she tugged the shirt up over Dylan's face to protect him.

She struggled to breathe and they both coughed. Each breath hurt. At the door, beyond the smoke, she felt cooler air, not the heat of a fire. "Go." She waved and pushed him. He yanked off the shirt and ran.

She was right behind him until something hard hit her from behind. Her knees slammed into the wood floor, sending her sprawling. Even as she cried out, she knew Dylan couldn't hear her.

A hand yanked her braid and pulled her head back. She saw a man's face, blurred through the smoke and the tears burning her eyes.

CHAPTER THIRTEEN

"BOSS?" SUSAN RAPPED on the door frame, which was strange. Normally, she had no concept of barriers.

"Come on in," Jason said.

She stepped into the room and sat down gingerly on the edge of a chair. "I need to talk with you."

He tried not to get his hopes up that she was quitting or had found a new job.

Jason leaned back in his chair, watching and waiting.

"I was wondering." She fidgeted with the hem of her blouse, then looked him straight in the eye. "I don't think I need to keep taking the sign language classes."

"Really?" He tried to keep his temper at bay. She might not need the skill on a day-to-day basis, but it was important training in understanding others. "Why do you think that?"

"Well, the only person I'm sure I'll ever need it for is that one woman." She sat up straighter. "And she's not even really a client."

"No, not technically, yet. But Maxine Nightingale?" He leaned forward now. "She was her foster mother, and has a great fondness for her. And Dylan? The young man from last week, he's a part of her life as well as being deaf himself. So she's not the only one."

"Chloe is handling that case. So, we won't work with *them* much, I'm sure."

"Them? Why would you think that?"

"I just don't think we should—"

"Stop." He cut her off. "Think before you say anything more."

Susan's eyes grew wide, and she leaned back in her chair as if he'd moved toward her.

"If your reasoning has anything to do with not wanting to work with people who are different or have disabilities, I don't want to hear it."

"But—"

"Yes?"

She glared at him then stood and walked out of the room. "Fine," she said, more to the lobby than him.

Susan had come with the job. When the firm had hired him, they'd given him this office and introduced her as his admin. She'd been friendly and accommodating, until about twenty-four hours into their partnership. She'd been one of the many challenges he'd faced trying to get his foot in the door here. Reaching partner seemed more elusive each day.

"You handled that well." Chloe's voice came in

the doorway, and she walked in without waiting for an invitation.

"Thanks. I think."

She laughed and took the seat Susan had just vacated. "She's part of the gauntlet, you know."

"What?"

"We've all had to deal with her. So far, you've lasted the longest."

"What do you mean?" Someone had actually managed to get rid of her?

Chloe laughed as if she could see the wheels turning in his head. "Most of us foist her off on the next new guy who comes along. Lucky for you, there's a new recruit coming in next week."

Why did that make him feel uncomfortable? "Is there a reason you dropped by, Chloe?"

"Yeah, actually there is. I just heard from the DA. Your friend, Dylan? They're dropping all charges."

"That's great." What a relief. "Thanks."

"You're welcome, but the facts of the case were what did it. He didn't do what they claimed. Plain and simple." She stood and headed out. "We just proved it."

He half expected her to pump a fist in the air. At the doorway, she stopped. "New recruit's name is Jim Ryan. You might keep that in mind." She tilted her head toward the lobby and Susan.

Once his office was empty, Jason texted Lauren and saw the message from Wyatt. He and Emily had arrived home just fine. Staring at it, he felt the distance. And suddenly he knew that he wanted to give Lauren and Dylan the good news in person. He glanced at the clock. Hopefully, he could get to the studio before she headed home.

"I'm leaving now," Susan said from the doorway, her jacket over her arm and a purse hanging from her shoulder.

"Have a good evening." He didn't say anything else.

"Yeah." She disappeared, and he heard the elevator open and close. He wasn't far behind her, heading out of his office and driving to Lauren's studio.

Part of the reason Jason had started picking her up at night was because so many of the streetlights in the studio's neighborhood were out. It wasn't quite dark yet, so the lights hadn't come on. The quiet, empty eeriness of the street only intensified his concerns.

Was this the same street that just last night had been lined with cars? Turning the final corner, Jason slammed on the brakes.

Flames shot into the sky from the back of the studio.

Jason parked almost on the curb, his phone already to his ear. He noted the glass shards scattered on the sidewalk. The front door was nothing but an open frame.

"9-1-1 operator. What is your emergency?"

"There's a fire at—" Jason stepped back to look

at the numbers screwed to the front of the building and read out the address.

The woman on the other end of the phone asked him questions, which he automatically answered, but didn't remember the instant after he spoke.

Smoke and flames lit up the night and Jason tried to see through the thick cloud of smoke streaming out the doorway. Where was Lauren? Had she already left? He glanced at his watch. What time did she leave when she didn't have the late class? He cursed.

Movement inside the smoke made Jason run to the door. He called for Lauren, then felt stupid. She couldn't hear him even if she was fine. "I think there's someone inside," he told the dispatcher.

"Sir, don't go into the building." The woman's voice rang out through the night. "Assistance will be there momentarily."

Jason saw a shadow. Lauren? "Like hell." He stepped through the shattered door, pulling his jacket collar up and across his face as best he could.

Light flickered ahead. The main studio? The auditorium? What was he seeing?

Dylan stumbled out of the smoke just then, coughing.

"Where's Lauren?" Jason asked, making sure Dylan could see his face.

Dylan coughed hard, bending over and pointing behind him. Jason directed him out the front door.

"Go!" To the dispatcher, Jason said. "One person's out. I'm looking for another."

"Sir, you really need to stay outside."

At the next doorway, Jason looked around. Nothing. *Wait.* Further back, on the other side of this smoke. Two figures.

Who the hell? "Hey!" Jason yelled.

The man suddenly turned and leapt through the smoke. He ran straight at Jason, and slammed into him. Taken off guard by the impact, Jason slipped on the polished floor. His phone went flying, clattering on the wood and skittering away. He registered the sound of the dispatcher's voice sliding away into the smoke.

Lower to the ground now, below the smoke, Jason saw her. On the floor. Crawling in the wrong direction. His heart froze. *Lauren!*

His original intention of chasing the attacker gone, Jason prayed Dylan was out where the man couldn't find him. He hurried across the floor to Lauren. She was leaning back now, her hands over her eyes. Tears streamed down her cheeks. As he reached for her, her bloodcurdling scream shattered the air.

She fought him. Kicking and trying to bite him. Thank goodness for all the roughhousing he'd done with his siblings. Lauren gave him a pretty good thrashing before he got his arms around her, pinning her between his chest and the floor.

She squirmed, until suddenly, she froze. Something about him must have registered as she reached for him and held on tight. He tried to ease away from her, but she flung her left arm around his neck, nearly strangling him in her panic.

Jason had to get them out. Heat against his back told him to move. Fast. His eyes burned from the smoke. Carefully, he loosened her arm and scooted away, never letting go. He couldn't tell her his plan to get out and with the smoky haze, she'd never see his lips or his sign.

He stood, trying to help her to her feet. The air was so thick with smoke, he nearly considered crawling out, but couldn't take the time to explain such action.

He grabbed her other arm to guide her and they both nearly fell to the floor when she crumpled in pain.

Ah, hell. Jason scooped her up, each breath agony. They were running out of time. She didn't protest as he ran toward the door.

Fresh air slammed him in the face as he reached the shattered door. His lungs burned, and he fought to control the hard cough that threatened to send them both to the ground.

Jason sucked in air, hoping and praying he didn't stumble. He had to get her farther away. Away from the smoke and the burning building. He spotted Dylan sitting on the curb across the street and headed toward him.

Blue lights strobed the night. The wail of sirens

pierced the silence. He tightened his arms around Lauren. She'd burrowed into his chest, hiding her face against his shirt. Her left hand curled into his jacket collar, holding on for dear life. Her other arm she kept tight to her side.

A harsh cough took him by surprise. He jarred them both.

The fire truck he'd heard approaching pulled to a halt nearly in their path. Half a dozen suited figures jumped out, yelling orders, grabbing equipment, creating even more chaos in the night. Jason went around the truck and crossed the street, letting the fire crew have the whole mess.

He knelt down and carefully settled Lauren next to him. She didn't let go.

A young man, wearing a paramedic's uniform, carrying what looked like a tool box knelt before them. A woman stood behind him, an oxygen tank in hand. "Here." She handed Dylan the mask, helping him put it on. Then turned to Jason.

"She needs help first."

"We'll take care of her." The man reached for Lauren, only to be met with the same fighting, biting woman Jason had found in the studio. Her fear vibrated through her, shaking Jason to the core.

The fingers of her left hand were flying. Jason recognized the sign for Dylan's name.

He pulled back, hoping that the dim streetlights and strobing emergency lights would help her see what was happening, help ease her fears. She fought his attempts to pull away. He ached to talk, wished she could hear him.

"Hey," Jason said softly, hoping she'd at least feel his voice vibrate in his chest. "He's right here." Carefully, he put her uninjured hand on Dylan's shoulder. The boy reached up and covered her hand, squeezing briefly. She relaxed slightly, still burrowing her face in Jason's shoulder.

Jason tried to pull back, but she clung tight, shaking her head in refusal. Something wasn't right. He leaned back and gently cupped her chin. He gasped, and despite her protests, carefully turned her toward the EMT. "What the hell?" Jason asked.

The EMT cursed as well. "Those are burns. Chemical, I'd say." He hollered over at the fire crew. One of the firefighters came over. "Hey, you guys need to know. There's some type of chemical in there." He showed the man Lauren's burns.

The man cursed and rushed over to his captain. Jason watched them talk, though he couldn't hear anything. The urgency of their movements jacked up his concern.

"What happened in there?" the EMT asked Jason.

Jason looked over at Dylan, who was leaning back, his eyes closed. He tapped the boy's arm and repeated the EMT's question so he could read his lips.

Dylan shrugged. "We were talking," he signed rather than taking the oxygen mask off. "Then *b-*

o-o-m. She—" He pointed at Lauren. "Pushed me to the door. I ran."

"They don't know anything," Jason told the EMT. "I got here to find the place already aflame. Damn it, just take care of her." His panic threatened to choke him.

Lauren had no idea what was going on. Her eyes were closed. The lids and surrounding skin were a ravaged red. When Jason wouldn't let her burrow back in, she tried to put her hand over her eyes. Protection.

"I think her right arm's broken," the EMT said. "But the eyes concern me more."

Dear God. The EMT reached up to touch her face and Lauren yanked away. Jason knew it was necessary, but he ached at the idea of forcing her to hurt.

"She's deaf," Jason said. "They both are." He tried desperately to come up with a way to explain to Lauren what was happening. What the hell was he supposed to do?

The stethoscope around the EMT's neck caught his gaze. He took her hand, waiting an instant for her to recognize his touch, to calm. Slowly, he guided her uninjured hand to the stethoscope. At first, she flinched at the touch of the cool metal, then he saw the realization dawn, and she relaxed. She nodded, telling him she understood.

She cooperated, only crying out when the man carefully opened her eyelids and shone a light in each eye. "Her eyes themselves look damaged. But they react to light."

Jason had no idea if that was good or bad. Time moved slowly, mired in the sizzle of the water on the flames, in the loud calls of the firemen, in the destruction of Lauren's world. The EMT put some type of medication and gauze over her eyes so even if she wanted to, she couldn't see the damage. That might be a small blessing, but Jason knew she'd eventually be heartbroken.

"Sir?"

The female EMT had an IV bag in her hand. Lauren was struggling again. The EMT seemed to think bullying Lauren would get this accomplished.

"Shhh." He gently touched Lauren's arm. They'd splinted her broken arm, and wanted to put the IV in her other arm.

She was trying to sign. He was so damned bad at this, especially when she could only use one hand. They'd put Dylan in an ambulance and were preparing to take him to the emergency room. He needed medical care, not to have to be an interpreter.

Jason focused. She spelled slowly, carefully. "*W-h-a-t-s h-a-p-p-e-n-i-n-g?*"

He couldn't talk to her. Couldn't write on something for her to read. Couldn't even sign badly to her. He took her hand in his. At least he could give her that message. She turned her hand, palm up and held tight.

Minutes ticked by as they placed the IV in her arm and prepared her to go in the ambulance. Then she slowly moved her fingers and spelled, "*D-o-n-t l-e-a-v-e m-e*."

How could he tell her he wasn't going anywhere? He leaned forward and tenderly kissed her. She tasted of smoke and pain. And sweet Lauren underneath. She kissed him back and leaned toward him. Giving in. Hopefully, not giving up.

PANIC DIDN'T LEAVE room for words. Lauren tried to swallow back the hurt, the fear, the darkness. But it was all there.

What had happened? Who was that man in the studio? Was there anything left of her beautiful dream? Was Dylan okay? She'd felt his touch, felt him move and squeeze her hand, but she still worried. Were his eyes hurt, too? Or anything else?

Why was Jason here? She didn't have a late class tonight. Whatever his reasons, she was glad he'd come. If he hadn't... No. She had to stop those thoughts.

Dear God, her eyes burned. She'd never felt anything like this. Someone, she thought it was the female EMT—the whiff of perfume was her clue as were the softer hands—put a plastic tube in her hand. An oxygen tube. Seconds later, she put it beneath Lauren's nose and carefully, avoiding the tender skin around her eyes that hurt so badly, looped it over her ears.

The panic returned. Were her eyes permanently damaged? They couldn't even tell her. She'd never survive that. Trapped inside her head...

No, she'd been able to see light when someone had flashed it in her eyes. It had hurt, but it had been there. Bright and real. She clung to that knowledge.

The same way she clung to Jason's hand. Damn. She shivered in the night's heat. She hated dependence, but what choice did she have?

Jason's fingers moved, his index finger moving skyward with her hand following. "Up?" Seconds later, she felt Jason's arms close around her, lifting her. She let herself enjoy the safe cocoon for a minute, laying her head on his shoulder as he settled her on what felt like a gurney. Someone put a blanket and straps over her legs. Then she felt movement, first upward, then sideways. They slowly rolled the gurney over what she assumed was the pavement since it was so rough. Then up again. An ambulance?

Jason never let go of her hand.

She leaned back, and tried to relax. Her breathing was fast and her heart pounded. She tried to tell her body to calm and slow down.

Instead, her fingers tightened on Jason's. He squeezed back and she leaned toward him, turning her face in the direction where he had to be. She ached to see him.

She pictured him in her mind's eye—the way

he'd looked last night. Totally out of place at the ballet with his cowboy brother. She tried to smile, tried to focus on the image. He'd looked so good, tall and strong.

Jason wouldn't let anything more happen to her. She trusted him. She had to.

SLOWLY, CAREFULLY, THE emergency room nurse washed Lauren's eyes. The gentleness of the woman's touch astounded Jason, but even with that careful touch, Lauren flinched and tears flowed down her cheeks. "The tears are actually good for her," the woman explained. "They clean better than any solution I can make up."

Lauren clung to his hand, as if he might slip away. He squeezed her fingers. He wasn't going anywhere.

"Can you show her this?" The nurse handed him a soft cotton pad, thicker than the gauze of before. At least this nurse realized she had to explain to Lauren what was happening. He put the pad in her palm.

"I'm going to put one on each eye. It'll block the light completely."

Jason nodded, tapping the cotton against Lauren's finger, then oh-so-carefully putting his index finger on her damaged eyelid. He waited for her to respond with a nod. Slowly, the nurse put a clean pad over Lauren's right eye. She winced but didn't fight.

"It'll be pitch black when I'm done," she explained. "The light is as painful as the burns. But for her, I think the dark will feel worse." The woman's compassion impressed Jason.

She secured the first pad, then waited, letting Lauren adjust to the deep black. When Lauren nodded, the woman lifted the other one. Jason's chest hurt. He hated that he couldn't do more.

Her grip on his hand tightened. He let her hold on. Once she was done, the nurse stepped back and took a deep breath. This was tough for her as well.

"Thank you," he whispered and smiled faintly. Lauren seemed to sense they were done and signed thank you—it was a welcome sight. He leaned over and kissed her forehead. He was so proud of her.

She tapped the pads over her eyes and signed, "How long?"

Jason looked at the nurse, repeating her question.

"Couple days or more."

How did he explain that? After a minute, he took Lauren's hand and made the sign for two, letting her feel it against her palm. Then he spelled out *d-a-y-s* letting her feel each letter, figuring that would be easier for her than using the sign.

She frowned then as if it hurt. She smoothed her brow. "Go?" she signed the question.

How the heck would he explain that the doctor wanted her to stay the night? He gently pulled his hand away, eliciting a faint gasp from Lauren. He leaned close to her so she could feel his presence beside her. He put his palms together and laid them beside her head in the sign of sleep.

"Here?"

He took her hand and put it next to his jaw and nodded. He tapped a single finger there, then formed her hand into the gesture of night. She sighed and nodded.

She pointed in his general direction and then spelled, "*S-t-a-y.*"

Jason's heart caught. The fact that she asked him to be with her told him how unnerved she was. Lauren didn't ask for anything. Her independence was taking a beating, but she was also strong enough to know this was a time to admit she needed help.

He once again nodded, with her palm against his jaw. Her thumb moved slowly across the rough stubble of his chin, finding his lips. He covered her hand with his own, turning his lips to her palm, relieved when she let herself smile. He saw her relax, her shoulders drooping just a bit, and her head fell back on the rough gurney pillow.

Sleep was her friend, but he wondered if she could even do that.

"Dylan?" she asked.

"The boy who came in with us?" Jason asked the nurse. "Where is he?"

"He's just a couple of cubes away. He asked us to call his grandmother."

Jason nearly laughed. Dylan didn't have a grandmother. He had to mean Maxine. As if on cue, the older woman's voice rang out in the emergency room. "My darlings. Where are my darlings?"

How the hell would he explain this to Lauren? Did he even want to try?

CHAPTER FOURTEEN

LAUREN STARED INTO the darkness. Pitch-black, heavy darkness. Not the darkness of night where a rim of light shone under the door, or the moon's faint glow peeked around the edges of a drawn curtain. No, this was weighted down, with pain, with bandages and fear.

Memories rushed in, and she was unable to bite back the cry of anguish that rose in her throat. She felt it escape from between her lips. The heat of the flames, the smoke, dark and thick, at first making her eyes water, then burn the longer she'd struggled to see where she was going. She shook her head to dispel the sensations, but froze as pain bounced around her skull.

She had no idea where she really was, though she'd been "told" she was at the emergency room. How long had she been here? Most of the time, Lauren hadn't been sure what was happening. Panic bathed her body in sweat, and she tried to sit up on what was likely a gurney. Something hard— a hand—settled firmly on her shoulder, pushed her back down.

She cried out again. She wanted to fight, longed

to have the ability to yell at them and tell them what she thought and wanted—and didn't want. She could sign, but they probably wouldn't understand her…or would they? A couple of choice gestures came to mind.

Then suddenly, another hand came out of nowhere, not to hold her down, but to curl around her fingers, warmly, gently. She knew this palm, knew the thick fingers and hard calluses of Jason's hand. She turned her hand in his, gripping hard, letting his touch engulf her and soothe her.

She'd never been able to know what the world sounded like, or what sound really was. But she'd been able to function by looking at it. She "heard" by reading lips and watching signers form words with their hands. Now she couldn't hear *or* see. Her greatest fears realized.

Was it gone forever, her only means of connecting? She felt as if she were trapped inside a coffin. The panic returned.

And then Jason's fingers moved. He was signing in the palm of her hand. Slowly at first, then more quickly, as he must have realized she understood what he was doing. She nodded, relief flooding her. He formed the letters he was just beginning to learn.

For her.

Her eyes burned, not from the smoke or her injuries, but emotion. She prayed the bittersweet tears could somehow wash away the pain and damage.

Lauren didn't have time to wallow in self-pity, though the temptation was strong. She had to focus. It was one thing to *see* a sign, another to feel its contours.

What was that? An *m*? An *a*, *x*. Maxine! Maxine was here? Another familiar hand, older, thinner, precious, curled around hers.

For the first time, Lauren understood Jason's frustrations at having to learn all this. Her chin up, she frowned, her concentration overpowering her fear.

She could do this. She'd find a way to make this work. No one was taking her life away, not if she had anything to say about it.

THE LOOK ON Lauren's face when Maxine took her hand might have been comical if she hadn't been so stricken. The bandages were stark white against her face, covering the piece of her that was the most expressive. Her eyes. But Jason knew her well enough now to read her body language.

From the nurse's explanation, he knew that she couldn't see a thing. Total darkness would give her eyes the chance to truly heal. Add that to the fact that she couldn't hear a thing…

Lauren immediately recognized her foster mother's touch, and she let the older woman hug her. Jason breathed a sigh of relief.

The nurse came back then. Her silly grin told Jason that she recognized Maxine, and along with the information she needed, he'd bet she'd ask for an autograph.

He let them have their moment, but once that was done, he stepped forward. "You're releasing Dylan?" he asked the nurse.

"Why, uh, yes. Here are some medications if he needs them tonight, and prescriptions to fill at your pharmacy tomorrow, if needed." She shook the packet she'd stapled to the discharge instructions and handed it to Maxine.

Jason really should let them know Maxine wasn't related to Dylan. He was, at the moment, a ward of the state. But the state wasn't here and wasn't going to take him home. Maxine would.

Dylan sat on the edge of the gurney, already anxiously moving his legs. He wasn't one to sit still long. Already, he looked better than he had all night. "Where's Tina?" he asked.

"She's with Hudson." Maxine spoke and signed. "They're meeting us out front."

Everyone nodded. Everyone except Lauren. She had no idea what was happening. The frown on her brow told him she wasn't happy about it. Her teeth caught her lip, her anxiety growing.

"Lauren's staying overnight," Jason informed Maxine.

The woman spun around from where she'd been talking to Dylan. "What?"

"The doctor wants to keep her for observation."

"Oh, dear." Maxine looked up at Jason, almost

too imploring, then back and forth between Dylan and Lauren, as if she had to choose. "What are we going to do?" This obviously hadn't been what she'd expected.

"Are you comfortable taking both kids?"

"Of course!"

"Then I'll take care of Lauren." He wasn't leaving her anytime soon, anyway. Until he figured out what *who* had caused the fire, he wasn't letting her out of his sight.

But how would he explain to Lauren? He reached for her hand, and she gripped hard. He had to force her fingers to let go. He slowly spelled *D-y-l-a-n*, then made the sign with her fingers for go and then guided her hands into the "home" sign. Then spelled Maxine.

Lauren puzzled it through, then nodded. Her brow smoothed slightly. She then pointed to her own chest.

He took a deep breath. Then put her hand on his chest and made the sign for stay. He was staying with her.

She shook her head. She signed that she couldn't ask him to do that.

"You're not asking." He kept the signs slow and simple, as much because of his own meager skills as for her. "No choice. I am staying."

Lauren bowed her head, then nodded. The slow way she made the thank you sign told him how much she appreciated it, *and* hated it.

When the nurse returned, Maxine signed the autograph with a flourish, then held the paper up and said, "This is my attorney. He'll be staying with my foster daughter."

She did take control of everything. Lauren wouldn't like Maxine doing that, but in this case it worked. And the nurse didn't even question her authority. He wasn't sure if it was due to awe or procedure.

He didn't care. Someone had tried to kill Lauren. They wouldn't get another chance.

Lauren was asleep. Jason stood in the doorway of her hospital room, staring at her. With the bandages, he couldn't see her expression. They'd taken her for X-rays and put her arm in a cast. How would she sign? He knew she could use one hand, but the signs were far from complete. Not all signs could be modified.

Mentally, he cursed, barely resisting the urge to put his fist through something or someone. If and when the cops found that guy, Jason hoped he didn't meet him. He couldn't promise to control the urge to kill the bastard.

Lauren moved, her legs shifting beneath the thin blankets. A soft whimper escaped from between her lips. Jason took several hasty steps, intent on comforting her.

And then, just inches from the side of the hospital bed, he froze, remembering her frightened scream at the studio. That had been the first real sound he'd heard her make.

As he stood there, she moved abruptly, startling herself awake. Her whimper of fear sent him the rest of the way to her side.

Jason tossed his jacket to the chair beside the bed as that sound came again—her small cry of terror. Carefully, so as not to jar her, or hurt her, he put his hand over hers and waited for the recognition.

She smiled and let her head fall back. Slowly, he moved away, watching as she tensed again. He lowered the rail of the bed.

He'd barely touched her again when she moved, sliding her hand up his arm, reaching for him. He leaned toward her. She wrapped her arms around his shoulders, burying her face against his neck. He pulled her in tight, rocking her.

Though he knew she couldn't hear him, he made all the appropriate, soothing sounds. "Shh, I'm here. You're safe now."

Lauren shifted, and he took the opportunity to settle next to her on the bed. Curling into him, she laid her head against his chest and pressed against him. What was she doing? Then it dawned on him.

As she'd blared the music in his car, feeling the beat of it, she was feeling his voice. His breath caught. He cleared his throat, struggling to get the words out, words that meant nothing to her, but which connected them. Intimately—closer than if they were lovers.

For the first time in his life, Jason was at a loss for words, but he'd be damned if he'd let her down now. He racked his brain for anything to say. "You know that I saw that last performance you did at the Alex Theatre?" He'd never intended to tell her, mostly because it was something he wanted to tell her, not explain impersonally in a text. "Your father was there. Pal. He came to see you perform. Dozens of times apparently. He was so proud of you." Someday, he'd have to tell her all of this again. Someday, when he could fully explain, and she could understand.

He felt her relax, though she was no closer to letting go than when she'd first reached for him. They couldn't sit like this, on the edge of the bed all night. She needed to sleep.

He shifted and her grip tightened. She remained silent and while he longed to hear her voice, he'd take silence forever rather than ever hear her pain again. "Come on, hon." He shifted her into his arms, closer.

Lifting her, Jason settled back on the mattress, stretching out with her, letting her lay her head in the center of his chest, where she could feel his voice and heartbeat.

"I'm not leaving. Not until you're ready for me

to," he said then shook his head. "Not leaving," he signed against her fingers.

Lauren signed her thank you, then something else he couldn't read, but he wasn't asking her to repeat it. He could see that the exhaustion, and the pain meds, were starting to take their toll. He closed his eyes, slowly moving his hand over her hair, stroking and soothing.

"My mom used to tell us bedtime stories. There was one I especially loved." He let his voice lower, speaking slowly as his mother had as a way to coax him to sleep. In his own mind, he heard his mother's voice, letting that calm permeate him and seep into Lauren. While he held her tight, he felt her breathing even out.

It was working. Peace soon wrapped around them. She'd fallen asleep. Thank God. He might never recover from the horror of tonight. Now that the activity had died down, the responsibilities had slipped away and she was safely asleep in his arms, the memories returned.

Of going to the studio to tell her and Dylan the news he still hadn't delivered, to pick her up for a music-filled drive—and perhaps pick up where they'd left off the last time they'd been alone—only to find her there in the flames and smoke. A man standing over her, her hair roughly falling from her ponytail, her face soaked with tears and angry red marks—from the smoke? The chemicals? What else had that man done?

The asshole had run as soon as Jason arrived.

If he hadn't appeared then…what would have happened?

Had the stranger intended more harm? Would they ever know?

The police wanted to question Lauren, but even they knew the futility at this point.

Anger, guilt and pain warred within Jason as he held Lauren.

The night stretched out as his thoughts chased his anger round and round inside his head.

WITH A SHEAF of discharge papers in her hand, wearing the new set of clothing Maxine had brought for her earlier that day, Lauren settled into the wheelchair. Jason was near—she could smell him—and his warmth settled against her back, reassuring. She'd have to wear the bandages for at least two more days.

Anger and fear choked her. Anger that someone had taken her independence so easily, and fear that she'd never get it back. The logical part of her knew she'd recover. The doctors had explained that—at least that's what she thought Jason tried so hard to communicate to her in simple sign. She still had to puzzle through it. And while she knew her body would heal, would she heal on the inside as easily?

How did you recover from fear?

Jason touched her shoulder, a signal they'd devised to tell her he was moving. The uneasiness only increased. She couldn't see where they were going, sensed only movement. She had to force her fingers not to tighten in a death grip on the wheelchair's arms. She concentrated on breathing evenly, smoothly.

Finally, cool air whooshed over her, and Lauren realized they'd gone outside. Up a slight hill, then down. A ramp. He slowly came to a halt.

Lauren sat still, not quite sure what he expected of her. Carefully, he tapped her knee, indicating she put her feet on the ground. Then he curled his big strong hand beneath her elbow and gently nudged her to stand. Air brushed the back of her legs. The wheelchair was gone. He put her hand on top of solid metal. A car door. She slid her fingers along the top, knowing the feel of his car.

Comfort and familiarity washed over her as she was able to slide into the passenger seat. She knew this car, this seat, this warm interior. She felt the door slam, and held her breath until the car dipped as Jason climbed in on his side. His door settled in place, signaling they were both in. They were here, alone.

Wonderful.

The engine roared beneath her feet, and she leaned her head back on the warm leather headrest.

The first thump of the music surprised her, startled her. Soothed her. The sensory deprivation of the past forty-eight hours had been too much, and Jason somehow knew she needed this.

Just as he'd known she'd found comfort in the vibration of his voice last night.

Bless him. She wanted to reach over and hug him. Instead, she let the beautiful beat move through her, let the music fill her. She ached to dance, to let her feet take her across the floor of her studio—

How badly was it damaged? She hadn't asked, and no one had told her. Not that it would have been an easy task. They'd had enough trouble just telling her how they were treating her injuries.

Her eyes burned, not from the anger or fear of her injuries. No, these were tears of grief. She knew it was gone. There was no way the old building had survived a fire that hot, that smoky.

Strong thick fingers touched the back of her hand. She hadn't realized she'd been gripping her own fingers tight. Her knuckles were probably as white as she imagined the bandages covering her eyes were. She forced herself to give in to the comfort of Jason's fingers gently holding hers.

JASON DROVE TOWARD his apartment. He knew Lauren would prefer her own place, and Maxine had pointed that out as well. But the town house's steep stairs and crowded spaces were too risky. Even something as innocuous as a trash can, unexpected at the end of a counter, could be a threat to a person who couldn't see.

The older woman had also pushed for Lauren to come to her house, but the kids' school schedule was plenty to keep Maxine *and* Hudson busy.

Not to mention that "someone" knew where Lauren lived. But Jason wasn't going into that with Lauren right now. He didn't want to scare anyone right now.

Somewhere in the middle of last night, when he'd awakened for the dozenth time, he remembered the text Lauren had sent him the night she'd received the flowers.

Had that asshole who attacked her sent them? He'd let the police know about the texts as soon as he could. Since the phone didn't survive the fire, he hoped the police could get the files from the phone company.

Fighting his frustration and anger, he focused on the road.

When he pulled into his parking spot and killed the engine he saw Lauren momentarily wilt, then go on alert. He didn't let himself think. If he did, he wasn't sure he could keep his distance. The need to fix things, the nagging sense of guilt that he should have been at her studio sooner, and the growing feelings he was experiencing toward Lauren would overwhelm him otherwise. She was a strong, independent woman. It was part of what he loved about her.

Loved? He stared at her. Yes.

The rightness of the answer didn't surprise him as much as he thought it should.

Patiently, she waited for him, and he hated her having to do that. "Come on." He wasn't sure who he was talking to. He climbed out and went around the car. She sensed the door opening and turned to climb out. She clung to the door's frame, hesitant.

Jason cringed, hating her fear and weakness. It was not who she was. He needed to get her back to normal.

Slowly, he led her to the elevator, fighting his own urge—again—to pick her up and carry her safely away from everything.

He put her hand on the keypad, the familiar round buttons, letting her know they were going into an elevator. She leaned against him as they rose up toward the twelfth floor. When they stepped into the hall, he wondered what she'd think if she could actually see this place.

He'd been overwhelmed and impressed when he'd first seen it, moving here from Texas. The chrome-and-blue color scheme was identical on each floor, each apartment a cookie cutter of the next. Some furnished, some, like his, not.

Again, she stood patiently as he unlocked his apartment door and guided her inside. He flipped the light switch, the can lights in the ceiling coming on to splatter pools of gold across the low-pile carpet. He led Lauren to the couch, guiding her around to the coffee table, having her touch the cool chrome and glass so she'd know it was there.

"Where are we?" she signed, facing him. Trusting him.

He paused, then took her hand and made the signs for "My place." He waited for her reaction. He was pleased when her lips turned up in a faint smile.

"Not fair," she signed. "I can't see your secrets."

He laughed, and too late, realized she still had her hand against his chest and could feel the vibration. He froze. She froze. As if she could actually see, she tilted her face toward him, questioning, inviting?

Disgusted with himself for even considering taking advantage of the situation, and fighting the ache to pull her into his arms and kiss away his own fears, he stepped back.

LAUREN WAS TIRED. So tired. But falling asleep scared her more than staying awake. Would the darkness still be there, as painful and oppressive when she awoke?

Jason had been wonderful. Last night at the hospital, he'd held her all night. That couldn't have been comfortable. But even if he'd complained, she couldn't have heard him, or even seen him sign. She'd missed so much.

She had to keep from crying. Tears burned. The ointment they'd given her helped a bit. Soon she'd have to apply more. Just before she went to bed.

She couldn't do it alone. The nurse had done it this morning. For a brief instant, she'd seen the blurred, shadowed image of the woman's kind face.

Tonight she'd need Jason's help. She dreaded that, too—dread mixed with anticipation.

What a mess.

The rhythm of approaching footsteps vibrated across the floor. He was near. She smelled the faded scent of his cologne. So comforting.

Jason touched her gently on her shoulder. Even with the warning, she jumped. "Sorry," she signed, knowing he'd want her not to feel sorry, but unable to help herself.

The side of the bed dipped as he settled beside her. Slowly, he took her hand, putting the tube of ointment in her palm, letting her feel the plastic's coolness. Then he softly tapped her forehead beside the tape. He was letting her know he was ready, letting her know he'd wait for her. Slowly, with her uninjured hand, she reached up and gently pulled at the medical tape, loosening the bandages.

Light stabbed her eyes, burning, painful. The damaged skin around her eyes tingled with the brush of the room's air. She blinked quickly, tears falling as her body tried to cleanse itself.

Jason had turned off the lights, all except one, clear across the room, but even that was too bright. Still, relief washed over her. Even in the dim light, she could make out his shadowed figure, could see the glow.

She needed to be patient, believing she'd be fine—in time.

Jason reached for the tube and nudged her chin back. She knew the drill, knew he had to help put it in between her lids. It was thick and gooey, and while it eased the pain, it was like looking through Vaseline.

As he lifted his hand to put the first bit on, she reached up and stopped him. She wanted to look at him, just for an instant. She took a moment to catalog his shadowed features. Her heart caught. He was so close, and, though out of focus, she let her hungry gaze drink in everything it could. She tried to put the blurry images together with what she knew. Her mind filled in the pieces, and she let herself savor the relief. She could see him clearly, at least in her mind.

Hesitantly, she reached up, laying her palm against the rough skin of his jaw. Slowly, she slid her fingertips toward his lips, and felt the softer skin move. Was he saying something? Then he paused, taking his hand and covering hers, pressing a gentle kiss to the center of her palm.

She lifted her blurred gaze to look at him, wanting to never stop looking at him…praying she'd be able to see him soon, clearly, in full light.

"Okay," she signed and tilted her head back. He nodded and moved closer, carefully, taking the tube and tilting it toward her eyes. Then once he'd recapped it and set it down, he took more gauze and tape to make her another mask.

Dread rocked her. The darkness threatened to overwhelm her. This time, he paused. The bandages in his hand, he reached out and cupped her chin, much as she had his. He didn't stop, however, but instead, leaned closer, closer still, and put his lips to hers. Gently, softly at first, and then with an insistency that thrilled and scared her. She returned his kiss, letting her eyes close naturally as she curled her fingers in the soft fabric of his shirt.

Lauren felt the vibration of him clearing his throat as he moved away. She didn't open her eyes, wanting to keep the kiss safe inside.

Oh, so gently, Jason put the gauze over her eyes and put the tape in place. The darkness wasn't quite so frightening this time. Maybe because she knew there was light on the other side of the bandages, light that she would be able to see at some point.

Or maybe it was because Jason slipped onto the bed beside her, fully clothed, and pulled her up against his chest, just as he had last night. She snuggled against him, not needing him as much as she had last night, but still not wanting to be alone.

She let sleep scoot in closer. Then she felt Jason relax and the soft vibration of his snore reassured her. If he was tired enough to sleep like this, he deserved it, and if he was comfortable enough, Lauren could, too.

CHAPTER FIFTEEN

SUNLIGHT POURED IN the windows. Jason had been so tired, and focused on getting Lauren settled last night, he'd forgotten to pull the drapes.

He looked down at her. She was curled up in the center of his bed, the blankets tucked beneath her chin, the bandages still firmly in place. Thank heavens. If she opened her eyes without them, the pain would be awful.

The skin on her forehead had been irritated by the chemicals, but this morning it looked much less angry and red. Hopefully, her eyes were improving as well. He'd take a good look when they put in the next dose of medicine.

It was still early, barely past sunrise, and while Lauren needed to sleep, Jason couldn't stay here with her. Not without his body betraying the feelings growing between them. He stood and closed the curtains.

Shadows fell over the room with the only remaining light coming from the reflection of the sunlight off the hall floor.

Leaving the bedroom, Jason made coffee and took a steaming cup out to the balcony. The twelfth floor wasn't up so high that he had an unimpeded view of the city. But between the buildings, he could see the distant hills and the city scattered beyond. The morning light slanted through and glinted off the rows of window glass.

He made a call to the office. His cell phone had perished in the fire, so he'd asked Susan to get him a new one. Thank God, it was company-issued—all he'd had to do was call IT, not deal with a phone company. He let Susan know he wouldn't be in today—he wasn't going anywhere, at least not anywhere that didn't involve Lauren. The idea of leaving her here, alone, made him shudder.

After he'd hung up, he finished his coffee and hustled to the shower. He needed to get ready for the day before Lauren woke up and needed his help.

Minutes later, Jason stepped out of the shower and froze. Lauren stood in the doorway. Slowly, hesitantly, she ran her hands along the door frame. When he'd first brought her into his room last night, he'd walked her around the floor plan. Odds were, she wouldn't remember much, but there were some essentials she'd needed to know about, a bathroom being one of them.

Lauren couldn't see him, but he hastily wrapped the towel around his hips anyway. She moved slowly, tentatively, as if trying to remember where everything was. The frown on her brow decided him. He reached out to her, his hand barely touching her elbow. Still, she jumped and hit her shoulder on the frame. Her gasp was soft, but definitely pain filled.

To keep Lauren from stumbling, Jason pulled her back to keep her steady. Lauren froze as her bare shoulder grazed his naked chest. Her sharp intake of breath was loud, vibrating clear through him.

Slowly, Jason put his hands on her shoulders—noting how her cheeks burned bright pink. He smiled. She'd apparently guessed his state of dress—or rather, undress—correctly. Carefully, he turned her in the right direction, and guided her to find what she was looking for. She nodded and closed the small privacy door.

Jason chuckled. She looked cute when she blushed. He had just enough time to grab clothes from the closet and cover the important parts. He was pulling his shirt on when she opened the door.

She'd never find her way back without help. She'd be covered in bruises if she hit any more walls. He hustled, barefoot, his shirt hanging open, and met her in the doorway. He touched her arm, and she let him guide her to the sink. By feel, she found the faucet and soap. He waited patiently, watching her, enjoying the view.

Even hindered with the cast, and unable to see, her movements were smooth and graceful. It was a bit disconcerting to watch her this way. He could look his fill, and he did. She had to know he was watching her. So why did he feel like a voyeur?

Even sleep-mussed, without all the trappings of

makeup and done-up hair, she was beautiful. Her hair hung to her hips in thick copper waves that had his fingers itching to touch. He didn't dare. He might never let her go.

The simple nightgown scooped low on her chest, clinging to curves he'd barely had the chance to explore. The other night in her office seemed like years ago.

Like most women, Lauren probably wouldn't believe him if he told her how pretty she looked. It didn't matter, though, since he couldn't tell her much of anything right now.

Not with words, anyway.

He intended to guide her back to the bed, but somehow, his fingers made a side trip to slip a stray curl behind her ear. The skin of her cheek was soft as down. Jason let his fingers linger.

Lauren leaned into his touch.

"*J-a-s-o-n*," she signed, then she swallowed hard. "I—" She tapped her chest, and then stopped. She tilted her head up, as if she could see him. Slowly, she reached out and touched her fingertips to his chest. Her fingers were small and cool against his bare skin. At first she froze, then slowly, painfully slowly, she slid her fingers upward, over his shoulder, along his neck to his still-rough jaw. She lingered there, her palm grazing his chin as her thumb slid enticingly over his lips.

Jason doubted she realized her tiny pink tongue

came out just then to run a damp trail over her own lips. Anticipation?

His heartbeat quickened, and while her hand was no longer against his chest, she had to feel the vibration that shook his entire body. After a couple of deep breaths to try and still it, he took her arm to lead her out of the intimacy of the bathroom.

But she didn't move. And he didn't guide her away. Instead, he pulled her against him, her warmth so sweet and soft. She was small, and while he leaned down, she still wasn't close enough. He bent and slipped his arm beneath her knees and lifted her up against his chest. He'd carry her back to his bed, rather than let her stumble around.

The cast rested solidly against his shoulder, but her other arm curled snugly around his neck, and she slid her fingers into the hair at the nape of his neck.

Jason should take a step, or two. He really should. But her lips were so close.

Lauren tilted her head and laid it against his shoulder. He called himself every kind of jerk for thinking about carrying her to his bed to do more than lay her safely down on the rumpled sheets—

Until her lips moved. Hot and soft against his neck, up along his jaw. Her tongue came out to taste him, tease him, torment him.

All he had to do was tilt his head just…so…

She tasted of early morning and sunshine—her lips soft and warm and welcoming. At first, he felt her thank you—but this was not simply a thank-you kiss. This was something more, something he craved and ached for.

Standing there, with her plastered across his chest, all the want he'd held back leapt to the surface. He was a man lost. Lost to Lauren's touch and his own desire.

LAUREN FELT THE groan in Jason's throat and his fast, hot breath brush over her skin. Though she couldn't see him, she had the taste, feel and scent of him. She'd never felt more a part of another person.

Her fingers moved, spelling absently against his neck, "*L-o-v-e m-e*." But even that thought process vanished as he kissed her. Long and deep.

Then suddenly, they were moving. Cool air wafted against her bare legs, and her toes brushed the edge of the door frame. The beat of his footsteps felt steady and strong. The bed's smooth sheets were cool against her back as he laid her down.

His bed.

She'd slept with Jason two nights in a row now. And he hadn't been inappropriate. Hadn't touched her. Hadn't—anything.

Had she misread the signals?

No. He wanted her. His heart beating furiously against her hand was proof.

Lauren slid her hand down, and felt the edge of his open shirt brush across her fingertips. She curled her fingers around the fabric.

She couldn't hold on to him and sign. Slowly, she pulled him closer, finding those sweet, firm lips again. Then she let her hand move, and in the center of his chest, where his heart pounded, she signed. "Love me. Stay with me. Want you."

Did he understand her? Would he—

The bed moved as he moved. What was he doing? Leaving? *No, please.*

Two big strong hands curled around her shoulders and gently pushed her back against the pillows. Disappointment lived for only an instant as those hands moved gently upward, caressing her neck, cupping her chin until his lips returned to hers.

Lauren melted into him, encircling his neck with her arm and guiding him back down to her. His body, hot and hard, settled over hers, pressing her down into the mattress, cocooning her in the scent of him.

She opened her lips for him, the feel of his tongue against hers insistent. As she slid her bare legs along his, the deep vibration of his groan shook her.

Her hand moved along the muscles of his back, exploring, touching, yet impatient. She tugged at the waistband of his jeans, hoping he understood.

His mouth left hers, traveling slowly down where his hands had been. She wore a simple nightgown and until this instant, she'd completely forgotten what she had on. With such a gentle touch, his fingertips grazed her collarbone, then slid over the exposed skin above her neckline, to dip inside and slowly, oh-so-slowly, slide into the valley between her breasts.

She hadn't worn a bra since they'd taken her smoke-permeated clothing at the hospital. She hadn't given it much thought, having slept most of the time since. Now she was glad for the lack of clothing.

His finger moved lazily to the right, then the left, teasing her, each time moving a little bit closer to the peak. Her skin tightened to the point of being nearly painful.

Then suddenly, it wasn't his finger teasing her, but the damp of his tongue. He slid the strap of her gown off her shoulder, and she nearly leapt off the bed as his lips closed over her nipple, tasting, teasing, pushing her to the edge.

She burrowed her fingers into his still-damp hair, holding him tight, silently begging him to never stop.

He moved away, slipping from her grasp. She wanted to protest, and then the fabric of her nightgown whispered lower, slipping off, the silky fabric a caress in itself.

She knew it was morning since he'd showered. Was there much light in the room? She remembered a set of windows along the wall. Could he see her?

The idea of him watching her made her self-conscious as much as it sent a thrill through her.

He was close, she felt his body heat. Was he looking…? Watching?

His hand settled on her hip, hot, scalding, then slid up over the curve of her waist, to tickle her ribs, then finally cup her breast. She arched into his palm, her breath quickly in and out, adding to the friction of his touch.

And then he was gone again. She reached out to find him, intent on pulling him back. His touch returned, as he put his hand in hers. Slowly, he spelled, making her stop and focus on the shapes his fingers made.

"*Y-o-u s-u-r-e*?"

She nodded, reaching out to follow the shape of his shoulders to the collar of his shirt. She pushed his shirt off, the fabric wilting lifelessly without his shape to fill it. She tossed it to the floor.

His laughter shook the bed. In response, he took her hand again, guiding her fingers to the waistband of his jeans.

Her entire body tingled. Carefully, she pushed the metal button through the thick denim, the zipper grinding against her fingers. The back of her fingers brushed hot, hard skin. And she melted.

Tugging his loosened jeans, Lauren hoped he understood she wanted him to help. One-handed, she couldn't take them off—and she needed them off. Now. She signed, "Off."

Cool air brushed her skin when he moved away.

What if he changed his mind? She couldn't reach for him if she couldn't find him. Where was...?

The bed shifted as Jason stretched out beside her. Heat rolled off him. Sweet heat. Unable to resist, she reached out, her hand finding him. She'd just leaned over when his arms slid around her. Running his hand first up, then down her back, he pressed her against him, molding each inch tightly to him.

And then he kissed her. Hard. His lips drank in everything she gave, and she gave it all.

She'd had lovers before, but none had made her feel so overwhelmed—and yet Lauren didn't feel lost. She felt cherished. This was where she belonged.

His touch was gentle, yet urgent. She needed more. This time when he pulled away, she greedily curled her fingers around his bicep.

He turned away, keeping one leg next to hers as if he understood her confusion. She felt movement, but couldn't tell what he was doing. And then he took her hand in his, placing a square packet in her palm.

THOUGH THE ROOM was nearly dark, some light slipped in from the hall and around the curtain's edge. Jason could barely make out Lauren's face, but he saw the comprehension dawn on it. He cursed the bandages that hid her beautiful eyes, but the way she gathered her bottom lip between her teeth told him she knew. The way she tore the packet open told him she wanted this.

Jason reached to take the condom from her, only to be met with a hearty shake of her head and the determined touch of her hands on him. He nearly roared aloud with the pleasure of her covering him, slowly, gently, protecting herself at the same time she nearly pushed him to his release.

There was no more waiting. He had to be in her. Had to feel her around him.

Pushing her back again, he rose above her, wishing he could see her more clearly. Aching for her to see him. He hesitated, wanting to be with her completely. His heartbeat shook them both, and her breath whispered over him. He held back as long as he could, waiting, wishing.

Suddenly, she planted her hand in the middle of his chest, the plaster cast solid and definitely immovable. He dragged deep breaths into his lungs. If she said no now, he'd stop. It would kill him, but he'd respect her wishes.

Using her good hand, she tugged at the medical tape at the edge of the bandages.

"No," he said then cursed the silence. Was it dark enough that her eyes wouldn't hurt? He didn't know. He understood her need to see, yet fear nearly made him pull away.

Lauren tugged the bandages off, and, blinking rapidly, she looked up at him. He'd almost forgotten how beautiful, how deep, how expressive her eyes were. He couldn't look away. He didn't ever want to.

She pulled her arm back and slid her uninjured arm around his neck, curling her legs around his hips, urging him closer.

Gently, he waited, poised until he knew he couldn't wait any more. She trembled against him, and he was done. With one hard thrust, he was deep inside her. Soft heat engulfed him as he moved, faster, harder. She matched his movements with the same urgency, driving him to the edge.

And then she fell over it. Her eyes drifted closed, and she arched into him, into his release as she tightened around him. And he kissed her.

SHE KISSED HIM BACK, deep and hot, finding a second release as he filled her. Would she ever come back to earth again? She hoped not. She didn't ever want to.

Carefully opening her eyes, Lauren still had her arm around him—his big body still covered hers. She didn't want to lose this connection.

Jason lifted his head, but otherwise didn't move. Slowly, he kissed each of her eyelids. The tenderness melted her heart and in that instant, she knew she'd fallen head over heels for this man.

All the things he'd done for her filled her mind. He was learning sign for her. He'd saved her from the fire and cared for her afterward. He'd taken

Tina out of a bad situation. He'd befriended Dylan and Maxine. And he'd made such sweet love to her.

Her vision was still blurred, but with what little light there was, she stared up at him, never wanting to look away.

And then he sealed the deal. He smiled at her. She'd never seen anything more wonderful. She had to have more, had to taste that happiness.

She knew then that she'd spend a lifetime never getting enough.

SOMETHING BUZZED. In the distance. Growing louder. Finally, Jason woke up. His phone. The one he'd sent Susan after to replace the one lost in the fire. It was vibrating against something. Somewhere. He hadn't set any ringtone.

With a curse, he hustled into the living room to grab it, feeling like an idiot when he realized it didn't matter. The sound wouldn't wake Lauren. "Hello?"

"What in the world are you thinking?" Addie's voice came loud and clear through the phone.

Jason smiled as he went back into the bedroom to grab his discarded jeans.

She couldn't see him, but somehow talking to his sister in the buff didn't feel right. "Hold on a second." He put the phone down and pulled jeans and a T-shirt on. "Okay, I'm back."

His oldest sister had always been a morning person, and he wasn't surprised that she was calling now. She often tried to catch him before he left for the office. She wouldn't know he wasn't going in today.

She wasn't a chatterer, like Tara or Mandy. She was the oldest, and was always in business mode. Even at DJ and Tammie's wedding, she'd let loose only so much. Briefly, he wondered if she'd ever let go and let herself fall in love. He couldn't remember her dating much in high school or since. Frowning, he walked back onto the balcony.

Addie's heart was in the right place, but she was never one to back off when she had a bone to pick. And she never called him without said bone in place.

"You didn't answer my question," she prompted too casually. He looked at the phone, then glanced back at the bedroom. Could she know? No.

"At the moment? Nothing. Thinking about having a cup of coffee." He knew that was an answer that would have gotten him a smack on the head years back. Now his older sister was a thousand miles away and couldn't touch him. Besides, he had no clue what she was talking about—the list of possibilities was too long right now.

"That's not what I meant, and you know it. Wyatt says you're working for the Haymakers."

"Sort of." That was still not an answer she'd like, but it was all he had.

"Dang it, Jason." He could hear her footsteps as she paced. "I thought you weren't going to."

"I never said that."

"Well, you should have."

Jason laughed. "I'm glad I didn't." Lauren's face came to mind. "Did Wyatt happen to mention Lauren?"

"Uh—the—ballet dancer? Uhm, yes." The silence was uncomfortable.

"It's okay, Ad. You can mention it. Yes, she's deaf."

"I... Jason, is she really Pal's daughter?"

He wasn't sure which part concerned Addie more. "What's really going on, Ad?" He didn't want to argue with his sister, nor did he feel as if he needed to justify his actions. She'd never stopped trying to be a mother to all of them, but something about all this was off.

"I just worry." She took a deep breath. "Trey Haymaker's resurfaced and he's been running his mouth off and..."

There was a tremor in Addie's voice and Jason's senses went on high alert. "What happened, Addie? Tell me."

"I—I was at the store yesterday. I didn't even see him. But he came up to me and grabbed my arm." Her voice shook, and Jason heard her take yet another deep breath.

"Who? Trey?"

"Yes," she whispered.

"Keep going. What did he say?"

"Oh, Jason. I know he wasn't sober. He reeked of

alcohol. I know Trey's not that kind of person, and in the past he's been the best of that family." Her words were rushed, as if she needed to say them quickly to get them out.

Jason took his own deep breath. "Addie. Focus." He felt like he was interviewing a reluctant witness. "What did he say?"

"He said—he said it so harsh—that he was going to kill her. This Lauren. Then yelled that he would go after you next. He—" Her voice hiccuped. "He was so angry. I've never seen him like that."

Jason froze. The man in the studio hadn't been Trey, had he? No, Jason was sure of it. Besides how could he be here in LA and there in Texas at nearly the same time? Then again, Trey had enough money to hire someone,

Jason was back to wanting to put his fist through something, or someone. "Did he hurt you?" He knew his anger was clear.

"No. Just squeezed my arm. A...a young man down the aisle was there and interrupted him. Oh, Jason, he seriously scared me."

As soon as they were off the phone, he would call Wyatt. He needed to keep an eye on Addie— and an eye out for Trey.

The sound of someone knocking on the apartment door made Jason frown. No one knocked on the door. He couldn't remember anyone he wasn't expecting ever showing up here. Even packages, which were few and far between, were delivered to his office. Not his apartment.

But with Lauren here, any number of people could be stopping by to see her. He'd told the kids and Maxine to come by whenever. "Hold on, Addie." Jason pulled his phone away from his ear. "Just a minute," he called, hoping whoever it was heard him.

Lauren was still in the bedroom, hopefully asleep, though he needed to help her with the medication and bandages soon. He hoped the vibration of the pounding didn't wake her.

He opened the door—and never saw the fist coming.

CHAPTER SIXTEEN

LAUREN NEEDED TO put the bandages back on. Even the small amount of light filtering in from the hallway burned. Keeping her eyes closed helped, but the conscious effort of doing that was draining. And not nearly as effective. She'd just swung her legs over the bed to reach for the medicine and gauze when the picture hanging over the headboard moved. What the—? She flinched away in case it was an earthquake. It didn't happen again.

Her injured eyes open, she saw the light in the living room shift. She grabbed the nearest piece of clothing, Jason's shirt that she'd tossed to the floor earlier. It was way too big, but it would do.

What was going on? Standing, she moved cautiously to the doorway and peered out. She could see Jason, his back to her, and beyond him, another man in the doorway. She couldn't quite make out the man's features. She shielded her eyes as she stepped farther into the painful light.

The stranger swung and hit Jason in the jaw. Jason stumbled back. Shocked, Lauren rushed forward, just as Jason got his balance back and grabbed the man. Jason was a big man, but so was the other guy. Jason shoved him out the door and pinned the man to the far wall with his forearm across his throat. The decorations hanging on the wall beside the elevator shook just like the picture over the bed had.

Jason was talking to the man, but his teeth were clenched, so from this angle she couldn't read his lips. She glanced around for a weapon, knowing she'd be worthless in a fight, but she had to help him. She had to—

The stranger saw her then, and while she couldn't fully meet his gaze and focus, she felt it. Anger. Pain. Something else, something dark, came at her. She shivered, and took a reflexive step back from the rage—and from the wicked scent of alcohol wafting off the man.

Jason turned his head then and saw her as well. The only other time she'd seen him angry was when he'd brought Tina away from the foster home. That had been indignant anger. This…this scared her. It was a rage.

Jason gave the other man another hard shove and stepped back, slamming the apartment door in his face. He twisted the lock with a harsh turn.

Even though the door was closed, Jason was still talking, probably yelling if his facial expression and body language were any indication.

When he finally turned around, she stared. Blood trickled from the left corner of his mouth.

JASON MIGHT BE a civilized corporate attorney, but he'd grown up in Texas. And somehow, the wilds of Texas had just shown up in LA, and not even Trey Haymaker got in more than one sucker punch. Especially a drunk Trey Haymaker.

Though the door was closed solid between them, Jason still didn't trust the other man. He waited, the last few minutes flashing through his mind as he fought to catch his breath.

A high-pitched voice somewhere in the distance called Jason's name. He looked around, knowing it wasn't Lauren. The phone was on the floor, and Addie was screaming from a thousand miles away.

Addie's words from earlier echoed around him. Trey had threatened to kill Lauren. Jason had to keep her safe.

Another sound startled him, and he looked back to see Lauren step farther into the living room. He prayed he could protect her. He'd slammed and locked the door, but he looked back now, just to make sure it remained locked.

A fist hit the other side of the door. "Get the hell out of here, Trey."

"Jason!" Addie's voice came from the phone still on the floor. He scooped it up, meeting Lauren's pain-filled gaze as he straightened.

"I'm fine, Ad. I'll call you back." He hung up on his sister, knowing there'd be hell to pay later, but the woman standing in front of him was more important.

Lauren stared wide-eyed at him, her injured eyes still red and watering. Or were those tears? Had she recognized Trey? Could she even see well enough to tell who he was? What was going through her head? She backed up. Afraid, or protecting herself from the pain of the light? He reached for her, but she scurried away.

He didn't know what he expected, but her ducking into the bathroom wasn't it. He heard the water running, and she hastily came back out to him. She lifted a damp washcloth, and cool water soaking the fabric, she pressed it to his lip. When she pulled it away, he saw the bright stain of his blood.

Shit. Trey had busted his lip. It wasn't his first, and probably wouldn't be his last, but he hated it now. Trey had scared the crap out of both Lauren and Addie for it. The man had talent.

Talent that didn't extend to enough smarts to know when he wasn't wanted. He pounded on the door again.

"Go away, Trey," Jason yelled. "I'm not letting you in."

"Is that her?" Trey's words were clear. He must be right next to the door. Jason clenched his jaw to keep his anger in check, and words he'd most likely regret from erupting.

"Let me in, Jason." Another fist hit the door. "This is between me and her."

Jason stalked to the door, curling his fingers around the doorknob, forcing himself not to turn it. Letting that idiot in might make him feel better, but it wouldn't help Lauren. "Get out of here." He squeezed the knob harder. "We'll talk when you're sober."

"You're one of *us*," Trey practically yelled the last word. "She's not."

Vague, muffled comments about Jason being a wimp and a chicken came through the thick wood. But they were fading. Hopefully Trey was leaving. Jason sighed, ashamed that this man was from the same neighborhood where he'd grown up. His brother actually considered him a friend?

"Was that *T-r-e-y*?" Lauren signed and Jason's heart sank. He would have to explain.

LAUREN RECOGNIZED TREY'S—albeit blurred—face from the pictures she'd pulled up on the internet when she'd first found out about her father. Her mind raced. Why was he here? Why had he punched Jason?

The blood on Jason's lip still scared her. She reached up to put the washcloth against his lip again, but he took it from her and did it himself this time.

Her eyes burned. The pain increased each time she turned her head. She needed to get back to the darkness, knew the risks of more damage to her eyes, but if Jason was hurt—

He started talking, and she tried to focus on his moving lips. But the bright sunlight pouring through the living room windows was like a knife. "I can't see enough," she signed, her panic too strong as he frowned, struggling to read her one-handed sign.

She swallowed back her frustration and fear, not sure if it was fear for her vision, or fear for this man who meant entirely too much to her all of a sudden.

Jason guided her back into the darkened bedroom where she sat down on the mattress. Carefully, he knelt in front of her, letting the light from the hall fall on his face and not hers.

"I'm fine," he said, and she was relieved she could see well enough to read his lips, though her gaze kept catching on the cut. "You need to take care of your eyes," he said as he reached up and touched her temple.

He picked up the tube of medication from the nightstand and their gazes met. She stopped his hand, shaking her head.

"What's the matter?" His frown was full of concern.

"What happened?" she signed. She saw the picture over the bed tremble again.

"Don't worry."

She frowned back at him. "You're nuts," she signed and pointed to the moving picture. "That—" What did she call Trey? Lunatic? Idiot? "He's still pounding on the door, isn't he?"

"Not for long." As if suddenly remembering the phone in his hand, he dialed. She saw the word *guard* appear on the screen. The picture moved again. His neighbors had probably beat him to the call.

"The guard's on the way up," Jason explained.

She waited only a second before signing, "Tell me."

"Tell you what?" Jason didn't meet her eyes, and she grabbed his arm to keep him from moving away.

"Tell me," she signed again, her motions harsher this time. "Why is he here?"

Jason looked down. Slowly, he signed, in sync with his words. She was almost too upset to notice that change. He didn't often do that, combining words with sign like Dylan and Maxine, like longtime signers did.

"I think." He touched his forehead for the sign and then rubbed it. "To hurt you."

"What? Why?"

Jason shrugged. "Addie, my oldest sister was on the phone." He lifted the phone he still held. "He told her that he was going to kill you. Then he said he'd come for me."

THE HURT AND DISAPPOINTMENT on Lauren's face was too much. Jason stood, pulling her against him. He'd never lied to her, and wouldn't start now. He knew she craved a family, knew she hoped that somehow these people she didn't know would accept her. This wasn't what she wanted.

Lauren pulled away then, picked up the scattered bandages and medicine and stalked to the bathroom. She closed the door and he heard the lock click in place. He'd leave her alone for now.

The pounding at the door had stopped and his phone rang. The guard. "We've got it handled, Mr. Hawkins." The man's deep voice sounded official. "Do you want us to call the police? Are you pressing charges?"

Trey would be even more ticked then. "No. Just send him somewhere to sober up." Jason couldn't do anything more about Trey right now.

Once he'd hung up, the phone rang again, and he looked down at the display. Addie. He cursed. He didn't want to talk to her right now, but she'd been nearly as scared by Trey as Lauren had. His older sister had always been there for him. It wasn't fair to ignore her now. "Hello, Ad."

"Are you okay?" He heard the tears, heard the panic and fear.

"Yes. We're fine."

"We?"

"Uh, yeah. Lauren's here."

"With you?"

He couldn't even begin to explain everything to Addie right now. He gave her the abridged version of the fire, of Lauren's injuries and why she was here. He left out the details of last night and this morning. But he heard his sister's suppositions.

"Do you think Trey had anything to do with the fire?" she asked softly.

"I don't know." And he didn't. After the wildfire in Texas that Pal had caused, and that had nearly been blamed on Trey, Jason couldn't see Trey being that mean, or that stupid. But the man was far from rational these days.

The bathroom door opened then, and Jason simply stared. Lauren stood there, all her copper curls wound up in a towel on top of her head. Another towel wrapped around her body. Barely.

She held it up with her casted arm. "Need your help," she signed.

Once again, Jason hung up on his sister.

LAUREN LOOKED AT JASON, wishing she could see more clearly and yet enjoying the muted view of him sitting there, on the edge of the bed, in the—thankfully—dim light. He looked less intimidating, less intense than the man she'd hurried away from moments before.

Not because she was afraid of him—but because she couldn't trust herself.

In the enclosure of the shower, she'd felt enveloped by him—his scent, the dark masculine color of the tile, the memory of all he'd done to protect her.

The mild-mannered lawyer she'd come to respect was a warrior at heart. And that confused her.

And intrigued her. She took a step forward and

froze when he looked up at her. Heat burned in his eyes. She swallowed the ache rising in her throat. "*I n-e-e-d* your *h-e-l-p*," she signed one-handed, having to spell rather than sign.

Jason nodded, the action seeming to bring the shutters down over his emotions. He moved toward her. Lauren felt the distance yawn between them, even though he was closer. Why was he shutting down and pulling back? Was he regretting taking her and all this baggage in? She barely resisted the urge to step back.

The hand that took hers, guiding her back to the bed, was warm, gentle, restrained. He paused.

Jason stared at her with such intensity, she felt the hot impact. "Oh, hell," his lips said an instant before he leaned down and kissed her—hard, hungry, wanting.

He didn't have to sign anything. She let the towel drop and leaned into him, her own adrenaline pushing her to him. She had to stand on tiptoes to reach him, but she didn't hesitate.

He tugged the towel from her head, letting her half-dry curls fall in damp coils down her back. She burned so hot that the coolness felt good, tickling and teasing her sensitive skin.

The love they'd made before had been perfect for a first time. But this? This was different.

This was hot, and harsh, and Lauren hung on tight for the ride she knew would be quick and rough and delicious.

There was no slow, sensuous undressing as she was already way ahead of him. He ripped his T-shirt over his head, barely giving her time to enjoy the view of all that naked chest before he shucked off his jeans. She could only stare.

Slowly, like a powerful predator, Jason pushed her back onto the bed, his knee already parting her thighs. She felt the cool mattress for only an instant before he rolled over her and pulled her with him.

Suddenly, he was on his back, his hands on her hips as he settled her over him. Her breath came in hot pants of need. Every inch of her ached to possess him.

Beneath her, Jason was a big powerful man who was still protecting her, still reining in his strength and his need.

Though she couldn't see his features as clearly as she wanted, Lauren watched in fascination as Jason threw his head back. His hands settled on her hips, his grip hot on her skin as he lowered her until not even air came between them. His jaw clenched, the muscles of his neck and shoulders went taut as he held back.

But Lauren didn't want him to hold back. She didn't need him to protect her, not now, certainly not from him.

Impatient, yet knowing it was worth it, she waited until he opened his eyes. The frustration there answered hers. Holding his gaze, she moved. She had to.

Now—now he was hers. This was how she wanted him.

Closing her eyes, the burning pain of her eyes receded, and she let go of her restraint. Every thought left her brain as he moved with her. Harder. Deeper. Farther.

The heat built, setting her afire a second before she exploded in a flurry of white-hot stars. He joined her an instant later, melting what was left of her sanity.

Spent, Lauren collapsed onto his chest, his arms coming around her, holding tight. She hid her face against the side of his neck as much to hide her eyes as to recover from the wild woman she'd become.

How could she possibly feel self-conscious? But she did, her cheeks warming with a blush.

Jason's lips, gentle and warm on her forehead, brought tears to her eyes with the sweetness of his kiss. She clung to him, not wanting the moment to end. Ever.

He wouldn't understand that, and she couldn't tell him. Her brain didn't seem able to send the signal to her hand to sign anything coherent.

He turned, settling her on the sheets and leveraging up on an elbow. "Your eyes," he said, misunderstanding her tears.

Reaching over her, Jason grabbed the medicine and slowly, as carefully as he'd ever touched her, he opened the tube and put the medicine in her eyes. Though the goo warped her vision, she couldn't look away. His hair, mussed from her touch, his injured lip, the line of his jaw…

Once he'd placed the first bandage, he paused. "You okay?" he asked, so close she could easily read his lips. At her nod, he kissed her, hot and sweet. She cupped his jaw with her hand, enjoying the rough feel of his skin.

Finally, he lifted the piece of gauze. She nodded and slowly lowered her eyelid, letting him know she was ready. She didn't want to stop looking at him, but the medicine and darkness helped ease the nagging pain in her eyes.

The darkness didn't seem as bad this time, especially when Jason settled back against the pillows and dragged her into his arms. He guided her head to rest on his shoulder, fitting her perfectly to him.

Moving her hand to the center of his chest, she felt his heart hammering beneath her touch. "This," she made the sign. "Feels," her middle finger slid down his breastbone in the next sign. "*R-i-g-h-t.*" She couldn't see him, and feared reaching up to feel his lips in case she hurt him, but she hoped— really hoped—he smiled.

DEAR GOD, HOW could the woman in his arms destroy and save him in the same instant? Jason held Lauren. And as she fell asleep in his arms, he let her, resisting the urge to have her again.

Adrenaline hummed hard in his blood, his heart

beat harsh against his ribs. He wanted her again. He'd never been like this with anyone else before.

Something inside him had changed since meeting this woman.

He'd moved away from his family for a reason. Away from, he'd hoped, that strong need to take care of them, and a fear of failing. He wasn't the oldest who'd learned to take care of things early, like Wyatt. He didn't have DJ's military training. He didn't even have his sisters' ability to cook.

That fear of failing multiplied with Lauren. He had to admit to himself that her deafness played a factor in his fear.

She was the most independent person he'd ever met. She didn't need him.

But right now, she did need him and that felt good. Damn good.

But who was he kidding? Once Lauren was on her feet again, and healed, she had one hell of a life to return to. A life of success and performances around the world.

A life that until recently had nothing to do with him.

The silence suddenly felt heavy around him. As one of six kids growing up, there was no such thing as quiet, much less silence in the house. And while he didn't mind quiet, there was something different about this. For the first time, he heard the emptiness.

Lauren's independence and resiliency were traits

he admired about her. And he wouldn't change that, not one bit. *He* had to learn to deal with it.

Because she made him want all the things he'd thought he didn't. Home. Family. Ties.

He looked down at Lauren. Slowly, softly, so he wouldn't wake her, he stroked the curls of her hair that tangled around her shoulders. While it was faint, the rasp when he rubbed the strands together was there. His ears sought out the sound—any sound.

Her soft breath. In. Out. Just a whisper. In the distance, the clock in the front room ticked, and the electricity to the appliances farther away in the kitchen, kicked on. Otherwise—nothing.

There was no conversation. Holding on to each other like this, even if her arm hadn't been in a cast, would have made conversation in sign impossible.

Could he be content with that? Could he adjust to the eternal silence—interrupted by the ear-shattering sound of music from time to time?

Would texting be the only true way to communicate complete ideas? Lifting his free hand, the one not wrapped around her, he stared at it.

Sign language was the hardest thing he'd ever tried to learn. It wasn't just about learning how to move his fingers, it was a whole different way of thinking. It wasn't an exact translation of English—it was more a way of getting concepts, intentions and meanings across. It was the purest of communication.

And yet, that simplicity was what stumped him. He loved the finesse of word usage. Enjoyed writing arguments to persuade or dissuade a person or jury. He relished debate. All those things were possible, but so much more difficult in sign.

Jason forced himself to slow his racing thoughts. Those things wouldn't go away. His job met most of those requirements. But they weren't things he could ever fully share with Lauren. Not in the same way. Was he okay with that?

She moved then, slipping away in her sleep to curl into the pillow rather than him. The empty air felt cool against his skin. Jason didn't pull her back to him, though he ached to do so. Maybe this was good. Maybe it was what he needed to clear his head, but right now, a clear head wouldn't help his heart.

CHAPTER SEVENTEEN

FINALLY, THE NEXT MORNING, the doctor removed Lauren's bandages. Except for the letter-filled square of light on the wall, which made her eyes hurt just glancing at it, the examination room was dark. Jason sat in a nearby chair. She kept her gaze down, surreptitiously watching his shadow out of the corner of her eye.

Even barely able to see him, she was aware of Jason. Of how his broad shoulders dwarfed the chair. Of the subtle scent of his aftershave.

The doctor brought her abruptly back to the present when he put a big black contraption with dials and lenses in front of her. She recognized the device from eye appointments in the past. He tapped a little cup where she knew she was to rest her chin. She leaned forward to do so.

She waited for what was coming. Light. She'd had this done before. But this time it would hurt. A lot.

The older man leaned around the frame and carefully touched her shoulder. She pulled back to look at him. He glanced over his shoulder at Jason, then awkwardly mimicked the sign for "Ready?" that Jason made.

She took a deep breath and nodded, resettling her chin. The beam of light seemed to cut clear through her skull, but she didn't pull away. Tears trickled from the corners of her eyes in protest.

He worked quickly, for which she was thankful. Finally, he turned off the painful light and moved the instrument back against the wall.

Jason stood, coming closer. She looked up, seeing him more clearly, his presence reassuring. The frown on his face, not so much. The doctor talked too quickly for her to read his unfamiliar lips. She only caught a word here and there. Jason listened, nodding occasionally. Once the doctor finished, Jason faced her, his form shadowed still, but he was signing slowly enough that even in the dim light she could read it.

"No apparent permanent damage." Every ounce of air whooshed from her lungs in relief. She had to gather her strength to focus. Jason's hands were still moving. "Still wait. Wear the *b-a-n-d-a-g-e-s* another two days. Keep putting in *m-e-d-i-c-i-n-e*."

Two more days? After these past two of essentially being trapped inside her own head, she was hungry to see.

Lauren's disappointment at having to wear the bandages longer threatened to eat away at her relief. "All the time?" she asked, and Jason translated for the doctor.

The doctor shook his head. He reached into a drawer and pulled out a form to hand to her. She tilted it toward the light. A schedule. Two hours on, an hour off, to start, extending the time off with each switch, leaving the bandages on all night for the next week, just to give her eyes a total rest.

But soon. Very soon she would be able to see all day. Her eyes watered, partially from the misuse, and partially from the joy of the confirmation she wouldn't lose her sight.

Lauren looked over at Jason. His smile showed even in the dim light. She couldn't look away. Couldn't stop her eyes from drinking in the images she'd feared she'd lost forever, at the face she'd kept trying to envision clearly in her mind, and never quite got right.

Except when she'd taken off the bandages last night... Maybe two days wouldn't be so bad. She hoped neither man saw the blush that warmed her cheeks.

ONCE THEY WERE situated in his car again, Jason took Lauren's hand and put it on the radio dial. Did she want the music? He didn't know how else to ask her with the bandages back in place.

She shook her head. Then pointed at her forehead and put her hands together in the double *g* for pain. "Head hurts."

He made the "okay" sign against her palm then started the car.

After a block, she reached out, her hand moving in the air, missing his arm by only a couple of inches. He stopped at the light before taking her hand in his. She nodded and pulled her hand back to sign. "My studio. I want to see it."

Jason just stared at her. The car behind him honked. After the jerk spread a layer of rubber on the pavement to go around them, Jason hastily pulled over to the curb.

He'd known this was coming, known she'd eventually ask. And she'd been sneaky. She'd asked in the car instead of at the apartment where he could more easily dissuade her. She sat there patiently, waiting for him to respond.

If the silence hadn't already weighed a ton, it would have knocked him over.

Jason reached out and put a hand on her knee. She turned to face him. Lord, he wished he could see her eyes, read her thoughts. He picked up her hand and, with his fist, made the nodding motion against her palm.

With a growing sense of dread, Jason pulled away from the curb. This was not what he'd intended. He couldn't guarantee he could keep her safe. He didn't know what was left of the place. If anything.

That same dread kept him from even meeting the minimum speed limit. The twist of her lips told him that she knew he was dragging his feet. She didn't say anything. But her body language silently called him on it.

Finally, Jason turned onto the street where just a few nights ago, the studio had glowed in the dark night. He shuddered as the memories flooded his brain.

In the harsh afternoon light, no one could miss the blackened shell of the old theater. Or the wide yellow strips of caution tape wrapped around the south end of the building.

As they drew closer, he saw the rest more clearly. Even after seeing it afire the other night, he was shocked by the damage. It was heavy on the one side, but thankfully not as much on the other.

Parking across the street, Jason killed the engine. He sat, staring at the building. Someone had boarded up the front entry. Thankfully the right portion of the lobby actually looked intact. He knew there'd be smoke damage, but it looked salvageable.

The doctor had said Lauren could take the bandages off an hour at a time. But they both knew she wasn't ready to deal with full sunlight. How would they do this?

She couldn't seem to sit still. Her breath was loud in the closed space of the car. She unfastened the seat belt and curled her hand around the door's handle. She paused, and he knew it wasn't fair to make her wait any longer.

Slowly, he explained that he'd come around and

get her, then lead her inside where he'd help her take off the bandages. He rummaged in his glove box to find a pair of sunglasses that he hoped would help if it was still too bright.

It took several minutes, and numerous tries at spelling and sign, but finally she nodded.

"YOU FOLKS GOT business here?" A man's deep voice came out of the cavernous blackness that had been the practice studio. Every muscle in Jason's body went on alert. He stepped closer to Lauren, gently putting his hand on her elbow as a tall man came in through the wall next to what used to be the front door. The same way they'd come in.

Lauren looked around, her uncovered eyes wide with shock and pain. She didn't need anything more to deal with right now.

"We might ask you the same." Jason faced the man as he stepped out of the shadows. "This is private property, and this is the owner."

The man actually grinned. He reached into his pocket and whipped out a badge. "I'm Detective Mark Capetti. I'm the fire investigator on this case. They said you were injured." He met Lauren's stare. Jason could tell she was trying to focus, without much success, on the man's lips.

"She's deaf." Jason signed what he could so Lauren could use both lips and hands to put the message together. "Normally, she reads lips well, but her vision's still diminished. We have to stay in the shadows as much as possible."

The man nodded. "I'd heard that. Sorry you were hurt, ma'am." He talked more slowly, thankfully not louder as so many people did. "I'd really like to ask you some questions. I've been waiting until you were better." Jason translated, much more slowly, and Lauren worked to focus on both men's lips and Jason's hands.

Lauren nodded. The man grinned again. Jason wondered how long he'd been on the job. Though he looked well into his thirties, he had a strong determination. And a friendly attitude. Jason wasn't sure why he'd expected something else.

"It may be slow," Jason cautioned. "She doesn't speak and I'm only slightly proficient in sign. You don't happen to know sign language, do you?"

The investigator shook his head. "Sorry. But you can help?"

"I'll try."

The man pulled his cell phone out and tapped it several times. He soon brought up a bright white screen. Jason hoped the man didn't plan to text with Lauren. She couldn't yet focus on a too-bright phone screen. Then he realized what he was doing. He guessed investigators didn't use those little wire-bound notebooks any more?

"Ready?" Jason asked Lauren, and she nodded.

"I know they asked for a statement. Has she been able to give that?"

Jason shook his head. "Ask *her* the questions directly. I'll explain if there's something she doesn't understand. She's good at reading lips, so moving closer and facing her when you talk should help."

The man's ears turned a bright pink, but otherwise, he didn't react to Jason's soft reprimand. The investigator nodded, then moved closer to Lauren and repeated his question. She shook her head in answer.

"Okay then. You'll still have to do that later. We were able to talk to the boy."

"*D-y-l-a-n*?" Lauren asked and Jason repeated.

"Yeah. But I haven't read it yet. I'll ask what questions I need for now. I may need to get back in touch." At her nod, he continued. "Do you have any idea how the fire started?"

Lauren worked to watch the man's lips, then slowly shook her head, looking away, as if she couldn't resist staring at the blackened walls.

"You were here the night of the fire?" Capetti asked Jason.

He nodded. "I got here after it started. A man pushed past me as I went inside." He met the officer's gaze. "I'd have gone after him, but I had to get Lauren out."

"Would you recognize him?"

Jason thought about that a moment. "Maybe."

"What'd he look like?" The detective pinned Jason with an intense stare.

Jason frowned, trying to bring back the memory. "Not as tall as me. Five-ten maybe?"

Capetti tapped on the phone screen, making notes. "Hair?"

"Dark. Kinda long. Scruffy."

Capetti stared at the screen for an instant. "You think he was homeless or a derelict?"

Jason had to think about that. "No." He shook his head. "I didn't get that impression." Then another thought occurred to him. Should he bring up his suspicions about the flowers Lauren had received the other night? With a sigh, he tapped her arm and spelled, "*F-l-o-w-e-r-s*?" She stared at him, a frown deep on her brow. Then he saw the realization dawn.

"My phone had a picture." She pointed at the blackened space where the office had been. "It was there. In my purse."

Jason pulled his new phone out and scrolled through his recovered texts and found the photo she'd sent him. He aimed the screen at her. She vigorously nodded and showed the investigator. He frowned and looked at Jason as she signed.

"Did you ever figure out who sent them?" Jason asked, repeating slowly with his hands. She shook her head.

"A couple of nights before the fire, someone— she didn't know who—sent those flowers."

The man took the phone, trying to make the picture bigger. He looked at Lauren. "Can you send me that?"

She nodded and handed the phone back to Jason. "Send to him?" she signed.

Jason nodded, and Capetti handed him a business card with his email and phone number on it. The soft ding of the message seemed loud in the empty building.

Lauren's hands were moving. "They should still be at my town house," she told him.

Mark frowned. "Where are you staying?" He looked at Jason, and Jason ignored the speculative gleam in his eye. "Not at home?"

Lauren shook her head. She lifted the bandages she held in the fingers of her casted hand. "I only have an hour break from this." Jason repeated her words, not elaborating. It was a challenge. This was her conversation. Her words. "I need his help." She pointed at Jason and looked up at him. "Can you explain?"

She gave him permission to elaborate and not just interpret. He took his time explaining her injuries and the limitations of her eyes. Mark tapped notes onto his phone's screen. He nodded occasionally.

Jason watched as Lauren wandered around. He was impressed with her strength—and her sneakiness. While he was busy explaining, she took the opportunity to explore while the officer was distracted. She was careful, staying where the floor was solid, though he still worried water damage could have weakened the wood.

"Be careful there, ma'am," Capetti spoke, then shook his head as he realized she couldn't hear him.

"Don't worry. We all do that." Jason smiled, feeling a sudden kinship.

"How long has she been deaf?" Mark asked.

"All her life."

"But I thought she was a dancer."

"Yep. World famous." Jason wondered if Lauren ever got a kick out of confusing people. Somehow, he thought so. Pride made him smile.

Lauren waved at them. She was signing. Jason focused on her question. "Where did the fire start?" he asked for her.

The investigator waved them over to follow him. He pointed at the remnants of a door frame. Lauren frowned as if trying to remember where they were.

"Storage," she signed.

"What was stored there?" Capetti was beside her, and she nodded as she could more easily read his lips. He poised a finger over his phone screen.

She was frowning, thinking. "Nothing." She shrugged and looked over at Jason and shook her head. Then her eyes widened. "The floor." She closed her eyes. "It's being refinished next week. Or was. Stripper was delivered last week." Her hand dropped to her sides.

"Refinishing it?" Capetti repeated. She nodded. "That explains the chemical burns." He pointed at

Lauren's eyes. "Excellent accelerant. Wouldn't take much to light it. Makes a nasty fire."

SITTING DOWN IN the middle of all this ash, filth and destruction for a good cry probably wasn't a bright idea. But, oh how Lauren wanted to. Such a loss. Thank God, she and Dylan had gotten out. What if there'd been others here? The kids? Her chest tightened at the thought. Staring at it all, she couldn't think straight.

Jason could explain everything to the fire investigator much more quickly than she could right now. She didn't normally shirk her responsibilities, or step aside for anyone to take over, but she was too overwhelmed and already, her eyes ached. She was running out of time, and she needed to see as much as she could.

There was a lot to take in, and soon there would be a lot to do, if she decided to rebuild.

And that was a big if.

She stared at the blackened shell of her office. Thank goodness she'd spent the day after the fundraiser getting all the checks and money counted and deposited in the bank. It was a lot of money, not nearly enough to fix this. But it could have all been lost—

Was that what that man had been after? Was that why he'd set the fire? Was he angry he didn't find the money?

She turned to the investigator and asked about

that. She saw Jason speak, repeating her sign. The man typed on his screen, but didn't give her an answer beyond a shrug. That wasn't much help, but then she probably wasn't much help, either.

She watched Jason. He stood with the investigator, talking and answering questions. She wasn't focusing enough to catch more than a word here and there. Yet, she trusted him to handle it.

She'd never trusted anyone like this before. Swallowing back the panic that realization caused, she headed away from the mess and went across the lobby to the main stage. The doors were closed and she carefully pulled them open. Other than the strong scent of damp and smoke, everything looked just as she'd left it.

Relief buckled her knees, and she sank into the familiar velvet of the end seat of the theater's back row. This was the heart of this place. The rest could be rebuilt, but without this historic stage, there would be no point.

In the safety of the darkness, she let her tears flow—tears of relief, of fear and uncertainty—until Jason's strong hands gently grasped her shoulders and pulled her into the comforting strength of his arms.

JASON LET LAUREN decide when to pull away. Finally, she stepped back, wiping the tears from her eyes and taking several deep breaths.

"Did you have the boards put up?" She pointed at the entrance.

He shook his head. "Who else would?" He should have thought of it, though. He'd been so focused on her, he hadn't considered all the details that needed taken care of in a crisis situation like this.

"Detective?" Jason called out to the hall.

Capetti glanced over his shoulder. "Yeah?"

"Do you know who put the boards over the door? Did your guys do that?"

"No." The officer laughed. "Not in the budget. Owners take care of that." Jason explained what he'd said to Lauren since the detective still had his back to them and there was no way she could see, much less read, his lips.

"I need a phone." Lauren glanced back at the destroyed office, a glint Jason didn't quite recognize in her eyes. "Need to text *M-a-x-i-n-e*."

"Why?"

"If not you—or the police—she stepped in."

Why did that make Lauren's shoulders droop? Why did she look defeated? He wouldn't ask now, but later, they'd talk.

"I'll be in touch, folks." Capetti stepped around the damaged walls. He turned back and faced Lauren. "Hope you're well soon."

Lauren nodded and waved as he left. Jason offered his phone. "Want to text now?"

Lauren shook her head and turned away. Slowly, she lifted the limp bandages and put them carefully back over her eyes. When she set the sunglasses on top to hold them in place, he guessed she was hiding, as well.

As they pulled away from the destruction, he couldn't help but glance over at her. Her silence was different this time. Not because she didn't speak, but because she couldn't—wouldn't. She didn't need to. Lauren's sadness filled the air.

Jason wanted to kick himself for bringing her there. He should have refused. It might have ticked her off, but it wouldn't have hurt her as much.

LAUREN AWOKE THE next morning, stretching and relishing the comfort of Jason's big bed. His side of the bed was empty and cool to her touch. She yanked off the bandages—hating them more with each passing minute, trusting that Jason kept the blinds closed. She wanted to see, not guess, where he was.

A good night's rest and the soothing effect of the medicine helped—a little. But she didn't think she'd ever enjoy nighttime again. Not the darkness anyway. Not really.

She stood and walked around just because she could. Something she'd always taken for granted—simple movement—was like a gift. Just last week, she'd been dancing across the stage, leaping and flying through the air. Now she was happy to be able to walk without help—or without running into a wall.

A smile exploded on her lips. Freedom—it felt so good.

Without Jason's presence, she took the chance to roam. She saw the line of light beneath the bathroom door down the short hall, so she knew Jason was taking a shower. The scent of coffee wafted in the air and reached out to pull her across the apartment to the kitchen where she fixed a big cup of the sweet brew.

The living room curtains were drawn part way, letting in enough light to see but not hurt.

She let her gaze drink in the sights. Half a week of the darkness behind the bandages made her hungry for light and color.

The whole place looked like something out of a designer magazine, all color-coordinated and perfect. Too perfect.

The open-concept design displayed it all—the smooth chrome in the kitchen was comfortable, and yet cool. The glass-top table was just as cool against her elbows as she leaned against it. She liked it—and yet, there was something missing. Something that didn't fit the man she'd come to know over the past few weeks.

She straightened when her gaze landed on a wooden chair sitting back in the corner. It looked out of place. Why was it here? The old-fashioned back, carved with flowers and scrolls, was worn, not damaged, but as if loving hands had frequently caressed the finish. The spindles were all intact, though they, too, looked worn in places. The seat was wide and welcoming.

She walked over to it. Though it was silly, she had to sit in it. She settled down on the chair, liking the wood's warmth instead of the cool metal against her backside. Suddenly, she realized what was wrong with this room, with this whole place. It didn't match Jason.

This chair. This was something she could associate with him. She smiled to herself, relaxing.

In her mind's eye, she saw this chair, matching a table and other chairs. In a house. A home. Where a family gathered around the dinner table. It made her think of things she'd never had. Things so out of the realm of possibility for her. Too much like the families she saw on TV.

In another life—

She froze, looking around.

This wasn't reality. This was a dream. Just like the odd chair, something was out of place.

Jason was being so kind. His strong sense of right and wrong and duty *had* to be what made him take such good care of her. He hadn't really answered her earlier question, but why else would he do all this for her? No one did such things without expecting something in return.

Jason came in just then, halting inside the wide doorway. His eyes widened in surprise as they met hers.

Lauren jumped up from the chair, the coffee

sloshing over her hand, thankfully cooled now. Her heart skipped a beat as she moved away from the chair to grab a napkin to dry her hand.

He didn't move, and she knew when she looked up she'd most likely see a question on his face. He had to wonder why she'd chosen that chair. She would if she were in his shoes.

And she wasn't in the mood to explain it to him. How could she explain the shaft of jealousy that shot through her, the longing that had made her want to curl up in the thing and get lost in its comfy hominess? Why, oh why couldn't she really trust him and take all this at face value?

She took her time rinsing out the cup and putting it in the dishwasher. Finally, she had no choice. She couldn't stand here staring at the kitchen sink all day. She turned to face him.

He walked across the kitchen to fix his own cup. Just cream, she noted. He leaned back against the counter, not bothering to sit in the cool uncomfortable chairs, either.

She finally gave in to her curiosity, hoping for casual, but sign language didn't do casual well. "Why the wood chair?"

He shrugged. "Mom's. We each brought one back after she died."

"We?"

"Brothers and sisters."

She'd guessed from the pictures in his office that

he came from a big family. "How many?" She took a step toward him.

"Six, including me."

She took another step, catching the whiff of damp and clean mingling with the coffee and sweetness. "Six? Where do you fit?"

"Number three." He always messed up three in sign, making the *w* at first, then remembering to use his thumb instead. It was a quirk she was starting to find endearing.

The frown settled deep between his eyes, a sign of his frustration. He took a sip of his own coffee, meeting her gaze. She was good at reading body language. She had to be. She'd learned from an early age the subtleties of a person's body and face. And the last two nights, she'd learned his unique traits.

He wanted to ask, she saw it plainly there in his eyes. "Go ahead," she signed. "Ask."

"You." He set his cup down and brought both hands up to sign. "Something's bothering you."

That was an understatement. She thought about lying to him. Yesterday had been full of so many things.

"Thank you," she signed, unable to resist drinking in the angles of his face, the breadth of his shoulders, the way the muted morning light shone off his hair. "For helping me."

How could she ever express her feelings? The man had done so much for her. Her years of fear and cynicism couldn't easily be discarded, though. *Why* was he doing this?

Finally, Jason returned her gaze, and she made the sign to ask him that question.

"Why what?" he asked in response, facing her so she could read his lips.

"Why are you doing this?" she signed.

"*D-o-i-n-g*?" he spelled. "Helping you?" He looked confused.

She nodded, breaking the flow of the conversation by looking away and throwing out the damp napkin. She looked up, watching him closely, as closely as her dim vision allowed. He shrugged, and she wondered what that meant.

"I don't know." He leaned back, not speaking further, not moving, not looking away. "Who else was going to help you?"

She lifted her chin. "*M-a-x-i-n-e*."

His eyebrow lifted, and she wondered what inspired that.

"What?"

He shrugged, then looked at her. "Yesterday. You weren't happy with her help."

She looked down. "She…takes over."

He nodded and smiled. "I see that. That bothers you?"

Slowly, she nodded, wondering how much she dared admit to him. "I've worked too hard to be independent." There were times she had doubted she'd ever get the chance to create her own life.

"You do well."

"Thank you." She saw a flash of emotion in his eyes. "You don't like that."

"It's not like or *d-i-s-l-i-k-e*." He shoved his fingers through his hair. "Your world. The silence—" He sighed deep, heavy.

He was struggling with the words, and she couldn't tell if it was his thoughts, or his skill with sign. She waited, trying, and failing, not to jump to conclusions. A few days and he was already pulling back from her? From them. The realization hurt. But she couldn't give up everything she'd worked so hard for, not even for him.

She lifted her chin and met his stare. "I need to go home." She couldn't stay here. Couldn't guarantee that she'd be able to resist much longer. Resist him. Resist—she hastily glanced over her shoulder at the wooden chair—resist the ache to have something she would never have.

"No." He shook his head, his smile fading. "You're safer here." He signed it with harsh movements that surprised her. "You can't hear someone breaking in, or see them coming. No," he repeated the last.

Jason was still learning sign, and the hardest piece for hearing people to understand was the emotional piece. The emphasis that came with sign. But he'd nailed it this time.

She glared at him, angry and hurt.

"That's it, isn't it? You think *you* can keep me

safer here. In your hearing world. But not my impaired one."

"What does that mean?" His sign was solid and clear without his lips accompanying. She wasn't sure he knew he was doing it.

"You." She stepped closer to poke his chest. "When Trey punched you, did he turn you into a macho Texas boy?" She knew she was insulting him, but he needed to understand she was strong. She could handle anything he, or the world, dished up. She'd done just fine without him before.

"You're not going anywhere." The anger in his face, in the way his hands smacked each other in sign told her more than his words. "Not yet." When she raised an eyebrow, some of his own macho stupidity must have gotten through to him. His jaw tightened, but he didn't sign anything else. Because he didn't have anything to say—or didn't know how to say it, she couldn't tell.

He signed slowly, less harshly now. "You don't trust me to keep you safe." He stepped closer, and she had to force herself to stand her ground. The pain in his eyes called to her. She had to consciously make herself look up. He suddenly seemed so tall. So out of her reach. He wasn't going to understand.

"This is my life. I run it. I take care of me. I do fine. I don't need you to baby me."

His eyes widened, then narrowed. "Really?" He stepped back, grabbed his cup and took a deep swallow. He was obviously gathering his thoughts and trying not to reply in anger. Her eyes suddenly stung. She knew him too well, and he wasn't even aware of it. Finally, the only part of him moving was his head as he looked over at her and shook it. She saw him holding back some retort.

He was a man who lived in a world of words. He knew exactly what and how he wanted to say it. It was part of what fascinated her about him. But he had problems being articulate in sign. And she knew that frustrated him.

Just one more thing to prove that she didn't have a place here with him. With one last glance at the homey chair, then up at the man, she headed toward the door. She had to pass him. And as she did, he reached out and snagged her arm, gentle, but firm.

Lauren stepped back, pulling her arm slowly from his grasp. His hand was like a caress down the length of her arm, her hand, her fingers. She backed up, stopping in the doorway. "Take me home." She paused in the doorway, then turned to meet his gaze. "Or I'll take the bus."

CHAPTER EIGHTEEN

JASON WATCHED LAUREN walk out of the kitchen, her head held high. The silence suddenly seemed heavy. Why didn't it feel that way when she was here, when they were silently talking with their hands?

He froze. What the hell had just happened? He almost caught himself yelling after her. In the space of a minute, something had definitely changed. He stared at his hands. Shocked.

They'd had an entire conversation—amend that, an argument—without him speaking. He'd signed, read her sign, and they'd understood each other.

But instead of jumping for joy, Jason cursed. Why the hell did his brain suddenly learn sign *now*? In the middle of arguing with her, he figured it out?

His frustration multiplied at not being able to discuss it with her. Not because he couldn't, but because her anger and hurt stood in the way. He ignored the nagging pain at the realization she didn't really trust him. He'd done a damned good job of keeping her safe. She didn't seem to appreciate that, either.

He wished Trey would come back so he could

pummel him a little more and release some of this frustration. Damn it.

Following Lauren, Jason proceeded to get ready for work while she dressed. Not signing. Not speaking. Not even facing her so she could read his lips if he chose to say something, which he didn't.

"Ready?" He finally faced her and spoke, the sign a single, simple gesture. Then, because he hoped she expected it, he leaned in, and none too gently, kissed her.

Lauren tasted of coffee and anger, and just a little bit of the passion he knew she was denying. It stirred him, and he felt her breath hitch as it stirred her, too.

He stepped back, staring at her for a long minute. She had the bandages in her hand but didn't ask for help. She gritted her teeth instead.

"Here." He reached down and took the package from her hand. He made short work of the process and she stood there, stiff and accepting. Her sign of thanks was clipped as her eyes disappeared from view.

Resting her hand on his arm, she let him lead her to the car. They drove in silence—no music, or sign or touch. Once he'd opened the front door of her town house and let them in, she reached up and took the bandages off again.

The look on her face almost made him give up his promise to go to work. There was more pain in her eyes than there had been—even at the studio. It was a different pain, though. It was a hungry pain.

"Go." She made the sign, aiming toward the door then tapped her chest. "I'll be okay."

He had to leave. Had to let her do this. Respecting her wishes at this moment went against every protective cell in his body. But he did it. And headed out the door and to his car without looking back.

As the day dragged on, Jason tried to put Lauren out of his mind, tried to focus on his job. It wasn't as if he didn't have piles of work to do. But nothing worked. She haunted him, her anger and pain nagging at him. Twice, he had to stop himself from walking out of the office and heading back to get her.

Finally, the anger Trey had ignited yesterday, that Lauren had stirred up this morning, exploded. "You did what?" he yelled at Susan. The woman had done stupid things before, but this topped the list.

"I... I..." She stammered and stepped back. The distance seemed to give her a smidgen of strength. "I gave him your address." She backed away a bit more.

At least that explained how Trey had found his apartment. "Why would you even think that was okay?" He tried not to yell. Really, he did.

"He said he was your friend." She wrung her hands. "He's from Texas, after all."

"Do you know how big Texas is?" The fact that

302 THE BALLERINA'S STAND

Trey had been a friend once upon a time didn't have any bearing at the moment. "I don't know everyone from there."

"But you know him."

"Oh, yeah. I know him." Jason curled his hands into fists. "He's why I have this." He pointed to his busted lip and right eye, the one that had turned a pale shade of purple overnight. "Tell me, do you like everyone you know?"

"Well...uh...no."

"Point made. Do not *ever* give my home address to anyone. Do you understand?" He leaned toward her, needing her to understand how important this was.

"Should I, uh, not have taken the file?"

"What file?"

"The one he brought with him."

"What file?" he repeated. "Where is it?"

"On...on your credenza."

Jason took a deep calming breath, as if that would help, forcing himself to turn away. A thick blue file folder with a huge rubber band around it sat next to his dad's belt buckle.

Dad had never known Pal, but Jason knew he wouldn't have liked him. Even at eleven, Jason had understood and emulated his father's strong sense of right and wrong. It still echoed in Jason's memory.

Something he didn't want to analyze settled in his gut as he stared at the file. Dread? Fear? *Hell*.

"I'm sure you have work to do," he told Susan with a pointed glare. The woman scurried out of the room, closing the door behind her.

The silence this time was heavy with anticipation. Pal had told him a courier would deliver the file. Why had it taken so long to get here, and why had Trey brought it? He was a bit surprised Trey had even bothered. Granted, it was part of the legal file, but Haymakers weren't above ignoring the law. Was there something here Trey wanted him to see?

Dismissing all those concerns, Jason picked up the file and settled in his leather chair. He stared at the blue cover. He waited. On himself? On what? This was stupid. He could, at least, finish *something* to end this wasted day.

Jason flipped open the file, and was surprised to find Lauren's publicity photo. He stared at her beauty for several long minutes, missing her.

Then he flipped the photo over, hiding it from view. What the—

The only thing legal about this file was the motion on top. Pal Jr. and Trey were contesting the will. Filed in Austin two days ago, the same day the studio had burned, it threatened to take everything away from her.

Jason envisioned himself flinging the file across the room, papers flying through the air. Though it would be mildly therapeutic, he resisted the urge.

There were no other forms to finish or read. This was Lauren's life recreated on paper. Not a court

304 THE BALLERINA'S STAND

document. The image of Pal's face, that night at the ballet, with tears on his cheeks, came to mind.

This was all Pal'd had of his daughter. What had he said about his life ending with Lauren's mother's death? Jason turned the page and started reading about the beautiful, injured woman he'd left on her own just a few short hours ago.

LAUREN HAD SPENT the day reacquainting herself with her world. She'd taken the bandages off on schedule, and managed to put them back on fairly successfully. The medicine was still difficult alone, especially one-handed—well one and a half since she could use her fingers, sort of, even with the cast.

She'd emailed Maxine, and the kids were going to stay with her until Lauren was completely done with the bandages. The caseworker had come to the mansion this morning, and was supportive of the decision. Lauren wasn't sure if that was because of Maxine's persuasion or the woman's relief at having less on her plate.

I'm here to help. Maxine wrote, I know there's a lot of work ahead.

Lauren appreciated the offer, and Maxine's caring. But she knew there was more behind the offer than just simple need. I'm not sure what I'm going to do yet. And that was true. She needed to talk to her insurance agent, and see what the adjusters had come back with. It could be weeks before she

knew the total damages. My insurance will deter-
mine a lot.

Such a nice man, that Ryan Davies. He'll be a
big help. He said you can start work, just let your
contractors know the claim number. I'm more than
happy to help finance this, dear.

Lauren cringed, her head throbbing. She'd forgotten that her insurance agent was also Maxine's.
Of course, she'd called him. Ryan was a good man,
but he made a lot of money from Maxine each
month. Lauren wondered where his first loyalties
were.

I'll decide. I'll let you know if I need anything.
Not that she'd ever do that. Thanks for helping with
the kids. She signed off the email and spent the
next hour waiting for the agent to return her email.

She didn't feel like going to his office and hope
he was available, *and* could get an interpreter. Ryan
Davies was one of the business people she dealt
with who hadn't bothered to learn even a smidgen
of sign. Maybe she should look for another agent.
One *she* picked.

Tomorrow, she had to replace her phone. Email
was not the best way to contact anyone. She could
call a service to translate through the phone, but she
only used them as a last resort. It was way too slow.

Going out—into the sunlight—alone—scared
her, but Lauren refused to give in to fear. Ever.

Her frustration high, and her head throbbing, Lauren sank down to the couch with a cool washcloth. She needed to relax and put the bandages back on. But not yet. The coolness soothed her painful eyes.

Her thoughts spun with her internal turmoil. Behind her closed lids, Lauren once again saw the images of the blackened shell of her studio. She swore she could still smell the acrid scent of burned wood.

Maxine's offer, while well intentioned, threatened Lauren's independence nearly as much as the fire itself.

And then there was Jason.

She couldn't think about him right now. Maxine, and the money it would take to repair the studio, sent her stress back through the roof. But thinking about Jason?

That was a whole different kind of stress.

JASON'S PATIENCE RAN OUT. All the nights he'd driven to the studio, all the times he'd taken Lauren home, he'd gone well below the speed limit, wanting to extend his time with her. Now, he forced himself to slow down, and not floor the gas pedal, or take corners on two tires. He was anxious to make sure she was fine.

He'd been too angry with Lauren this morning, and she'd been too distant, for him to remember she didn't have a phone. Not that he'd have called her, but he could have texted to make sure she was okay.

Finally, her town house came into view. The sun was already at the horizon, stretching shadows around the neighborhood. The lights in the living room were on, but otherwise, the place was dark. Made sense if she was there alone. The kids were probably still at Maxine's.

He jerked to a halt outside, not bothering to pay attention to the meters or the hydrant out front. Sitting there for a minute, he took a deep breath. He was being ridiculous worrying about her. But without a phone how would she call for help? He should have thought of it earlier.

Jason took the front steps two at a time, nearly skidding into the front door. He ached to pound on it, but she'd never hear him. He hoped she had put on her bracelet and would see the lights flash when he hit the doorbell. All dozen times.

Lauren yanked open the door, alarm on her face. She stared up at him, her eyes wide. "What is wrong?" she signed. "Everyone okay?"

Relief washed over him. She stood there, staring at him like he was crazy—looking better than anything or anyone he'd seen all day.

Comfortable that she was okay, Jason held up a finger signing, "One minute." He went back out to his car and pulled out the file. She stood in the doorway, her hands on her hips. She looked totally confused.

Inside, Jason locked the door and ushered her back into the living room. She curled her legs up and settled in the overstuffed chair. Her hair fell around her shoulders where the light glowed against the copper. She picked up a cup of something warm she'd left on the side table, staring at him expectantly.

Carefully, he lifted the file, looked at it and gently set it on the coffee table. He didn't sign or say anything. He simply sat down in the chair opposite the couch. And waited.

"What's that?" Palms up, she frowned. She couldn't miss her name written on the tab in Pal's cowboy chicken scratch.

The file Pal had created, that Trey had given to Susan. That Trey, and most certainly Pal Jr., had read. While Lauren couldn't avoid it any longer, that didn't mean she'd embrace it.

"It was Pal's." He paused. "They are *c-o-n-t-e-s-t-i-n-g* the will."

She took another sip from her cup, staring at the blue file, drinking slowly for a dozen or so long minutes. All the while, Jason sat watching her. Waiting.

LAUREN STARED AT the file on the coffee table. The dull ache behind her eyes told her she needed to rest them more. Soon.

But now Jason sat in the chair facing her. "Tell me what's inside," she said, trying to avoid looking at it. Not sure what was in it. Knowing it was more than just legal papers.

He simply shook his head. He didn't speak. Didn't sign. Just waited.

Was it so horrible? She shivered, despite the warm mug in her hands and the heat of the tea sliding down her throat.

Her father had held it. Had looked at those same pages. Had he created it?

Jason seemed as nervous as she was. She could see it in the lines around his mouth and the way he kept bouncing his foot. Had he looked inside? Surely, he had.

Lauren sat forward, set the cup down and flipped the file open. She hadn't been aware of Pal Haymaker until just weeks ago. How long had he known about her life? Had he watched from afar? Or had he been ignorant of everything she'd faced? And now, frowning, she wasn't sure she wanted to know anymore.

She was surprised to see her publicity picture under the legal paperwork, but none of the rest was a surprise. She knew and remembered every one of the foster homes listed here. She swallowed back her anxiety.

Jason leaned forward, and she looked over at him. He signed slowly, asking if she was okay. She nodded, lying to them both.

"How did you get all this?" she asked.

"Pal hired a *d-e-t-e-c-t-i-v-e*. Trey dropped it off at my office."

Her father had hired a private investigator? He

seemed to have tried to find her and piece together her life. He'd found all this. Surely—

She shut off those thoughts and went back to the file.

As she flipped pages, something fell out. A photo. It landed on the floor and slid away. Jason jumped up, almost too quickly, to grab it. He stared at it before extending it to her.

"Who?" he asked.

She took the photo, and gasped as if a fist had slammed into her chest. Kenny. Not the Kenny who had tormented her all those years ago. Not the wild boy who had been hell on wheels and then some.

No, this was a man. An evil-looking man. A mug shot. She could only stare. She'd have never recognized him. But that stare? She'd never forget that. Finally, putting the picture to the side, she fought the temptation to turn it over, but that would be giving in to the bullying Kenny had excelled at.

Hastily, she pawed through the file, looking for the rest. Finally, she stared at the papers that went with the mug shot. The rap sheet of charges and convictions. Plural.

She froze. Reading. All the things he'd done. Her stomach turned. Jason's palm settled warm on her arm, startling her, and she realized he was slowing her down.

"What's the matter?" he signed.

"It's him," she answered. "*K-e-n-n-y.*" Her fingers shook so badly, she could barely form the letters. The photo slid off the table and landed face down on the floor this time. Something about that face vanishing gave her room to breathe.

She gulped in air, realizing a panic attack was close. She hadn't had one in years.

She shot off the couch and walked away, pacing. She didn't want to see the memories. Didn't want to remember any of it. She closed her eyes, the darkness behind her lids easing the pain of both her injuries and her mind.

Who else had read this file? Her father. He'd seen the police reports. Of her attempts to run away. Of what Kenny had done to require a mug shot. Did he think Kenny had done something to her? Or did he think she was like Kenny, being a foster kid?

Was that why he'd never come to get her?

KENNY, WHOEVER HE WAS, was the key to Lauren's past. Jason had gotten that impression from the copy of the rap sheet that Pal's investigator had put in the file and the look on Lauren's face when she saw it. Jason's stomach tightened. He had read about the man's crimes. Lauren wasn't listed as one of his victims. But that didn't mean she hadn't been one.

Jason managed to make her stop and take a minute, but her curiosity and other emotions he couldn't identify, soon dragged her back to the file. She stared, flipping the pages back, forth, rereading them.

When she looked up, there were tears in her eyes. "What?" he asked.

Her fingers flew and he couldn't catch everything. He'd thought he'd gotten the hang of sign this morning. But it dawned on him now that he'd probably be taking classes for the rest of his life.

He ached to understand her, to know what she really felt. He wanted to talk with her about everything—about this—without having to use technology or an interpreter. He didn't want anything between them. He tried to catch more.

"He did this." She pointed at the page and extended it to him. "He hurt them." Her signs were simpler now. Direct. Harsh. Easier to read. She poked at the page with an angry finger, nearly punching through.

Jason nodded and sat down beside her on the couch. "That's why, this." He flashed the mug shot. "They caught him."

She waved her hands in the air, a sign he knew she'd created herself, as if she were erasing their conversation from a chalk board. "I." She jabbed the center of her chest. "Should have helped. He tried with me, too."

Jason had feared that when he'd first read the file. Had Pal wondered if the same things that had happened to those girls had happened to his daughter?

"Tell me," he signed slowly, partially because of his ability, and partially to give her time to think and decide what she needed to share with him. He wanted to know—and yet, he didn't.

"I didn't do anything. He tried to—" She waved at the list of women Kenny had attacked. "I got away before he could. I ran like hell." She paused, her gaze distant as if she saw the events of that day. "For hours." Her hands slowed now. "And hours. I got lost."

He imagined the young girl he'd recently seen photos of in the case files. "How old?"

She paused, looking down at the papers, then back up at him again. "Thirteen. I never told anyone."

The same age as Tina. The need to punch someone or something roared through him. "You were only a kid." He tried to soothe her, but it didn't work.

She looked back at the papers, now scattered over the table's surface. He wished he'd never seen the damned thing, wished he didn't have to answer the question he was pretty sure she was going to ask.

"My father knew all this?" She waved her hand over the mess.

Jason hesitated. "In the end? Yes." He faced her, making sure she could clearly read his lips. "I don't know about when you were a kid."

Her shoulders slumped. She made the now familiar sign for "thank you."

Jason reached out, needing to touch her. Holding

her hand hindered her ability to sign, so instead, he traced the soft edge of her jaw with his thumb. "For what?"

"Your honesty."

Jason frowned and shook his head, not sure what she meant.

"For not sugar *c-o-a-t-i-n*-g things," she explained.

"This." He waved at the mess. "Not your fault."

Time froze and the air warmed as their gazes locked. Dear God, he was so proud of her. That scared young girl who'd grown into this strong woman, had run.

His mind filled with the image of the first time he'd seen her, running across that stage and leaping into the air with such ease and grace. Even when she'd been hurt, when she'd had to accept his help, she'd done it with strength and grace. She sure as hell hadn't learned that from her parents. Maxine? Perhaps.

Or maybe it was just who *she* was. He liked that idea. It was her strength, her ability, pure Lauren.

Jason suddenly understood what his brothers and sisters had all experienced. What they'd warned him would happen. What he could have sworn didn't really happen.

He was falling in love with her.

Time stretched out as Lauren sat staring at the scattered file. Jason watched her.

Then, suddenly her eyes widened and she stood.

Her breath came in gasps as she yanked another photo to the top of the pile. An old Polaroid.

She stabbed it with her fingers. "What is this?"

Jason stood, walking around to see it more clearly. He'd read through most of the file, but it was all out of order now. The faded image of a log cabin nestled in a thick grove of pines was a splash of color against the white pages. She stabbed at the image with her finger again, demanding his answer.

She'd gone pale, her frown creasing her entire brow. When she looked up at Jason, her eyes were wide with confusion. "I feel—" Her finger lingered on her breastbone. She set the picture down. "It is *f-a-m-i-l-i-a-r.*" Her frown deepened. "I do not remember—" She rubbed her forehead.

He had no clue what to say or do.

"Where is it?" Lauren stared unblinking at the photo. "Where?"

Jason moved pages around, looking for the deed to the property. He found it at the bottom of the scattered pile. He handed it to her, knowing it was up north, deep in the Cascade Mountains between California and Oregon. "It's yours now."

"Mine?" The look on her face was a mixture of wonder and terror.

What was she thinking? What was driving her panic? He remembered some reference to the cabin in the will, but couldn't fully recall. Where were those papers? He looked through the scattered pages without success and finally asked Lauren for her copies. She went over to a leather bag that sat by the door.

She extended the papers he'd originally given her. He stared for an instant. Had that really only been a few weeks ago? He looked at her, not sure he remembered not knowing her.

He found the paragraph he'd remembered in the document and showed it to her. He was pretty sure the sign she made wasn't for pleasant company.

Pacing, she turned several times, and he could almost swear he saw the wheels turning in her head. "It's valuable, isn't it?"

"I—I think so." Jason wasn't sure where she was going with this. Was that why the Haymakers were contesting the will?

"Can I sell it? Use the money for the studio?"

Ah, that made more sense. "I suppose."

THIS COULD SOLVE everything for her. Except something about the picture nagged at her. Something teased at her emotions. She couldn't look away.

Then Jason handed her another piece of paper. Absently, she looked at it. Then she looked at it again. The deed. Owner listed as Rachel Ramsey. Her mother. "What?" She looked up at Jason.

Flashes of light and memory cut through her brain. She closed her eyes, hoping maybe it was her eye injuries. But the dark behind her eyelids was filled with the same images. Only clearer.

Of sunlight pouring through a kitchen window

framed with blue gingham curtains. Of wood paneled walls. Of a big, round braided rug and a fireplace with river rock around a carved, wooden mantel.

Lauren shook her head, a dull throb growing behind her eyes. Fatigue or emotions, she wasn't sure.

Jason touched her arm, startling her. She looked up at him. "Don't decide now. Let me call this man." Jason lifted a business card.

She frowned reading the man's name. "Who is he?"

"The caretaker at the cabin." He pointed at a property management title under the name Harley Stapleton.

"I can—"

"I know you can," Jason interrupted.

She could see he wanted to do this, that he was trying, and failing to tamp down the need to take over. The fact that he tried to hold back made her stop and consider.

"Okay, only because I don't have a phone."

"We'll get you one tomorrow." He stepped closer, crouching down in front of her. "We'll decide after I talk to him." He shook the card.

Lauren nodded. She didn't dwell on the fact that she was letting someone else take over. At least he'd asked.

This close she saw the irises of his eyes widen. She wasn't sure if he moved slowly, or if time itself slowed.

She reached up then, touching her palm to his cheek before pulling back to sign. "You can't keep taking care of me." She shook her head, her curls dancing around her shoulders.

"Why not?"

They stared at each other. Lauren truly didn't understand his need to do exactly what she didn't want.

He leaned in and his lips, warm and strong on hers felt right. She let him pull her close, into his arms.

And then it didn't matter who was in charge or in control.

None of that mattered at all.

CHAPTER NINETEEN

Lauren awoke with the comforting sense of a warm body beside her. Jason. She smiled and peeled away the bandages. For the first time in nearly a week, the morning light didn't stab at her eyes. She looked around, enjoying the simple view of her bedroom.

It was also the first time she'd had a man spend the night here. She looked over at Jason's broad shoulders and bare back, remembering the feel of both beneath her hands last night.

Her smile grew, and, as if he could feel her stare or hear her thoughts, he awoke. He turned and shifted, stretching like a cat. She enjoyed the view until he turned and his gaze met hers. Then there was no looking away, no denying she'd been watching him.

"Morning," she saw his lips say.

"Morning," she signed as he reached for her. The rough stubble of his morning beard scraped her neck, sending chills through her body. Such a masculine thing. And yet, his lips were a soft contrast as they found hers.

This was the perfect way to wake up. Wrapping

her arms around his neck, careful not to be clumsy despite the cast on her arm, she returned his kiss.

Jason moved his big hands over her body, touching and warming her everywhere. At first slow, savoring, then more quickly—urgent.

As if he could read her mind, he seemed to know exactly when she needed him closer, deeper. And then he was there, moving inside her, taking her to the one place only they could go together.

His lips found hers again and with one last thrust, he sent them both over the edge.

Once her heart rate nearly returned to normal, she moved, but Jason had other ideas. His arms tightened. Rolling over, he took her with him, settling her head on his shoulder. She snuggled in close, savoring the intimacy.

This was how she wanted to wake up every day for the rest of her life—

Her eyes flew open, and Lauren resisted the urge to pull away. Instead, she looked up at the profile of the man she'd fallen in love with.

And she had fallen—hard and deep. He already took up space in her life. She'd never thought anyone could do that.

Did he feel the same? What *did* he feel for her? They hadn't talked about that.

Lauren wasn't stupid or naive enough to think sex equaled love, but the rest? The way he took care of her? Was that love, or just his chivalrous need to be in control?

Now, here in his arms, was not the time to puzzle through this. Not with his body so close and his touch so warm. Later, she'd think. Now, she just wanted to feel.

JASON STARED AT his reflection in Lauren's bathroom mirror. He looked like hell, but Lord, it felt good.

She'd gone downstairs to figure out breakfast and he headed to the shower.

Something had changed about Lauren this morning. The anxiety of last night was gone, and she was smiling. The fact that her eyes were nearly healed and she was free of the bandages, had to be a big part of it.

She came up the stairs just as he was finishing his shower and handed him a steaming cup of coffee. Hers was already on the nightstand, so she must have made a couple of trips. The cast was still a hindrance.

Dressed in a bulky blue sweater and dark pants that hugged her shapely legs, Lauren looked beautiful as she curled up on the bed and leaned against the headboard. She looked every bit the confident ballerina. If he didn't have so much to do…

His phone rang on the nightstand, and he stalked over to it, intending to silence it. The number on the screen made him answer instead. "Hello."

"Jason Hawkins? This is Harley Stapleton. You left me a message last night."

"Yes, I did."

"Sorry I didn't hear my phone. I was at dinner with my grandkids, and they're pretty danged loud."

The man had a Texas drawl as thick as any Jason had ever heard. It shouldn't have surprised him since the man had worked for Pal, but it did.

"Thanks for returning my call, Mr. Stapleton." Jason turned so Lauren could at least see his lips and "hear" his side of the conversation. Her eyes grew wide, and she carefully set her coffee cup down, as if she were afraid of spilling it.

She focused on his face.

"Please call me Harley, it's a much better fit than mister anything." The man laughed.

"I'm glad you called, Harley. Lauren Ramsey and I would like to see the Haymaker property, if that's possible."

"Sure is." The man's enthusiasm came through the phone loud and clear. "It'll be mighty nice to see that little girl again. Pal kept me informed on all her doin's over the years, but it ain't the same."

"You knew Lauren?"

"Last time I saw her, she was a little tyke, cute as could be. But, yeah." There was an instant of silence. "Guess she's all grown up now." There was a sadness in the man's voice, but he quickly cleared his throat to banish it. "When would you like to come up?"

"Today?"

"Sure, though I need to warn you, you get here

to town, it's another couple of hours on horseback to get to the cabin."

"You're kidding."

"Nope, wouldn't kid about that." Harley laughed. "Pal refused to build any roads. He was paranoid about anyone findin' the place."

"Why was that?"

"Don't know why, just was." As if that were explanation enough.

Jason frowned. That didn't sound like Pal. The man hadn't been afraid of anything. Or so Jason had thought.

Had there been threats? Jason thought of the file downstairs. Maybe there was more there. Looking at Lauren now, if someone threatened her—or his family—how would he react?

"If you want to come up today, I could get a reservation at the B&B for you, then we could head up in the morning," Harley suggested, breaking into Jason's thoughts. Jason repeated the suggestion to Lauren. She frowned, but nodded.

"Sounds good."

"Great, I'll have Lillian who owns the B&B set up a couple of rooms."

"Thanks, Harley. We'll call you when we hit town." Jason ended the call, taking a minute to frown at the phone and collect his thoughts.

Lauren's anxious stare nudged him to explain. "We have to ride horses to reach the cabin." He'd laughed when they'd learned animal signs in class. Now he was glad for it.

"Horses?" Her eyes were wide. "I don't know how."

"You can do it." Jason actually looked forward to the prospect of sharing something with her from his world.

"How far?"

Jason shrugged. He hadn't asked distance. "A couple of hours. Hey, you can always ride with me." He wiggled his eyebrows, which broke the tension and found him with a pillow aimed at his head.

He laughed, glad she'd set down her coffee when he launched himself, and the pillow, back at her.

WHILE JASON RAN to his office to finish a few things and clear his calendar, Lauren had gone to the store to get her new phone. Jason had offered to help, but she sent him away. She'd done this before.

On their way out of town they stopped at the mansion. Maxine had both kids on the dance floor.

"Of course they can stay until you return." Maxine threw her hands wide, dramatic as usual. But the spark in the older woman's eyes told Lauren Maxine was thoroughly enjoying herself. And so was Dylan. Though Tina looked less than thrilled, she wasn't running away or arguing.

A short while later, Jason and Lauren were headed up the coast highway. Sunlight glinted off the polished hood of the car, and Lauren was glad for her dark sunglasses. Her eyes were hungry for sights now that the bandages were off. She drank in the bright blue sky and the sharp browns and greens of the earth's edge where the winding gray ribbon of highway cut into the hillside.

She rolled down the window, the cool air fingering through her hair. For the first time since the fire, perhaps since she'd met Jason, she felt like herself.

By the end of this trip, her eyes would ache, but they were healing well. She'd be fine. This was how she lived her life. Feeling happy and in control, she settled back to enjoy the ride.

The Mountainside Bed-and-Breakfast looked like a dainty fairy-tale house. Lauren thought it would be beautiful with holiday lights and a fresh coat of snow on its eaves and gingerbread trim. Maybe they'd come back around the holiday time.

"Anything look familiar?" Jason asked once he'd parked in front.

She shook her head. She'd wondered the same thing as they'd driven into town. If she'd been here before, wouldn't she remember *something*? She was disappointed that she didn't.

Harley met them for dinner in the B&B's small dining room. It reminded Lauren of the chair in Jason's kitchen, and she knew she was right. This type of setting suited him better.

The caretaker of her father's cabin definitely looked like someone who lived in Texas. His big cowboy hat, worn jeans and dusty cowboy boots fit in here, but she could tell he'd come from the Lone Star State. He could have stepped out of the pictures she'd first pulled up on her computer of Pal and Pal Jr.

"You grew up mighty pretty," Harley told Lauren. Jason had to translate as she struggled to read the older man's lips. His accent was, according to Jason, deep Texas and he talked as if his jaw was wired shut.

When Jason explained about her lipreading, Harley pulled the toothpick from between his lips, thinking that was the problem. "Sorry about this." He waved it in the air before putting it on his empty plate. "Picked up the habit when the missus made me give up my smokes."

Lauren nodded. She'd have to rely on Jason, which was fine. He was getting quite good at sign.

She watched Harley for a long time. This man knew so much. Did she want to know what he could tell her? Where did she start asking?

Then he saved her. "Can I tell you some things I think you should know?" After Jason finished repeating what Harley had said, Lauren met the man's faded blue gaze and nodded.

"First, the cabin belonged to your mother. Pal built it for her, to thank her for takin' care of him." At Lauren's frown, the old man explained how Pal had been in Vietnam, and had fallen from a helicopter. His injuries had left his legs damaged, requiring him to need surgeries and treatments all through his life. Rachel was a nurse who worked with orthopedic patients.

She'd been much younger than Pal, but that hadn't mattered. "Apparently, somethin' happened. You're here." Harley smiled.

A nurse. Somehow, Lauren knew that. She didn't know how she knew it, but she did. "Did they—we—ever live at the cabin?" Wouldn't she remember that? The sadness that blanketed Harley's face when Jason repeated her question told her maybe she didn't want to remember.

"Your mother was one of those people who lit up the whole world, you know." He paused for a long time.

She met Jason's gaze that held as many questions as her mind did.

Finally, Harley spoke, but he looked down, and Lauren wanted to scream as she had to wait for him to finish so Jason could translate for her. "She told Pal that she had cancer when they were up there." Another long pause as Jason talked to her with his lips and some sign.

"She wanted to die there, but he wanted to take her all over the world for treatments."

Lauren had known her mother had died from cancer. As a nurse, she'd have known what her chances were. She'd have known more of the realities than other patients. That made sense.

"What happened?" Lauren asked.

Harley looked up at her then, his eyes filled with a deep, sad pain. "She wouldn't go anywhere. She moved you in there for a while. Up until her last day, she refused to leave here. All she wanted to do was be with you. And she never stopped loving Pal." Harley fidgeted with the salt and pepper shakers. "But Pal was an angry man. He thought if he left her, she'd change her mind and follow him."

"She didn't." Lauren made the sign, knowing even from the view of a five-year-old's memory that Rachel had made her decision and stuck with it. Jason curled his hand over hers.

Harley nodded. "After that, I don't know that I ever saw Pal happy again. He wouldn't forgive *her* for leaving *him*."

Jason was nodding and she tilted her head, questioning his action. "What?"

He shrugged. "That describes how Pal was when I knew him. Angry and mean." He looked at her. "Sorry."

It might have hurt *if* she remembered or had known the man.

But she didn't. Not at all.

The conversation dwindled, and Harley headed home. "See you folks at 8:00 a.m." He'd already given them the map to the stables, and a vague description of how they'd get to the cabin. It wasn't far as the crow flies. But they weren't crows, so they'd have a two-hour trek through the pass. "Should get us there before noon."

JASON COULDN'T REMEMBER the last time he'd felt this relaxed. Part of him felt slightly guilty, but not enough to make him change things. Being away from the office, on horseback, with Lauren. What more could he ask for?

He and Lauren had spent the morning getting her acquainted with the little mare, then following Harley's lead out of town.

It wasn't likely that they would make it back by nightfall so the old man had packed for an overnight trip with saddlebags and bedrolls. "Precautions," he said as he strapped a rifle in its scabbard to his saddle.

Lauren frowned and Jason translated Harley's explanation. "We're going into the *w-i-l-d-e-r-n-e-s-s*. Never can be too cautious. Lots of hungry critters are coming down from the high country because of the drought."

Harley pointed out sights and animals along the way, explaining the lay of the land with an intensity that reminded Jason of his brother Wyatt and his passion for his own land. A herd of deer fascinated Lauren until something spooked them, and as one, they bounded away and disappeared over the next ridge.

The cabin, this land, sat smack in the middle of prime, high-country land. Jason realized how undervalued the place must be. The lack of utilities, and a road to the property, were primary reasons. He could see where a man could get lost up here—and Pal and Rachel had done just that, for a while, anyway.

He almost envied them. Looking over at Lauren, he'd love to have that with her.

The sun was high in the sky now, and Jason knew they had to be close. They reached the top of the next ridge, and Harley pulled his mount to a halt. He waited for them to catch up, and Jason saw why as he pulled up beside him. The view was phenomenal. He turned to watch the wonder spread over Lauren's face when she saw it.

There, on the opposite side of a wide, high meadow, nestled against the thick arms of the pines, sat the cabin. The old Polaroid hadn't begun to do it justice. Harley was right—no one would have ever found this place without knowing it was here.

Time stopped as they sat there, looking, enjoying. The scent of sage, pine and cool air filled his lungs and filtered through his body and mind. It smelled right, like belonging and welcome home. Sweet and wild.

Lauren took her own deep breath, and they shared a glance. She pulled forward, anxious, he could tell, to be there.

If she'd been a more experienced rider, he'd have challenged her to a race across the field. He wanted to take off and run, let the horse have a bit of freedom, but it would be a while before she could do that. He was assuming by the smile on her face that she liked the ride. Wait until she got down. Though they'd taken several breaks, she wasn't used to riding like this.

As they moved across the field, the sun played in her hair, and she looked as at home on a horse as she did on a stage.

Yeah, he could stay here with her for a *very* long time.

DREAMS DIDN'T COME TRUE. Lauren knew that, but she had to keep reminding herself of it.

The warm sunshine had cooled the higher they'd climbed, and the air had grown thinner the deeper they moved into the wilderness. Jason sat on the dark horse as if he rode every day, which he had as a kid. A faint trail led them through the stands of pine and aspen. Mottled sunlight fell through the branches, across the breadth of Jason's shoulders. Lauren didn't want to look away, but she needed to focus on riding.

The bright sunshine in the field had caressed him, and she'd finally given in and watched him. She let the mare follow the others, the reins warm in her hands. The scents of the forest, horse and leather seemed so natural and comforting. She actually felt like she was getting the hang of this.

Harley led them to an old-fashioned hitching post at the base of the cabin's steps. "You folks go on in." With a grin, he tossed her a set of keys. "There's a stable out back. I'll get these guys settled in."

Once Harley was gone, Jason joined her on the front porch. "Ready?" he asked.

Lauren frowned. Was she? What was on the other side of that door? The past? Memories? She was strong, she knew that. She'd been on her own, alone in her silent world since her mother's death. Yes, she'd been housed in foster homes, but she'd *lived* only with herself. With only herself to go with her each time they moved her.

Her belongings from her mother—her clothes, the little pink princess suitcase, the toys, the books, all of them had vanished at some point. Either by falling apart, being replaced or being forgotten.

Nothing, and no one, had been with her through it all.

She didn't need anyone. Or anything.

But today... Today Jason was here, standing behind her. He'd become her friend, and so much more. Today, she needed him to be the something more.

Slowly, she touched the rough-hewn wood of the front door. The hand that she prided herself on being steady and strong, trembled as she turned the key in the lock and pushed the door open.

The room was exactly like what had flashed in her mind. Exactly as she remembered when she'd found the picture in the file.

She'd been here before, but the memories had been blocked for some reason. Had something horrible happened here that she couldn't remember? She shook her head and forced herself to step through. Oddly, her fingers didn't move. Her thoughts and words stilled.

The wood had been polished to a high gleam when she'd been here before. A thin layer of dust now coated everything. She'd been a child, and the angle was different now that she was nearly two feet taller.

Frowning, she turned her head from side to side, drinking in the sight of the huge stone fireplace whose chimney shot up and through the log roof overhead. An antique deer-antler chandelier hung from a thick black chain, the chain now wrapped in white cobwebs with strands that shot out to bounce off the tips of some of the antlers.

She felt the stamp of a footstep vibrate through the wood and she glanced back at Jason as he came up behind her. She saw his brow knit and his lips pucker in a silent whistle as he glanced around. For a brief second, he captured her gaze. She'd never heard the sound of a whistle, though she'd read descriptions of it in a book. She cocked her head, lost in her wonder.

Why did he make her do that? Why did he, of all things and all people, make her want more of the world? She'd learned in foster care not to expect too much. Wanting only led to disappointment.

She shook her head and tore her gaze from him. She had more to look at here, more to think about. The great room encompassed the living room, dining area with high ladder-back chairs at a dusty table, and a small kitchen. Old appliances, white and chrome, looked out of place in the rustic kitchen.

Lauren's mind filled, memories falling over her, nearly overwhelming her. Blue gingham curtains, wafting in the breeze from an open window slammed into her thoughts. Her mother washing dishes, staring, smiling out at the woods. Sunlight had poured in, mottled by the aspen leaves beyond. Now the bare branches were on the other side of the glass. The curtains limp, the bright colors dimmed by dust and time.

A set of wooden stairs, narrow and rough, disappeared up into a dim hall. She knew that upstairs was a loft, and she looked up to see the rail that hung at the edge, not so far above her head as it had been when she was five. The master bedroom was up there. Her mother's room. She backed away. His room.

Her mother had loved this place. Pal had built it for her, built her dream up here in the isolated mountains. Sadness whispered over Lauren. Not loneliness, but grief for the mother she only had as a memory.

A group of framed photos sat on a side table, a painful surprise. Lauren's throat ached, nearly choking her. The largest one was a different pose, but it had been taken the same time as the photo of Rachel that Lauren had lost as a child. Her vision blurred, the cool air chilling her tears, making her eyes feel rimmed in ice. She blinked, trying to clear her vision, fighting the sadness.

She should be joyous that she had the picture again. That she'd regained the memories of her mother from this place. But she wasn't. It hurt too much.

Maybe the emptiness of her memory was better. It was certainly less painful.

A cold breeze wrapped around her from the still-open door. She pulled her sweater tighter. Walking slowly, carefully, she walked from room to room, what few there were, seeing the past as if it were playing on a movie screen.

Her mother had been so young, so pretty, her hair long and flowing, much like Lauren's was now. Was that why she'd never cut her hair like the other girls? She hadn't ever considered that before. She could see Rachel standing there, at the top of the narrow curved stairs, smiling down.

Not at Lauren. No, her mother's smile in this memory had been for Pal Haymaker. For the man Lauren realized now, was her father. A man whose heart had blackened to ash when Rachel died. A heart that had turned so solid, he hadn't left any room for his daughter.

Lauren shook her head, fighting the images that followed. The anger, the arguing, the emptiness after her father had left. She remembered that sometimes they forgot that while she couldn't hear, she could read their lips.

They'd hurt each other. Pal Haymaker hadn't had room for anything that wasn't perfect in his world, or in his heart.

The cancer that had taken Rachel hadn't been her imperfection. That had been the stubbornness that came with her red hair.

Lauren saw through adult eyes the man's harsh judgment, saw clearly the reality and depth of his loss. She tried to understand it. But that little girl, the one who'd come here, excited to see her father, hadn't seen his pain. She could only feel her own hurt. Feel her own heart breaking when he left them. Left them here alone to face the horror of Rachel fading away.

Had he even bothered to worry about the fate of a motherless little girl?

Lauren moved haltingly down the short hallway beneath the stairs to the small bedroom in back. The room that had been hers. It seemed even smaller now. The single log-framed bed that used to have a pink comforter on it was now cloaked in a serviceable gray bedspread.

Obviously, he'd never thought of her again.

She turned, stumbling over her own feet and into a strong pair of arms that engulfed her. Arms that were here now—and whose comfort she gladly took. But for how long?

CHAPTER TWENTY

JASON GUIDED LAUREN to the big leather chair and made her sit down—before she fell down. He took the bright-colored afghan, folded on the ottoman, shook out the dust, and settled it around her shoulders. The cabin was still cool, and the leather cold and stiff. He hoped it would help as he started the fire.

Harley, or someone, had laid logs and kindling in the grate before leaving last time, and Jason lit it with matches he found in a kitschy brass holder on the hearth. Soon the room would warm.

Lauren was pale and in shock. Something had upset her, and while he wasn't certain, he could guess at the memories assaulting her.

She had that look he knew well. Growing up with three sisters had its perks. She was either going to fall apart into a puddle of tears, or explode in a fury of anger. His bet was on the latter. The woman who'd survived everything she had wouldn't let this beat her.

The question was, how ticked would she be? And how long would it take to surface?

The flames had just caught, and were licking

around the thick dry logs, when he saw her move. She struggled for an instant to slip her arms free from the blanket.

Her gaze was dry, and she stared into the growing flames.

"My father," she signed slowly, as if to herself more than him. "He was a weak man." There was no frown to indicate she was asking a question. Just a statement of fact.

Jason wasn't sure what she wanted or needed from him, so he waited, sitting on the raised brick hearth facing her. One thing he knew, she wasn't someone who had to "talk" things through. Her deafness, the limitations of sign, made her that way.

But that didn't mean she didn't *need* to talk things out sometimes.

"Tell me what you need from me. To listen? Or do something?" he signed, sensing it was easier for her to focus on one means of communication right now.

Her smile was bittersweet, distant. "Thank you." She waved at the fire and the blanket, then pointed at her wrist. "I just need time."

"You got it."

The silence grew, neither of them signing or moving. Finally, she shifted, facing Jason. "This—" She pointed at the chair where she was sitting. "Was his favorite. I remember sitting on his lap." She frowned down at the chair. "Here. By the fire. He read me a book. Using sign."

Her face held pain, and a bit of wonder lurked in her eyes as she stared at the flames. "It was *The P-o-k-e-y Little P-u-p-p-y*." She looked at Jason. "Why do I remember that?"

What could he say? "I don't know." The contradictions of her father had to hurt. This memory didn't fit with the anger and pain Pal Haymaker had left behind him when he walked away. The memory she'd become most comfortable with.

Slowly, Lauren stood, pulling the afghan tighter around her shoulders. She came over to sit beside him on the wide hearth. Leaning her head on his shoulder, she sighed. He slipped his arm around her shoulders, letting her lean on him.

Not surprisingly, she didn't stay next to him long. Would she ever let him really take care of her? Did he really want her to? Her independent spirit was one of the things that attracted him to her.

He'd have to think about that.

He was still thinking about it later that night when the storm he'd been anticipating hit.

"Why did they even have me?" Lauren's sign was harsh and big. He'd learned that her precision faded when she was emotional.

She'd gotten ready for bed and Jason was already sitting against the rugged headboard in what had been her mother's room up in the loft. According to Lauren, it looked totally different now. Everything of Rachel's was gone. It was a double-edged sword—the loss hurt her, but the difference probably made it possible for her to be in here. Was that why Pal had done it?

"This is not the dark ages." She paced barefoot, oblivious to the cold wood floor. "They had options."

She turned to glare at him. His brain clicked into legal mode and the challenge of arguing Rachel and Pal's case intrigued him—perhaps too much.

"Did they really have a choice?" He spoke it, too, to help her understand and think.

"Money wasn't an *i-s-s-u-e*."

"True." Jason stacked his hands behind his head, pondering. "Religion?"

Her brow arched.

"What?" He lowered his arms to make the sign. "It's a viable question."

"They were having an affair."

"Good point."

She faced him, her hands on her hips. "Whose side are you on?"

He tried to smile and ease her tension. "Yours. I want to help you."

"You're not—" She slashed her hand through the air. "Helping."

"Looking at all sides doesn't help?" That was such a foreign idea to him. He was actually surprised. Looking at an issue from all sides was second nature to him.

"No." Lauren stared at him. "You *c-o-n-f-u-s-e* me."

Jason waited to see what she did next. Finally

she stopped pacing and yanked back the covers to climb in beside him. Once settled, she sat, staring.

He touched her arm to get her to look at him. "Maybe they really did want you."

She turned to look at him. "I wish I knew." Her hands shook, and she clasped her fingers together as if to get them to stop.

Finally, she started signing again, her hands gentle and flowing. "All I ever wanted was a family. I would lie awake at night, imagining what it would be like." Her hands stilled.

"What did you wish for?" he prompted.

"Dinner at a table with people every night." She closed her eyes as if seeing those distant childhood dreams behind her eyelids. "Of someone to come home to, who I could tell about my day." Jason watched her, concerned. Her eyes opened and she looked at him. Something that looked a lot like self-pity flashed in her eyes, but he couldn't be sure as she looked away so quickly. That was so unlike her, and yet he understood the reaction. He reached over and tilted her chin up, making sure she could see his lips. "Look. I believe they cared deeply about you. Even Pal. He read to you, remember?" That was an image Jason struggled with.

She nodded slowly. Something else was bothering her. Could she even explain it? Did she understand it herself?

"Talk to me," he urged. "What's going on in there." He tapped her forehead gently.

She shrugged. Jason waited.

"Why?" She paused again, then signed so quickly he almost missed part of it. "Why do I remember him? Not her—here?"

Guilt flowed out of her. "Him teaching me sign. Sitting on *his* lap. Him playing with me. *H-a-r-l-e-y* said we stayed here." Tears spilled over Lauren's cheeks. "Why don't I remember *her* here with me? Nothing but a couple flashes."

Her sign was so harsh, her frown so deep, it was the equivalent of yelling. She pounded the mattress with her fist. "Why?"

A shrink he was not. But he did study people. And he remembered his own mother, so busy surviving that the details got lost.

But how to explain his thoughts to her. "My dad died when I was eleven." He almost grinned when he got the number sign correct the first time. The numbers still plagued him and focusing on that shut out the pain he always felt about his dad. "My mom got *c-a-u-g-h-t* up in day-to-day stuff, she lost the little extras. Your mom took care of you. Played sometimes. But *P-a-l* probably always played."

She nodded.

"But why can't *I* remember?" She was beating herself up about it. No arguing would help, so he backed off. "It's not just forgetting her." She paused. "Dylan and Tina need me to know how to do mom things. And she did them. I know it. But

I can't remember how." She looked around. "No. This place. It has bad memories."

"Come here." He pulled her into his arms, knowing it wasn't a solution. But it was all he could do to comfort her.

"What if—"

He saw her sign from the back this time as she wasn't facing him. It was easier to read, more like he was doing it himself.

"What if they *did* want me—until…" She slowly touched her ear then her jaw. The sign for deaf.

"No!" Jason cried, the vibration of his voice startling her. He pulled around and grasped her shoulders. "Don't ever think that. I knew Pal. Even he wasn't that rotten."

"You don't know." She shook her head.

What could he say, or do to prove to her that she *was* wanted and loved? He was at a loss. "You're right. He didn't care about anyone. But he kept that file. He went to the ballet to watch *you*."

Jason bent down and tried to catch her eye.

Leaning forward, he kissed the top of her head. *"I—"* He tapped his chest. "Want you." And he knew as he said it that it was the truth.

And he proceeded to show her how much.

THE CABIN WAS empty when Lauren woke up the next morning. Jason and Harley had planned to leave early to ride the property line. Jason wanted to see where the boundaries were and how they were marked. Ever the legal mind, tying up the loose ends. They'd need all that when—if—she put this place on the market.

They'd invited her to come along. She could tell he had loved riding yesterday, but she was still deciding. Her legs and backside were weighing in on the decision today. If she kept the cabin, there had to be a road put in.

She didn't necessarily want to sell this place, but she might have to. Visions of her damaged studio threatened to taint her day.

Outside, the sky was blue, with wispy clouds overhead. From the height of the sun in the sky, she'd slept a long time. A restful night helped clear her mind. Why had she let herself get so upset yesterday? That was so unlike her. Silliness. She dismissed her overreaction, blaming it on all the stress lately—the kids, the fire, her eyes and the added strain of the trip.

Stretching, Lauren headed to the small bathroom, showered and threw on jeans and a sweatshirt. Simple, relaxing clothes. There wasn't anyone to dress up for, no one to impress. Jason had seen her much worse than this.

As she walked past the mirror, she smiled at herself. Without makeup, her hair curling naturally without any fancy styling, and hanging loose down her back, she was surprised at how young she looked. Approving, she went to the kitchen to grab a quick breakfast. The warm scent of coffee still mingled its warm aroma with the wood and outdoorsy scents that permeated the entire place.

Resisting the call of the outdoors was no easier for her than it had been for Jason, though she wasn't interested in riding through it. She wanted to walk.

Sunlight shone through the thick pine branches, the deep blue sky beyond was rich and bright. She slipped her sunglasses on as she stepped outside, almost reluctant to mute the brightness, but still not ready to risk any pain to her eyes.

The air was cool, and she swore she could taste the crisp, mountain air. No wonder her mother had loved it here.

A narrow dirt path led down the hill and through the trees. Another memory. Pal holding her tiny hand, guiding her along it. Pointing to things, much as Harley had yesterday, only Pal had slowly shown her the signs to match. *Tree.*

Bird.

Flower.

She knew that just a short distance down the hill there was a pond. There he'd taught her *water* and *fish.* She made her way along the trail, winding through the thick trees and shadows. Enjoying the simple beauty.

Finally, she reached the clearing she remembered. The trees seemed to crouch closer, the grasses seemed thicker. The pond's water was crystal clear, the surface still, and as she dipped her fingers in it, ice-cold.

It looked undisturbed. Peaceful. She found herself making the signs her father had shown her, as if talking to him. Or her younger self.

Lauren stood there a long time, drinking it in, enjoying the light and scent of it all. The sun lifted higher, warming her.

A wide boulder sat at the edge of the water, the sun warming its surface. She climbed up, enjoying the heat the stone gave off. From here, lying on her belly, she could peer into the pond's clear water and watch the fish. She was as mesmerized as she'd been when she was five.

She knew she needed to head back. Jason and Harley would be back soon, and she had things she had to do. She wanted to look through the entire cabin, see what was here, see what she remembered. See what she wanted to keep—if anything. She hoped that she'd have a decision made by then.

What did she want to do with this place? Keep it? Sell it? Would she ever come here? Could she stay away?

She slid off the boulder, her feet landing with a soft thump on the water's edge. A shadow moved in the trees, and she turned to look up the hill, smiling at Jason.

Except it wasn't Jason.

Lauren instinctively stepped back, fighting to keep her balance and not fall into the water.

The man looked vaguely familiar, but with the

sun in her eyes and a baseball cap low over his eyes, she couldn't see his face clearly.

There were only a few people who even knew this place existed. How had he—?

He moved toward her. "You still talk like a moron, princess?" The man faced her to speak, making sure she could clearly read his lips, as if he knew—

How...? She tried to step away, but he was too quick. Thick, hard fingers dug into her arm. Realization dawned quick and painful. The bus driver? The one who drove so wildly? It couldn't be... Kenny! She struggled to get away, but he was too strong.

"You didn't recognize me, did you, princess?" He looked rough, rougher even than he'd looked driving the late-night bus. His jaw was unshaven, his hair long and shaggy. Anger and frustration rolled off him.

He was right. She hadn't recognized him. She'd simply been focused on her life, on riding the bus home.

His hot breath brushed her face. "All those times on my bus? You were in *my* world." He laughed, poking at his chest, to gloat. Though Lauren couldn't hear, she recognized that sneer. She shivered.

"Ever wonder why I drove like I did?" He laughed again. "All that perfect balance you got? I controlled you. Made you bump into a seat. Stumble."

Was that what a cackle looked like?

Lauren trembled and cringed, knowing Kenny felt her fear. She had to think.

She glared at him, not able to sign, unable and unwilling to do anything else. He glared back and the years fell away. She saw him as he'd been— the bully bent on making everyone, especially a hearing-impaired girl, feel like less than dirt. She had to get away. No one was going to save her. The guys had no idea where she was. Why hadn't she stayed at the cabin?

Jason. Her heart skipped a beat. He'd blame himself if something happened to her. He took responsibility so seriously.

She shook her head to dispel such thoughts. She couldn't worry about him now. She had to worry about herself. She couldn't tell Jason how she felt, how much she appreciated him if Kenny finished what he'd told her all those years ago he wanted to do to her. That he'd done to those other girls. Her mind fell backward to that awful day.

She'd gotten away from him then. She'd been thirteen. Surely at twenty-eight she was just as capable. *Think,* she told herself. What happened back then? What had she done?

Sweet-talking wasn't an option. Despite the cringe that shook through her, she relaxed and leaned against him. She watched the grin spread over his thin lips.

Lauren had to look at Kenny to read his lips. But

making sure her expression didn't give away her true emotions took everything she had. All those hours of practice for the stage blessedly came to her rescue. She forced her lips into the best smile she could fake.

"You got it." He nodded. "You. Me. Alone here." He leaned closer, too close. "Did you like the flowers?" She resisted the urge to gag. His grip loosened, just like it had in the school yard back in middle school. She was expecting it, but he wasn't the teen he'd been then. As she pulled back, she watched the dark take over his eyes. She had to act. Now.

She yanked free, feeling dirty fingernails cut along her arm. She focused. And pulled harder. This time when he reached for her, she was ready.

She lifted her arm. The thick cast that had driven her crazy for a week glowed bright white in the midday sun. She smashed the hard plaster into the bridge of his nose. For an instant, she actually felt his scream of rage.

She didn't stick around to find out what happened next. She ran. Just as she had when she was a kid. Her feet found purchase on the uneven path. Branches scraped her face as she ducked under the trees. Was he behind her? Would he catch her? She couldn't let him.

This path, while familiar, was also unknown. As a little girl, she'd been more interested in the tall man beside her. But if she stuck to the trail,

Kenny would know where she was headed. Was there another way?

She took a chance and turned into the trees. Praying she was headed the right way.

If she wasn't? She'd rather perish in the woods than let Kenny ever touch her again.

The edge of the cabin's roof appeared over the hill. She couldn't let her relief slow her down. It wasn't in the cards to be Kenny's victim today. She pounded up the hill.

She focused on her destination, heading toward the cabin. A tree root seemed to leap out of the ground. As if in slow motion, she fell. Her palms hit gravel the same instant her knees pounded the dirt.

Hard fingers grabbed her ankle and yanked. Her shirt slid up as he dragged her backward. Gravel and pine needles scraped her skin. Anger bubbled up inside her. She kicked without looking, her foot connecting with solid muscle and bone. She didn't think it was his nose again, but she hoped so. He didn't let go. Instead, he flung her over, making her lie there on the ground, staring up at his bloodied, angry face.

"Bitch," he spat, words and blood. "You ruined my life. Tattling to that damned caseworker. You'll pay for the mess you made."

What mess? She thought of the rap sheet she'd read in Pal's file on her. That wasn't her doing. He'd done it himself, but he didn't seem to see it that way.

Seeing his fist raised in the air, the forest dark behind him, she cringed at the hatred on his face.

Ballet required a limberness she knew he didn't have. Toe shoes put calluses on her feet that were now a blessing. She aimed. And kicked. He wouldn't be having children anytime soon—or ever. His mouth widened in a scream. He let go.

Scrambling to her knees, she crawled a few feet, then levered up. And ran like hell—again.

The hill was steep. She'd just emerged from the trees when she caught sight of something she didn't expect. A bright red Hummer sat in front of the hitching post.

The unblemished clearing that had yesterday been filled with wild grasses and flowers had been torn apart by the vehicle's big tires. Her heart pounded, her mouth went dry. Anger flooded through her. How dare he!

She reached the cabin's steps, her feet pounding the wood. She tried to turn the handle, but she couldn't get a grip. Finally, it turned and she stepped inside.

The cabin was still empty. She was on her own. She slammed and locked the door. It was solid, but it wouldn't hold long if Kenny came after her. She had to find a weapon, had to reinforce the door. She spun around, looking for anything.

For a heartbreaking instant, she froze. Kenny had been in every room. She knew because he'd thrown everything around. Pillows and cushions from the couch. Upending chairs.

The pictures. Her heart broke. They'd been knocked to the floor. Her mother's picture was intact, but the glass cracked across Rachel's face. The other one, the one of Pal, was more than cracked. He'd flung the frame to the floor. The way the glass spider-webbed over Pal's face showed he'd stomped on it. Destroying the glass, breaking the frame, and nearly obliterating Pal's face.

Lauren's eyes burned. She might be angry at her father, but how dare Kenny?

They might not be perfect memories, and she might never know all the answers, but they were hers. Not his. She wasn't letting him, or anyone, take them away now that she had them back.

Anger spilled into an adrenaline rush. The big heavy couch—she had to move it. She shoved. Again and again. The legs scooted against the wood, vibrating through her. Inch by tiny inch it moved. Finally, she leaned against it. It was tight against the door. The couch would slow him down, but it wouldn't stop him.

She needed a weapon. The fireplace poker and two knives from the kitchen would have to do.

Minutes, maybe hours, passed. Trembling, she felt her anger—deeper and hotter than ever—boil inside her. She rummaged in her purse, seemingly untouched by Kenny, and grabbed her phone. Damn it. No battery and no electricity to charge it.

Where was Kenny? What was he doing? Where were Jason and Harley? She'd be damned if she'd let Kenny win. *Or* hurt either of them.

Her thoughts raced. And understanding dawned. *This* must be what Jason felt for her. This need to protect, to take care of things and people she loved. She couldn't turn it off any more than he could. And she didn't want to.

As she waited, she set to work cleaning up everything, and sorting through the chaos in her head. Bus driver? Really? Had he set the fire, too? He must have. Just to manipulate her, or kill her? She stamped her foot, wishing she could stomp Kenny.

Lauren took the pictures out of the frames, tossing the chards of glass. She'd have them restored. She put the pillows back on the couch, which looked ridiculous with it shoved up against the door. It didn't matter how ridiculous anything looked.

She was taking control.

"How long have you known Lauren?" Harley asked. They were about halfway around the property. He'd shown Jason two of the cornerstones. They were buried, but intact.

"Not as long as I'd like." Jason smiled. "I've known the rest of her family since I was a kid."

Harley nodded, then turned in his saddle to look at Jason. "Did anyone know Rachel or Lauren even existed?" The pain in the old man's eyes was deep.

Jason shook his head. "Not as far as I know."

They rode in silence for a minute. "I don't even remember a Mrs. Haymaker. I know she was there." He thought back. "But she was pretty invisible."

Harley nodded. "Beth was a very timid woman. If she knew her husband had another family, I doubt she'd have ever said or done anything. She was scared to death of him, but even more scared, I think, of bein' on her own."

They rode to the next marker without talking. Back up in the saddle again, Jason was the one to ask the question this time. "How did Lauren get to LA from here?"

Harley didn't look surprised by the question. "I took her." Harley's voice broke as he looked over at the horizon, in the direction of the cabin. "We buried Rachel out by the pond. That's what she wanted. There's a small marker there." He rode in silence for a minute. "I took Lauren down the mountain on horseback after Rachel passed."

His voice broke again. "That little one was so lost. She kept crying for her mama, until she finally fell asleep."

Jason felt his own throat tighten. "Where did you take her?"

"To Pal. But the bastard was so drunk, he couldn't think straight. Couldn't even stand up. The dumb shit. He came after me when we went to leave. He fell down the stairs and broke a hip. That's when he had to start using the canes all the time." Another long silence. More questions flew around in Jason's head, but he didn't think Harley was up to hearing them.

"Me and the missus kept her as long as we could. But the county got wind of us having her. The social worker at the hospital where Pal was called social services. They took her."

That made sense. Not a pretty image, but reality.

"He didn't even fight to keep her." Harley was angry now. "He let the system take her. And we couldn't find her. We weren't family, so they wouldn't let us know what was going on." His voice cracked, and while Jason couldn't see his face, he knew the anguish he'd see there.

"I think Rachel would have appreciated you trying." He would never know the woman, but he knew the love Lauren felt for her, even if her memory was vague, the bond was solid. Maybe the pain she'd felt here was what kept her from remembering?

He thought of his own mother and all she'd done for them after their father had died. "Thanks, Mom," he whispered, his head tipped up at the blue sky above.

They finished the last section of the ride in silence and headed back toward the cabin. He'd wondered what Lauren had done with her morning. She'd been adamant that she was fine, and he gave her the space she asked for. Now he was anxious to see her and hear her decision. There was no rush, but she'd been the one to decide that she was making up her mind today.

"Oh, hell no!" Harley's voice echoed across the wide field as they came over the ridge. The older man kicked his horse into a run. Leaning low over the horse's neck, they raced across the grass.

Thick tire tracks cut across the pristine field. What the—? Jason soon caught up with Harley.

THE COUCH MOVED. Just an inch. Hurrying to the window, Lauren saw Kenny kicking the door. She'd been right, the door wouldn't hold long. He was yelling something, but she couldn't read his lips.

Should she run? Or stay by the door and hit him with the poker? Could she actually stab him with a knife? Panic threatened.

The thumping stopped. Where was he? Had he given up? The Hummer was still there. He was out there, somewhere.

Suddenly, he was there, on the other side of the glass, glaring evilly at her. She took a step back, holding the poker like a baseball bat. His fist came toward her, through the glass. Blood and glass flew everywhere. She prepared to swing when he suddenly froze.

He stumbled backward. Then crumbled into an unmoving heap. She scooted away, surprised when a shadow fell over him. Confused she glanced out at Kenny. And then at the shadow.

Harley stood at the top of the steps, his face dark

and menacing. His weathered old frame was out-
lined by the daylight as he lowered the rifle he'd
aimed at Kenny.

Kenny didn't move. A wide stain of dark red
grew on the fabric of his shirt.

Suddenly, there was movement everywhere. The
couch slid. The door flew open. Strong, familiar
arms wrapped around her, lifting her. Holding tight.
Jason's scent permeated the air, engulfing her, the
poker and the knives clattering to the floor. She
threw her arms around Jason's neck.

She trembled and Jason moved, taking her away
from where Harley knelt beside Kenny. Jason sat
down in the big chair, not letting her go. Pulling
her tight against him.

She had to know. She struggled back from Jason's hold, staring first at his face, at the agony
there, and then beyond him. To the open doorway.
To where Harley was wrapping the colorful afghan
around Kenny's shoulder, holding the blanket tight
against his wound. The bright colors soon turned
dark red. He didn't cover his face, though. He was
still alive.

Harley was on his phone. Calling for help. She
let herself feel a smidgen of relief. Kenny was alive.
Would that mean she had to fear him? Would he
come back someday? She trembled, and Jason
turned her away from the view. He was still taking care of her. But this time she let him. Now that

she understood, it didn't seem quite so overbearing. She curled into him then.

He was talking. She felt his words. It was like in the hospital when she'd burrowed in to feel the vibration. She savored the comfort, but then pushed back, aching to see his face.

Their gazes met. "I almost lost you," he said, and somehow, she knew it was in a whisper, though she'd never actually heard one. She felt the pain that stole the strength from his voice.

As if suddenly embarrassed by the display of emotion, Jason broke their gazes' hold and began taking stock of her injuries. He stared at the bright red stain on her cast. He frowned and she moved her unbroken hand to spell "*h-i-s*." She nodded toward Kenny and tapped her finger against Jason's nose. His eyes grew wide, and he turned to look at the injured man.

"That's my girl." He smiled, his pride shining through the worry.

She couldn't hold back any longer. She wrapped her arms around his neck, and pulled his lips down to hers. She had to have him. Had to taste his caring. The saltiness of his lips surprised her. For her. He shed tears for her. This strong, intense man— cried for her.

CHAPTER TWENTY-ONE

ADDIE WAS BAKING. Not good. Jason watched his sister out of the corner of his eye. Everyone loved her cookies. But they all knew that when she was baking—something was up.

He and Lauren had arrived at the ranch last night. The hearing to resolve the contest to Pal's will was tomorrow, so he'd convinced her to come early, to meet people and be prepared.

"What's up, Addie?" Jason ventured, noticing that Wyatt paid extra attention to his coffee.

"Nothing." She put another cookie sheet in the big industrial oven, then started making more round balls of dough.

"Then why are you making all those cookies?"

"Because you all love them."

"We do." Jason nodded. "Thanks for making them. So what's up?" he repeated.

"Uh-oh." Wyatt shifted in his seat.

"Don't you go uh-ohing me, Wyatt Hawkins. You have the same concerns I do."

"I do?"

"Don't play stupid." She shook the wooden spoon she'd been using at them both. "Tell him."

"Tell me what?" Jason settled at the big kitchen table. He knew this had something to do with Lauren. Addie never could resist meddling in anyone's life.

Wyatt took another drink and didn't say a word. He didn't have to.

"Do you love her?" Addie and the lethal spoon faced Jason.

"I don't know if that's any of your business. But, yes."

Another half dozen cookies found their way to the cookie sheet. "Have you told her?"

"I'm going to."

Addie huffed and finished filling the tray. Wiping her hands on the dish towel, she poured herself a cup of coffee. She sat down to face her brothers. "You want to make it permanent?"

Jason felt like a teenager again, and he didn't like it. Wyatt and Addie had been as much parents as siblings to him after their father died. But they just couldn't shake that role now that he'd grown up. "Yes."

"And you brought her *here*? She's a world-famous ballerina. She travels all over." She waved that spoon again, this time encompassing the whole room, and probably beyond.

Jason looked at Wyatt, who was still focusing on his coffee, but he seemed to feel the weight of Jason's stare. He looked up then at Addie. "Now, Ad—"

"What's wrong with here?" Jason asked.

She rolled her eyes. "Are you kidding? She doesn't fit here. This is not a five-star anything."

"I resent that," Wyatt said, finally joining the conversation.

"Because she's a ballerina?" Addie was being so irrational. This was insane.

"She's *the* ballerina. Have you ever seen her perform? It's amazing."

Addie was in awe. He'd never seen his sister like this. Jason grinned with pride, and pleasure. He knew better than to laugh. The spoon was still in reach. "Yes, I have seen her perform. You're right, she's amazing. But she's an even better person."

Addie nodded. "I understand that. It's just... I'm worried." The timer went off then, and she returned to the stove to take the cookies out. The even rhythm of the spatula between the cookies and the metal cookie sheet was a familiar, comforting sound from Jason's childhood.

"What are you really worried about, Addie?" Jason stepped over to his sister and snatched a cookie. Also just like his childhood.

"I—" She stopped scooping cookies. "Do you know what you're getting into with her disability?"

"I know the hurdles. I don't care that she's deaf."

Addie turned and faced him, a glare and spoon at the ready. "Now that's a blatant lie."

She surprised him. "What?"

"You most certainly do care. You wouldn't have learned sign language if you didn't care."

"She has a point," Wyatt actually spoke—then hastily returned to his coffee when they both glared at him.

"Okay, I care. But I can't let it come between us. Others have done it."

Addie beat more cookie dough into submission before speaking again. "Are you being realistic?" She looked over, expecting an answer.

He knew she said all this out of caring for him—nothing against Lauren. He put his hands gently on his sister's shoulders. "I have thought this through. Lauren is deaf. She will always be deaf. There are hurdles." He took a deep breath. "It kills me that she and I can't talk this easily."

Jason moved away and stared out the window at the wide fields that were just coming back to life after the devastating fires.

"I know when she travels, we won't be able to talk on the phone. We'll text." He shrugged. "If we have kids—" He had to clear his throat before going on. "She won't hear a baby cry in the middle of the night." The list he'd mentally written got longer each day. "The idea of mothering the teens, Dylan and Tina scares her. Heck, it scares me. But you know what?" He turned to alternately look from Addie to Wyatt.

Addie stared back, wringing the life out of the dish towel in her hands. "What?" she whispered.

"Despite all that, my life would be far worse without her." The silence hung there, as if to remind him of Lauren's world—one he was just beginning to understand.

"Don't worry, Ad." He knew that was an impossibility but he had to lighten the mood. He heard Wyatt laugh. "Look." He took the dish towel and set it aside, making sure she was focused on him. "I'm a grown man. If things don't work out, it wouldn't be my first broken heart." Though it would be, by far, the worst.

"No, that would be Lisa Adams," Wyatt mumbled.

"Don't remind me." Addie frowned. "You were in such pain."

"I was fourteen!" Jason snatched another cookie. He gave his sister a peck on the cheek. "Thanks for caring, Addie," he whispered and headed out to find Lauren.

"You were no help, Wyatt," Addie said, her voice following Jason down the hall.

"Yes, I was," his brother responded. "He is still speaking to you, isn't he?"

"Oh, hush." Jason heard another cookie sheet slide into the oven.

LAUREN HAD NEVER been to a ranch before. She and Jason had arrived last night to a house full of people—his siblings, their families and ranch hands.

People who didn't know sign language, but tried so hard to be polite to her.

Her world felt a million miles away.

Footsteps thumped on the floor behind her. The only person who would approach her was Jason.

Lauren stood at the veranda's rail, but turned to look over her shoulder and fought the urge to smile. The city-slicker attorney was long gone. Jason wore a blue cotton work shirt and worn jeans. Weathered boots peeked out from the stack of denim at his ankles. It reminded her of the night they'd gone dancing.

"Country looks good on you," she signed.

He laughed, and not for the first time, she wondered what small piece she was missing by not being able to hear it. She seldom felt that way, but lately, with Jason she questioned everything. She turned back to the view of the valley spread out before her. It was nearly as stunning as he was.

Wyatt Hawkins's ranch house was big yet homey. She could imagine a family growing up here. Kids running wild across the wide prairie, riding horses hell-bent-for-leather, climbing trees and swimming in rivers when their parents weren't watching. All the things she'd read about in books and seen on TV. *And* that Jason had shared with her about his childhood.

Nothing remotely related to her growing up in LA.

Jason stepped closer and after catching her gaze,

he pointed north, his arm sweeping from left to right across most of the horizon. She frowned, questioning him. He'd told her about the devastating fires, but the land was recovering. What was he showing her?

"*H-a-y-m-a-k-e-r* land." He signed. "All the way to the next county."

She could only stare. If her father had claimed her while he was alive, would she have grown up here? Something inside her ached.

Movement on the horizon caught her eye, and she watched, mesmerized as a herd of cattle ambled up from the edge of the earth and headed toward them. Half a dozen men on horses were behind them. Dust rose up from the multitude of hooves and the sun shone off the floating dirt.

"Who?" she asked.

"*W-y-a-t-t-s* men." He pointed to the bluff. "Old pasture. Time to move them in closer."

"Why?"

"*B-r-a-n-d-i-n-g.* Fresh food." He tilted his head and took her hand. Leading her down the steps, Jason headed toward the big barn. The doors stood open, and the scent of animals wafted out of the wide doorway. Curious, she followed.

It took a minute for her eyes to adjust to the shadowed interior, but she trusted him. Finally, he stopped, and she joined him at the edge of a stall. A colt, black-and-white with thin legs and big beautiful eyes stared at them. Curious about them as well.

"Name?" she asked, her fingers hitting together in the sign.

"*D-o-m-i-n-o*," he spelled and she smiled.

It was a perfect name for him. The colt moved closer to the gate, and Jason gently stroked the horse's nose, slowly moving up to his ears. She stood back, not sure what to do. Her only experience with a horse had been when they'd ridden up to the cabin. Jason and Harley had taken care of everything then. She shivered, drawn to the animal.

She wanted to touch the horse and yet, what if she did it wrong? She held back.

Jason smiled at her, gently guiding her closer, pulling her hand forward with his. She was so enthralled. The beautiful animal stared at her with such wide, friendly eyes.

The fur of his nose was soft beneath her fingers, as were his ears. She was surprised that the long strands of his mane weren't as soft as she'd expected. And yet…she loved touching him, loved the feel of Jason beside her, his arms protecting her as the horse accepted her affections.

She'd never felt closer to anyone than she did this man. And for the first time, such closeness didn't scare her.

Suddenly, Jason stepped back, leaving her alone with the colt. She turned to look at him and was surprised to see him pull a folded piece of paper from his pocket.

"What's that?" she signed.

Jason looked at the paper. After a long moment, he extended it to her. As she took it, he signed. "Kenny's confession. It explains a lot."

"How did you get this?"

"Helps to know connected people." He grinned. "*C-h-l-o-e* faxed it this morning." His colleague who had helped Dylan. Lauren must remember to thank her.

She quickly scanned the page, her throat going dry as she read his confession. He'd stalked her for months. How had she not noticed? He'd crossed paths with her by chance in the beginning, when he'd covered a coworker's shift, but after that, he'd calculated everything.

He'd attended the ballet and learned what nights she taught late. Watching, waiting. When Jason showed up to give her a ride home, that had put Kenny over the edge. Something had snapped. He had to have her, had to make her pay, he'd told the police. Lauren shivered.

"He admitted to setting the fire." Jason cringed. He moved closer now that she'd finished reading the paper and folded it. "He found you in the mountains by pinging your phone."

She didn't even know that was possible, or that Kenny was smart enough to do something like that.

"How?"

Jason shrugged. "I don't know how it works. Your phone is on the table. I *d-i-s-a-b-l-e-d* that feature after reading this." He lifted his chin, as if waiting for her to dish out some of her usual indignation for him doing that. She didn't.

"Thank you. You take good care of me."

And he did. She just wasn't sure what that meant for the future, for either of them.

"Take that—" He tapped the paper. "To court tomorrow. It can't hurt."

She nodded slowly, planting her hands on his broad chest, almost wishing he'd added a cowboy hat to finish off the look. "Kiss me," she signed and lifted up on her toes. Almost high enough.

Rather than kissing her, Jason looked into her eyes as if searching for something. He cupped her chin with his big hands, his thumb sliding over her lips. "I—"

Why did he hesitate? Then he bent his head, just a little, to meet her lips and she ignored everything except the rightness of it.

THERE WEREN'T MANY people in the courthouse this early in the day. Why would there be, she wondered. It was a small town. She'd met the judge last night when he'd been at the restaurant they'd all gone to for dinner, for heaven's sake. The man was actually Emily's boss.

Life in a small town was very different from Los Angeles. Jason had dropped her off out front, while he parked the car. She was glad for the time alone to gather her thoughts. Now, sitting here, on a bench outside the courtroom, waiting for Jason and the Haymaker family—her family—she felt lonely.

When had she stopped feeling independent? When had she stopped relishing her solitary time?

A movement at the end of the hall made her look up. The morning sunlight poured in onto the highly waxed linoleum. She could only see the silhouettes of the three people who approached.

As they drew closer, Lauren gasped. Maxine, Dylan and Tina stood there, their arms linked, as if blocking anyone else from coming through. The older woman smiled and, they all walked toward Lauren.

She didn't bother to stop herself from opening her arms and letting her foster mother enfold her in a warm hug. They clung together for a long minute before Maxine pulled away. She didn't sign, she spoke, making sure Lauren could see her lips. "We're here to support you." She pointed at each of them. "*We're* your family. Today."

"Every day." Tina stepped closer.

Lauren blinked away the tears, hoping to—to what? Show them she could do this on her own? She couldn't, and it was time she admitted it to herself and the rest of them. Jason had shown her that she could lean on someone and still be strong.

And it was a lesson she needed to make sure both these kids learned.

The light changed again, and she looked up. Where Maxine had stood a moment ago, Jason entered. He looked as surprised as she felt. She let out a breath that she hadn't realized she'd been holding when a smile spread over his face.

"Now this is what I like to see," he said, and signed. They all shared hugs.

The bailiff stuck his head out of the courtroom's door just then. "Five minutes."

Jason nodded. "Thanks, Bill." He looked around, a frown replacing his smile. "Have you seen the Haymakers?" he asked the group. Lauren shook her head and the others joined in.

As if on cue, Trey came through the closed door at the other end of the hall. Another man who Lauren recognized as Pal Jr. followed him. Both men glared at her. Her heart sank.

She'd never needed anyone before, never let herself want to need someone. So why did their snub hurt? Why did she want them to want her?

Maxine's arm around her shoulder helped.

Trey and Pal Jr. walked over to the door, brushing past the bailiff as if the older man wasn't even there.

Bill frowned, then shrugged and propped the double doors open. "Might as well come on in."

Jason gestured for them to precede him. As Lauren went to follow Maxine and the kids, he stopped her. She faced him, not sure what he was stopping her for.

Jason leaned in and slowly, carefully kissed her.

She wished they were alone, where she could step closer and slip her arms around him. Hold on tight.

Vibrations made her step back, and she looked over Jason's shoulder at the herd of people headed their way. Wyatt and Emily. Mandy and Lane with little Lucas in his baby carrier. DJ and Tammie—minus Tyler who was in school. Tara and even Addie were here.

Wyatt clapped Jason on the shoulder. "I like the way you argue a case there, little brother." She read his lips as he winked at her.

Jason actually blushed. "What are you doing here?"

"We're here to support you." Addie stepped forward and took Lauren's hands in hers. "Support you both." She said it a bit too slowly, but Lauren would forgive her.

Jason took her hand and led the way into the courtroom. Lauren felt all those footsteps follow her.

Trey looked up from his seat at the front of the room, his frown deepening as everyone came in. "What's this?" she saw him say.

She turned to face him and signed, "Family."

"What'd she just say?" He stood, his hands fisted.

Though Trey wouldn't understand, she turned to face him and finger spelled, "*F-a-m-i-l-y.*" She plunked down in the chair at the front of the room.

Lauren left Trey sputtering and confused and

Jason let her. He joined her at the front, with his family and the important part of hers seated in the gallery behind them. He grinned at her as he sat down beside her.

JUDGE LITCHFIELD HAD been the head of the family court here since Jason was a kid. He ran a good department and had been one of the reasons Jason had gained an interest in the law. He respected the man, and was glad he'd been assigned this case. Looking over at Pal and Trey, whose lawyer had just hustled in, Jason didn't see any smiles on the other side.

"You think you could have been any later, Jackson?" Pal Jr. grumbled at the man.

The tall silver-haired man with the polished silk suit met Pal Jr.'s stare. Jason barely resisted the urge to shake his head. The man had been Pal's lawyer for nearly fifty years. Like Pal Jr. or Trey was going to bother him?

"I could turn around and go back to Dallas if you'd like." The man's stare was intimidating. "Would that be late enough for you?"

Ouch. Trey and Pal Jr. were contesting the will this man had drawn up at Pal's direction. He didn't look like someone who took kindly to being questioned. Jason wasn't sure why he was sitting on their side.

This was going to be an interesting day. He looked over at Lauren, wondering how much she was getting just reading lips. He couldn't sign and explain at this point. Where was the interpreter?

Judge Litchfield's court was minimally formal. "Let's get started," he said, looking first at Pal Jr. and Trey and then over at Lauren. Jason couldn't read his expression.

"I've read the document, and I'm aware of all the parties, including Pal Sr." He pinned the Dallas attorney with a stare. "I don't see anything to make me overturn it. Do you have anything to explain?"

The attorney stood, formal despite the casual environment. "I drew up the document, but my clients, who are the primary beneficiaries, feel there was some issue with the last set of changes Pal Sr. requested."

"Did you draw up that part?"

"I did."

The judge frowned. "Do you feel it was appropriate?"

"I didn't have a problem. Pal was competent at the time. My clients can perhaps explain more clearly." He waved at Trey.

"Go ahead." Judge Litchfield sat back in his big chair, its leather frame creaking. "This ought to be good."

"Don't I even have to be sworn in, or go to the witness stand?" Trey demanded.

Litchfield's lips minutely turned up. "Son, this is probate court. No one's on trial. But if it would make you happier, be my guest." He waved at the seat on the raised platform beside his desk.

As Trey strutted toward the seat, Jason stood. "Your honor."

"Yes?"

"My client is deaf, and while we tried to get an interpreter, she hasn't arrived. May I sign for my client?"

"Of course. Is there anything from before we need to repeat for her?"

Jason signed the question to Lauren, but she shook her head. Relieved that she was keeping up.

"How do we know if he's not telling her the truth?" Trey stopped and asked.

This time Litchfield actually rolled his eyes. "Why would he do that? You're the ones contesting this will. Not her."

Trey barely paused before taking the seat. "I still don't trust him."

The judge ignored him. "Okay, counselors, proceed."

The Dallas attorney remained behind the table, though Jason came around to the front, facing Lauren so she could see him and read what she could of Trey's lips.

"Why does he have his back to me?" Trey asked. The judge still ignored him.

Jason saw Lauren smile. Guess she *was* able to read his lips. Still, Jason prepared to sign, waiting for the questions to begin. This would challenge his skills, but he'd do his best. If he couldn't do it, he'd ask the judge to let Dylan give it a shot. But Jason *wanted* to do this.

Jason moved closer to Trey. "Better?" Trey simply glared.

"Would you please explain why you think this will should be dismissed?" Jason asked.

"She's lying. She obviously got to Grandfather and tricked him somehow."

"Can you prove it? The file, your honor, marked exhibit A, is pretty solid."

"Looks good to me," the judge said.

"She has to be lying. My grandfather never mentioned anyone else. He might have been a harsh man, but he loved my grandmother."

"No one's arguing that, son." Litchfield actually seemed sorry for Trey. "This is about Pal's competence and the document." He turned to Trey's lawyer.

"Do you have any questions, or information we don't have?" the judge asked Trey's lawyer.

"No, your honor. My client's dug himself a deep enough hole without my help." The man faced Lauren, smiled albeit stiffly, then grabbed his briefcase and headed to the door without another word to anyone.

"He can't do that." Trey stood up, pointing at the attorney.

"He just did," the judge said.

"But—"

Lauren stood and faced the judge, signing slowly. Jason spoke, translating exactly, not interpreting for her. "May I speak?" she asked.

"Of course." The judge smiled at her. "Step down, Trey. You've had your turn."

"But—"

"Now."

Lauren settled in the seat Trey vacated.

"Go ahead, my dear," the judge said.

"Hey," Trey protested. "You didn't treat me like that."

"Look pretty funny for me to start calling you dear at this stage of my life, Trey." Everyone laughed.

"Go ahead."

Lauren took a deep breath and faced Jason. "I didn't know anything about any of you until Jason came to see me." She pointed at Jason and she saw him repeat her words. "I grew up in California. I've never been here before. I was in foster care from the time my mother died when I was five until I turned eighteen." She paused and faced the Haymakers. "I didn't come looking for any of this.

"All I ever wanted was a family." She looked over at Pal Jr., who looked down and squirmed in his seat, and Trey who frowned but didn't look away.

Jason swallowed, taking a step forward. She lifted up a hand. "Let me say my piece." He nodded and stepped back. Lauren took a deep breath and faced him. He waited, ready to translate her sign for the court. She lifted her chin and confronted her fear. She'd come too far to let the past or Kenny or any of the other hurdles in her life get in the way. This was what she wanted.

"Your Honor," she signed and saw Jason's lips form the shape of the words. The judge looked at her, while he listened to Jason.

"It's true. I never knew my father. I have vague memories from when I was five. I didn't know about the ranch. The money. None of it." She glanced at Pal Jr. and Trey. "I didn't know them. I––" She stopped her hand against her chest. "I still don't."

The judge held up a hand to stop her. He turned to Jason and spoke. She watched, waiting for Jason to repeat the question. "Have you talked with them?"

She shook her head. The older man frowned. "Continue."

"I didn't know any of this until the day Jason came to my house." She looked at Jason then, catching his eye. "You—" She pointed at him and he frowned, knowing this was shifting. "You gave me my family." She turned to face the judge. "I didn't know about any of this. And I still don't care about most of it."

"What do you care about?" The judge faced her and she didn't need Jason to sign. She could read the old man's lips.

"My family."

The judge frowned, looking confused. "I don't understand."

"Blood doesn't make family," she signed. "The cabin gave me back the memories of my parents." She faced Jason again, seeing all those faces behind him. "Maxine Nightingale took me in as a kid. I have a huge family of kids at my studio. All of you—" She waved at Jason's siblings, all sitting there with Maxine and the kids. "You've given me more than my real family." Slowly, Lauren stood and walked over to Jason. Stopping in front of him, she reached up and put her hand against the rough edge of his jaw.

She took a deep breath, then carefully moved her lips to form the words. Her voice needed a lot of work, but she'd already decided to do this. She'd practiced. She spoke. "I love you."

Jason stared. He'd stopped translating for her—probably in shock.

"This is ridiculous!" Trey shot to his feet, startling everyone.

Judge Litchfield's gavel slammed down on the desk, and even Lauren felt the impact. She stared at the older man, surprised by the anger on his face.

"That's enough," he said to Trey, his enunciation distinct with his anger. "Trey and Pal Jr." He pointed the gavel at them. "I've known you all your lives. Your family has wreaked havoc in this community. I knew your father better than I'd like, and he robbed the legal system of the chance to bring him to justice."

Pal Jr. stood and Lauren looked back at him. "Now, Warren—"

"No, we're done here." Litchfield slammed the gavel again, and several people jumped. "The will stands. Case dismissed."

Jason turned to face her, his smile wide. "You won."

She smiled back. "We did." She waved at everyone.

"Your Honor?" Jason said, not looking away from Lauren.

"Yes?" The old man had stood, preparing to leave.

She saw Jason swallow. "You got time for a wedding?"

Slowly, Jason got down on one knee, his heart in his eyes. "Will you marry me, Lauren Ramsey? I love you, too. I always will."

For the first time in what seemed like ages, happy tears filled her eyes and she let them. She nodded and gently tugged on Jason's hands, for him to stand. "Yes. Now." She looked over at the judge, who smiled and nodded as well.

Everyone they both loved was here. Everyone who mattered… Lauren turned and looked at Pal Jr. He was her brother. Her brother! She pulled away from Jason and walked over to the Haymakers. She might never get the chance again to reach out—to maybe find some connection with her flesh and blood.

"Would you—" she signed and knew Jason translated when Pal Jr.'s eyes flicked to someone behind her. "Would you stay, and give me away?"

Pal Jr.'s eye grew wide and color swept his cheeks. Slowly, he nodded. Was that emotion in his eyes? She walked around the table, to slip her arm around his. She looked at Jason. "Ready."

More movement and suddenly Tina was beside her, a dried bundle of flowers from the vases at the back of the room extended to Lauren. She took the offered bouquet.

"Now you're ready," Tina signed and said.

And she was.

* * * * *

LARGER-PRINT BOOKS!

GET 2 FREE LARGER-PRINT NOVELS PLUS
2 FREE GIFTS!

♥ HARLEQUIN®

Romance

From the Heart, For the Heart

LARGER-PRINT BOOKS!

◆HARLEQUIN

Presents

PASSION
GUARANTEED
SEDUCTION

GET 2 FREE LARGER-PRINT
NOVELS PLUS 2 FREE GIFTS!

YES! Please send me 2 FREE LARGER-PRINT Harlequin Presents® novels and my 2 FREE gifts (gifts are worth about $10). After receiving them, if I don't wish to receive any more books, I can return the shipping statement marked "cancel." If I don't cancel, I will receive 6 brand-new novels every month and be billed just $5.30 per book in the U.S. or $5.74 per book in Canada. That's a saving of at least 12% off the cover price! It's quite a bargain! Shipping and handling is just 50¢ per book in the U.S. and 75¢ per book in Canada.* I understand that accepting the 2 free books and gifts places me under no obligation to buy anything. I can always return a shipment and cancel at any time. Even if I never buy another book, the two free books and gifts are mine to keep forever.

176/376 HDN GHVY

Name _____ (PLEASE PRINT) _____

Address _____ Apt. # _____

City _____ State/Prov. _____ Zip/Postal Code _____

Signature (if under 18, a parent or guardian must sign) _____

Mail to the Reader Service:
IN U.S.A.: P.O. Box 1867, Buffalo, NY 14240-1867
IN CANADA: P.O. Box 609, Fort Erie, Ontario L2A 5X3

**Are you a subscriber to Harlequin Presents® books
and want to receive the larger-print edition?
Call 1-800-873-8635 today or visit us at www.ReaderService.com.**

* Terms and prices subject to change without notice. Prices do not include applicable taxes. Sales tax applicable in N.Y. Canadian residents will be charged applicable taxes. Offer not valid in Quebec. This offer is limited to one order per household. Not valid for current subscribers to Harlequin Presents Larger-Print books. All orders subject to credit approval. Credit or debit balances in a customer's account(s) may be offset by any other outstanding balance owed by or to the customer. Please allow 4 to 6 weeks for delivery. Offer available while quantities last.

Your Privacy—The Reader Service is committed to protecting your privacy. Our Privacy Policy is available online at www.ReaderService.com or upon request from the Reader Service.

We make a portion of our mailing list available to reputable third parties that offer products we believe may interest you. If you prefer that we not exchange your name with third parties, or if you wish to clarify or modify your communication preferences, please visit us at www.ReaderService.com/consumerschoice or write to us at Reader Service Preference Service, P.O. Box 9062, Buffalo, NY 14240-9062. Include your complete name and address.

HPLP15

REQUEST YOUR FREE BOOKS!
2 FREE WHOLESOME ROMANCE NOVELS IN LARGER PRINT
PLUS 2
FREE
MYSTERY GIFTS

❋❋❋❋❋❋❋❋❋❋❋❋❋❋❋❋❋❋❋❋❋❋❋

H E A R T W A R M I N G™

❋❋❋❋❋❋❋❋❋❋❋❋❋❋❋❋❋❋❋❋❋❋❋

Wholesome, tender romances

LARGER-PRINT BOOKS!

GET 2 FREE LARGER-PRINT NOVELS PLUS
2 FREE GIFTS!

Ⓗ HARLEQUIN®

INTRIGUE

BREATHTAKING ROMANTIC SUSPENSE

HILP15